Judgment Day

Jonathan Martin

ISBN-10: 0692463364
ISBN-13: 978-0692463369

DEDICATED TO

Alexis Eileen Adams
1963—2014

I will never forget what you did for us all.
We miss you.

CONTENTS

ACKNOWLEDGMENTS

Mom, Sequoya, Patricia, Will, Gerald, Ilsa, and my fiancé Austyn. Thank you all so much for your help and support in writing this. I appreciate it all.

1
The Lone Lycan and the Mysterious Man

It is a dark autumn night in Drake City. The sun has just set, and the industrial city is coming alive. The city natives are out mingling, some headed to work, others stirring up trouble. From a cold, dark alley connected to the main street, emerge the sounds of tussling and a dog yelping out in pain.

A gang of guys is jumping on an overgrown wolflike creature, a Lycan, a fur-laden creature who stands primarily on its hind legs. It is too small to be fully mature, a little muscular but a runt, really. Its fur is black and dirty brown, but that is obscured by being soaked in its own blood. The thing has been beaten to hell, has several broken bones, and is bleeding from its mouth, nose, and ears. The leader of the gang has pinned the Lycan against a trash can and has begun to choke the life out of him.

The leader whispers to the Lycan in a cocky tone of voice, "We're going to make an example out of you, you overgrown mutt." He pulls a bowie knife from his belt and holds it against bloodied Lycan's neck. The Lycan, with a lifeless expression, eyes the pale man's lips with his blurry vision.

The leader of the gang yells, "This is Drake City! You diseased, bottom-feeding, overgrown rats are not welcome here!" The rest of the gang continues to watch while cheering their leader on, obscuring the view of many curious bystanders passing by.

"I am going to cut you up into tiny kibbles and bits and mail your furry ass back to Puppyland where your own species will eat you without thinking. Mindless mammals you all are!" the leader exclaims with a sick, sadistic smile on his face. The Lycan looks in the leader's shining eyes and, without hesitation, spits his own blood in his opponent's face, sternly saying, "Do your worst...parasite!"

The leader, disrespected, rears back his hand wielding the bowie knife and then punches and breaks the Lycan's jaw. The Lycan falls to the ground, writhing in pain. Knowing it would only hurt more to move, he stays as limp as possible. The gang's leader wipes the blood off his face and tastes it. With a disgusted snarl and glare, he then begins giving the Lycan another vicious beating. The creature tries to scream, but moving its jaw is too much pain to handle.

"Dirty canine, I've tasted better pig's blood!" the leader yells mockingly while his gang continues to laugh and cheer. "Blood Pack! Remember that in the afterlife, you worm!" the gang leader yells as he stops kicking the Lycan in its tender ribs and readies to sever its spine. He raises the bowie knife in the air with an evil laugh and shouts, "Goodbye, Lassie! It was fun!"

In a flash of light, the gang leader's hand holding the bowie knife hits the ground in front of the Blood Pack's grunt members. It is no longer attached to its owner. The Blood Pack's members freak out, yelling.

The area quickly fills with a thick fog. The Blood Pack's scared members peer through the fog and see two men coming towards them. The first one lunges at them as if he has been thrown. It is their leader. He lands on the underboss. He is in shock and is clutching the wrist where his hand once resided. The rest of the gang looks on at the second ominous man in the fog.

The man's eyes begin to glow a deep purple, and an angry voice echoes from the fog. "Take your leader and go if you don't want to end up like him." Swiftly, they grab their leader, pull him out of the alley, and make their way up the main street, frightened and knocking pedestrians over. The beaten Lycan hears the commotion, peeks over, and sees a blur of a shadow man in the thick of the fog. The man walks towards the Lycan out of the fog, but before seeing his face, the canine creature blacks out.

A few days later, a man wakes up in a small, dark tent, lying on a small cot. He hears crickets chirping. He smells and hears crackling, burning wood. He lies there gathering his thoughts, feeling lost, light-headed, and starved. He then sits up, immediately feels a sharp pain in his ribs, and remembers the beating he took from the Vampyr gang.

The man gently lays a hand on his abdomen, anticipating pain, and feels some type of cloth. After examining the cloth closely, he realizes it is a bandage. He feels his legs. They as well are bandaged. The rest of him is naked. He has returned to his tiny, frail human form. Wondering where he got the bandages from, he remembers the man in the fog. He hears the crunch of light footsteps on foliage-covered grass, finds the tent opening, and peeks through it. He sees the dark woods lit up by a tiny campfire. A tall, shadowy figure feeds it more wood and then sits down on a stump in front of the fire. He hangs his head down and lets out a sigh of relief.

The man then quickly looks up at the tent. The Lycan inside becomes nervous. The hair on his tail and the back of his neck stands up, and he freezes up, hoping the tall man will forget about the tent. The tall man grabs something next to him, stands up, and slowly walks around the fire. The Lycan, fearful of what might happen, quickly jumps out of the tent, totally disregarding his injuries, and tries to confront the man.

"Ouch! Oh hell, that sucks!" The Lycan falls to his knees, writhing in pain. The dark, shadowy man quickly walks towards the Lycan, who, not knowing the man's intentions, takes a swing at him and collapses. The man springs backwards, and in continuous pain, the Lycan yells, "By the Spirit!"

"You believe in that Mumbojumbo? Well, at least your jaw is back to normal," the mysterious man says, bending down to assist the Lycan. "You need to rest. You haven't healed all the way yet."

The Lycan hears the concern in the man's voice, and it angers him. He stands up, trying to see past the shadows, and realizes what happened before he blacked out. He yells at the mysterious man, "Why did you do it?"

The man, confused, replies, "What?"

"Why did you interfere?" the Lycan screams while growling.

The man thinks for a moment and then gives a tiny chuckle and states, "Because you were getting your ass beat?!"

The Lycan's golden skin quickly sprouts fur, his face forms into a muzzle, and his limbs grow out as he transforms into his Lycan form and barks loudly at the mysterious shadow man, "I did not ask for your help! I can handle myself on my own!"

The shadowy man pauses for a moment, turns his head in confusion, and replies, "They were going...to kill you!"

The Lycan responds, "What's it to you?!" He is too weak to fully transform and recedes to his man form.

There is an uncomfortable silence for a few moments. Even the crickets have stopped chirping due to all the yelling. But then the mysterious man begins shaking in anger. He breaks the silence. "You ungrateful shitbag!" he yells, balling his fists. "I had more important things to do than saving your nutty ass and nursing you back to health! My only family is in jeopardy and I take the time to help you, and it turns out you're just a waste of time and flesh!" he says to himself, turning his back on the suffering Lycan. He throws the things he had prepared for the Lycan on the ground and runs off, disappearing into the thick of the woods.

The Lycan, after cooling off, thinks about what the mysterious man said. Being hard-headed, he dismisses the man's words. While still in pain, the Lycan realizes how cold it is in the woods and walks towards the fire to keep warm. He steps on the thing the man had thrown to the ground. He picks it up, curious, and continues his path towards the fire. He sits on a hollowed-out log next to the fire, examining the object. It's a bag. He opens it up and begins feeling around for what's inside. He feels something mushy and warm. He smells blood and tastes it as well. There's no mistake. He pulls out a fresh slab of cow meat.

The Lycan immediately devours the meat from a freshly butchered cow while huddling up to the fire as closely as possible. Even then, the autumn breeze gives him uncomfortable shivers and goose bumps. He is still too weak to turn Lycan and use his fur to keep warm.

He sets his sights back on the bag and sees that it is not yet empty. He loosens the tightly closed drawstrings and looks inside. It contains clothes: an old leather coat that belonged to a member of the Blood Pack judging by the insignia on the back, a newer pair of sweatpants, and beach slippers from about a century ago.

The Lycan quickly puts the clothes on. The sweats even have a hole for his tail. It makes him think about the mysterious man. Then he begins to think about his past and how in the last several years, no one has cared about him enough to salvage anything for him. He began to think of the loneliness he has endured all these years and suddenly regrets the things he said to the mysterious man.

Later on that night, back in Drake City, the recovering Lycan, in wolf form, stalks the mysterious man who seemed to be searching for something high and low, causing disruption in the area. The man has asked around of some of the more friendly locals and even interrogated some of the lowlife city gang member grunts.

The Lycan, waiting for the perfect moment to reveal himself, follows the mysterious man nonstop from roof to roof, from basement to basement, catching only darkened glimpses of his face. The mysterious man shows no signs of slowing until he stops on the roof of a building to scope out a very popular Blood Pack hangout below, on the outskirts of the city. That is when the Lycan chooses to reveal himself, but before he can, the mysterious man calls him out of hiding.

"Had a funny feeling I was being followed," the man says out loud while watching the Vampyr grunts below party and dance to the loud, catchy music.

The Lycan steps into the light, surprised, and asks, "How did you know?"

The mysterious man replies, "Your footsteps are kind of heavy. Don't think you're fully healed." The mysterious man slightly turns his head over his shoulder and asks, "Why are you following me?"

The Lycan looks at the man sternly and responds, "I'm not a waste of flesh, asshole." The mysterious man chuckles and redirects his attention to the Vampyrs below. "And I've come to help make up for some lost time I caused you," the Lycan continues.

The man yells back, "It was my choice! I do not need your help!"

Frustrated, the Lycan quickly replies, "Really? Is that why you've been running around incoherently searching everywhere? Interrogating everyone with no real leads, no clues, because you don't need help? If I were you, I'd take all the help I could get. This is a big city, and I bet you haven't covered ten percent of it."

The mysterious man hangs his head, ashamed of his progress, and responds, "You're one to talk about help. So what do you want for your help?" He chuckles, "For me to end you?"

The Lycan steps forward, smiles, and quickly replies, "I can smell someone from a mile away."

The mysterious man laughs as he jumps off the roof ledge. The Lycan runs over to the ledge and watches the mysterious man drop into the middle of the crowd of Vampyr gang members

Most of the Vampyr are too drunk to notice the mysterious man wearing combat gear and a hood over his face. He yells to get their attention, but no one can hear him over the loud music. The mysterious man becomes aggravated and blasts the stereos with lightning from his hand. The music stops, and all attention is directed towards him. He sweeps back the hood, revealing his face. He is a young, deep dark brown male with a wide nose and thin lips. His charcoal-colored hair is short and curly and seems to wave in one direction. He has a serious look in his coffee-colored eyes, a look as if he is ready to kill or be killed.

"A woman went missing from Old District about five nights ago! I've asked around this city for answers, and everyone seems to point their fingers at the infamous Blood Pack!" he yells. Some of the drunker gang members respond with cheers at the young man's somber speech. He grabs one of the gang members swiftly, shocks him severely, and drops him.

"Anymore bloodsucking assholes want to interrupt me?" the man yells, surrounded by the crowd looking at their peer unconscious, smoking on the ground. "Now all I need is a name, and you all can go back to enjoying your miserable bloodsucking lives!" the mysterious young man continues.

"Not if you destroyed the tunes, man!" one drunk and disgruntled gang member yells, trying to be humorous.

The young man clenches his teeth, grabs the gang member grunt by the collar, cocks his right hand, and readies to give him a lightning-charged punch to the face when the member quickly sobers up, signaling no to the young man, frightened. "Blaine!" the grunt yells.

"What about him?" the young man replies aggressively. "If anyone knows about taking humans from that village, it's him!"

The Vampyr grunt quickly squeals, fearing for his life. The young man drops him and walks away from the party towards the least populated street. The Lycan jumps down and follows the young man.

After catching up, the Lycan asks the young man, "You want my help or not?"

The man looks at him, smirking, and replies, "Can you smell the name Blaine?" trying to imply that the Lycan is useless in this situation.

The Lycan responds, "No, but I can smell Blaine."

The young man stops, turns, and looks at the Lycan. "You can smell Blaine?"

"Yes!" the Lycan responds.

"How?" the young man asks.

"Well, let's see. Well, I'm a Lycan! Oh yeah, and I am a Lycan," The Lycan responds sarcastically.

The young man says, "No, I mean how? Like, have you come in contact with Blaine?"

"Yes!" the Lycan answers.

"How and when?" the young man asks quickly, anxious to hear the answer.

"Blaine is the guy you stopped from killing me," The Lycan responds.

The young man lunges back, surprised, and immediately becomes angry. He punches the building they are beside, cracking the concrete wall and injuring his hand. "Damn it!" he yells.

"You have serious anger issues!" the Lycan says jokingly.

The young man turns to the Lycan, gives him an evil stare, and walks towards him as if ready to hurt him. "Do you think this is a game?" the man says while gritting his teeth. Eyeing the Lycan, he continues to advance aggressively.

"No!" the Lycan answers, stepping cautiously backwards.

"It's been five days...five days since they came and took Marie!" the young man yells. "Three of which I have wasted nursing you back to health! The others I've worked, all the way up right now!" He rambles while the Lycan stops backing up and takes more of a hostile stance towards the young man. "If you're going to help, then help! The last thing I need is funny little comments and remarks," the young man yells, coming face to face with the Lycan.

"OK, I'll ask again. Do you want my help or not?!" the Lycan asks sternly while looking the young man in his fired-up eyes.

The young man replies, "Yes! Now, please lead me to him."

"I can but I can't," the Lycan replies quickly. The young man, ready to give the Lycan an earful, swells up with anger, but the Lycan stops him. "Hold on, macho man; hear me out!" The Lycan begins his explanation. "Blaine is probably somewhere far on the other side of the city, judging by his faint smell. We could run there, but even then, by the time we reach him, the sun would already be out."

The young man calms down a little after hearing this but is still anxious about the situation. "So what do you want me to do? Wait until tomorrow?" he asks while balling his bloody fist, eager and anxious.

"Yes," the Lycan answers in a way that puts the young man at ease.

"What do you have in mind?" the intrigued young man asks, raising an eyebrow.

"I know the building where Blaine and his branch of Blood Pack sarcophagi are," the Lycan says, giving the young man a smile. The young man smiles back but still shows some concern for his family member. "Look," the Lycan continues, "during the day we can't get into the building because it's bolted shut, but the moment they leave, you can capture Blaine and ask him whatever it is you need to ask him."

The young man nods. "OK! Sounds like a plan!"

The Lycan laughs and replies, "Does it?"

"Yes, it does," the young man responds.

The Lycan steps back in relief and says, "Good, because a second ago you looked like you wanted to bite my head off."

"Well, you're the Lycan!" the young man replies comically while giving the Lycan a serious look.

"Ace," the Lycan says, revealing his name while sticking his hand out, gesturing for a friendly handshake.

The young man accepts the handshake and responds, "Anarchious."

2
Black Satin

The Lycan, Ace, leads the mysterious young man to the Blood Pack's hideout. Their base is on the abandoned side of the city where most of the lowlife Vampyr slumber during the day. The two hide across the street in a dusty old abandoned factory, camping out during the day, awaiting dusk. They sit on the third floor next to some old dusty windows and machines, figuring they will get a better view up high.

During the stakeout, Ace, curious about their quest, begins to ask Anarchious questions. "So Anarchious, this Marie—what's the relation?"

"She's… family. That's all you need to know," Anarchious responds while bandaging his swollen and bloody right hand.

"Oh yeah, well, that's a great way to get to know someone who's trying to help you," Ace replies in a sarcastic but jolly way while Anarchious continues to wrap his hand up.

"Get to know? So what are we, on a date now?" Anarchious responds, grinning, still paying intense attention to the bandages.

"Well, Anarchious, how do you expect me to trust you when I don't know anything about you but 'Marie is the only family I've got!'?" Ace says mockingly, imitating Anarchious's low, gloomy voice. The young man ignores him, balling his fist to test the firmness of the bandage. "I've got an idea," the persistent Lycan says. "I'll tell you something about me, and you tell me something about yourself, OK?"

Anarchious nods. "Yes," he says, expressionless, testing his handiwork by punching his injured right hand into his left hand.

"OK, well, let's see." Ace begins to rub his chin, pondering. "Well, I am a Scorpio, my favorite food is medium-rare steak, and I love chasing my tail," Ace says, laughing and hoping that his stupid statement will lighten up the mood.

Anarchious looks up with a serious face and asks, "Why did you try to get yourself killed?"

Ace's face drops from being happy to being ashamed. He responds, hanging his head, "To ease it." Anarchious eyes Ace as he pauses, causing a long, awkward silence. "The loneliness was too much," Ace continues. "Losses..." He picks his head up and makes eye contact with the now-curious Anarchious.

"Loss?" asks Anarchious.

"I lost my family when I was young, and ever since, I've been alone," Ace explains, then breaks eye contact with Anarchious.

After hearing Ace's story, Anarchious looks at the sun through a dirty window and daydreams of the human soldiers coming to his village when he was younger. He envisions his kid-self at a playground alone. It was a beautiful day, the sun was out, it was warm, and the wind was brisk. The season had just changed to spring. He remembers it vividly—the newly blossomed flowers, the stunning colors.

Anarchious snuck away from his mother, who was in a conversation with someone nearby. His mother called for him. He heard her voice and back, but before he could turn the corner to where she was, he realized he had left his red-twist candy behind. He then heard his mother call out to him once more. He needed to hurry, and in a crackling flash, he was back on the playground near his candy. He walked over to it and looked up. A human soldier was hovering over him. The look on the soldier's face was frightening; he pulled out his knife from his sheath and quickly grabbed young Anarchious.

"So what about you?" Ace asks, waking Anarchious from his daydream.

"What was that?" Anarchious replies while trying to wipe the stress from his face.

"I've told you a little about myself, so tell me something about you, man," Ace responds.

"What do you want to know?" Anarchious replies.

Ace immediately asks, "What are you?"

Anarchious looks at Ace with a confused expression while raising his right eyebrow.

"I mean, I know you're definitely not a Lycan or a Vampyr," says Ace. "A Broom Hopper wouldn't have helped me, and humans don't jump off six-story buildings and survive."

Anarchious reclines with his hands behind his head, staring at the old, unkempt ceiling of the factory. "Honestly, I don't know what I am," he explains. "Marie always said we were Mutants."

"What do you mean 'we'?" Ace inquires.

"People like me. 'We' were once called Mutants," Anarchious replies as if he made a mistake. He didn't, but he was thinking of his family.

The Lycan, confused because he's never heard of such people, pushes further. "Were? What are you referred to as now?"

"Extinct," Anarchious replies, glaring at Ace, ending the inquiry.

The two camp there all day, taking turns napping, getting rest as they await dusk to fall. As the sun sets and shadows begin to grow, Anarchious wakes Ace as the Vampyr city is awakening from its twelve-hour slumber.

Ace and Anarchious are watching the building across the street like hawks, hoping for Blaine to emerge, when suddenly a tiny mass of Vampyr grunts rolls up to the building on old-style motorcycles. They park in front of the building, aggressively creating a large half-circle barricade.

"Who the hell are they?!" Anarchious says to Ace, trying to keep his voice down.

"New recruits," Ace responds.

"Yes, I see that, but why so many?" Anarchious asks.

Ace, big-eyed, is worried about the situation. "I don't know. They gather like this only when they decide to pull humans or to defend someone." Ace watches the biking grunts closely. "Look!" he exclaims.

Anarchious looks out the dusty windows and sees two of the grunts dragging another one into the building. "He's your 'you ruined the tunes' guy," Ace proclaims, mocking the Vampyr grunt from the night before. After a few more minutes of waiting, they hear someone yelling from the other building.

"What's that?" Anarchious asks Ace as he begins to listen closely.

"It sounds like someone is pissed the hell off," Ace says, still listening. Then, in a surprised motion, Ace cocks his head back and yells, "Blaine!"

Anarchious reacts, saying, "What's hap...?" But before Anarchious can finish his sentence, they both hear glass crashing from the building where the frightening screaming took place.

Something or someone is falling from the building windows. There are two beings, one seemingly strangling the other, and in midfall, one of them bursts into flames and disintegrates into ash. The other being lands on his feet victoriously. He is a tall, pale man wearing a Blood Pack leather jacket. He has green spiked hair and is dressed head to toe like a punk.

The green-haired Vampyr yells furiously and spits on the ashes, sneering, "Good riddance! Bloody snitch!"

"Blaine!" Ace exclaims.

"Hell, that was so weak. I'm going to kick his ass worse now," Anarchious says while laughing and cracking his neck and knuckles. "Shoot, there are a lot of them, though. You got my back?" Anarchious asks while he continues to limber up. Ace looks at Anarchious with reluctance. "What, man?" Anarchious asks while smiling. "Hope you're not scared of these guys because of what happened a few days ago. C'mon, we'll get a little revenge."

"That's not it!" Ace responds as if he is ashamed and looks away, seemingly distressed.

Anarchious stops stretching and gives Ace a serious look. "What's up?" he asks the Lycan.

"I can't fight," the Lycan replies to the eager Mutant.

Anarchious continues to glare at the Lycan. He then cracks a smile and begins to laugh. "It's not that hard for you, I assume. Punch, kick, bite, and repeat as many times as needed. Maybe add some claws," the Mutant states to the Lycan.

"No, not that! I can fight if I choose to—duh—but I refuse to be a mindless brute!" Ace responds, balling his fist and turning his back on Anarchious and walking towards a back exit.

While Ace walks away, Anarchious's mood falls, and he becomes serious again. "Fighting for something isn't wrong, you know." Anarchious begins to explain. "I'm not a very violent person at all, and I don't like to fight. Sure, it's fun, but purposely taking joy in hurting a living being isn't fun." Ace refuses to turn around. "Look," continues Anarchious, "sometimes you have to fight when you don't want to, and other times you shouldn't fight when you want to." The discouraged Lycan is still heading towards the exit. "I am going down there with or without you!" Anarchious exclaims, but it falls on deaf ears as Ace exits the room, leaving Anarchious to fend for himself.

Meanwhile, below, Blaine is commanding and rallying his gang. He calls his underboss over and whispers to him, "Go tell Zera we've got everything under control." The underboss nods yes, hops on his motorcycle, and rides off towards the busy part of the city.

"You will spread out in this city and find this renegade! Once you find him, do not engage him. Report to me, and we all will get a piece of him!" Blaine yells to his disciples. They all begin to cheer and clap.

Suddenly, a big crash echoes from above them. A man rapidly descends and lands on his feet in the middle of the gang's circle across from Blaine. It's Anarchious. With a fierce look that could kill, he glares at the leader. Blaine steps back, afraid, then steps forward and readies himself in an aggressive fighting stance, trying to hide his initial reaction as the rest of his gang watches.

"I'm right here. No need to look for me," Anarchious snarls to Blaine in a very dark tone of voice. "We can avoid all of this. All you have to do is tell me where my aunt is, and we'll forget all about this." Blaine rolls his eyes, smirking back at Anarchious. "Oh, so you want your ass kicked! OK! I can arrange for that!" Anarchious says as he becomes annoyed at the Vampyr gang leader's cocky gestures.

Blaine laughs and holds out his right arm, displaying the stump where Anarchious had cut off his hand a few days earlier. The gesture signals, Bring it on! Anarchious doesn't pay attention to the cockiness or the fact that Blaine's hand has grown back so fast, but he does notice the long, silky black scarf Blaine has wrapped around it. It looks familiar; Anarchious recognizes the weird circular symbols stitched in it.

"That's Marie's scarf!" Anarchious points out, becoming enraged.

"And what are you going to do about it?" Blaine replies, grinning. "You're surrounded! You walked right into your own execution party. Blood Pack! Kill him!" Blaine yells, ordering his gang to do away with the surrounded Mutant.

Anarchious, not backing down, shoots forward and knocks down Blaine with one punch to the nose. The rest of the Vampyr gang attacks the Mutant left and right. He defends himself, punching, smacking, and kicking the swarming Vampyrs one by one. Blaine gets up and tries to make a run for it.

"Come back here, coward!" Anarchious yells as he sees Blaine trying to get away. Anarchious viciously knees an attacking Vampyr in the gut, bringing him to his hands and knees. The young man then quickly jumps off that Vampyr's back into the air and lands on Blaine's, forcing him to the ground. He turns Blaine around and grabs him by his leather collar. "Where is she, you fucking parasite?" Anarchious yells to Blaine in his face.

Blaine glares back and tries to choke Anarchious as the rest of the gang members try to pull the Mutant off their leader. They continue to try to pry Anarchious's death grip off their superior. As Anarchious becomes more enraged, his body begins to surge with electricity.

"Where the hell is she?!" Anarchious yells, infuriated. He releases his electricity, shocking the group of Vampyr tugging at him and Blaine, sending everyone flying back, striking other Vampyr and motorcycles, destroying and knocking them down.

Blaine passes out, and Anarchious lets out a long mighty roar as he is surrounded by the remaining Vampyr. There are too many of them, and Anarchious realizes he used a vast amount of energy by shocking the gang members. He stands up, readies himself, and, breathing heavily, fearlessly yells, "Bring it, suckheads!"

The Vampyr begin to attack the lone Mutant once more. The Mutant finds himself with enough energy to defend himself only by dodging, but it's no good. Eventually he is in the clutches of the Vampyr grunts. They jump and beat him, punch, kick, and stomp him repeatedly. Anarchious tries to fight back and shock a few, but he has worn himself out, and they only kept coming. The Vampyr pin him down to the ground as he struggles. One of the Vampyr pulls a machete from his leather coat and hovers over Anarchious with a disturbing look on his face. It's the man the Mutant had shocked unconscious the night before.

"So I bet you thought what you did last night was funny, huh?" the Vampyr, still twitching, yells at Anarchious.

Anarchious pauses and glares at the Vampyr as if he's crazy. Anarchious regurgitates blood, spits it beside of him, and then breaks out in a frenzy of laughter while the Vampyr look on, amazed at the Mutant's arrogance.

"Son of a bitch! Hold him down!" the Vampyr furiously screams at the fallen Mutant as he raises the machete above his head, ready to hack at Anarchious's limbs.

Anarchious feels numb. Most of his senses are shutting down, but he's still anticipating the pain, so he looks away, closing his eyes, able to smell only the leaking gasoline from the wrecked motorcycles.

Just then, an immense roar echoes from above. Everyone freezes and directs his attention to it. An ominous figure is rapidly descending from the sky towards them. The frightened gang grunts release the weakened Anarchious and retreat from his trampled body as the figure lands at their victim's head.

The Mutant, realizing that he has been released and that the grunts have stopped their assault, opens his eyes, lifts his head slightly off the gasoline-covered ground, and looks towards the deep violet sky. He sees someone standing over him. Anarchious, realizing who it is, relaxes his head back onto the ground and says aloud, "So cliché!"

It is the Lycan, Ace, and like a bloodthirsty predator, he begins to circle Anarchious's body, creating a perimeter around it while glaring at the Vampyr grunts. A bold grunt aggressively steps forward, testing the Lycan. Immediately, Ace lets out a violent snarl, and the Vampyr makes a hasty retreat back into the crowd.

"Leave now and there won't be any more bloodshed!" the Lycan shouts to the Blood Pack members.

"Ha! Empty threats! You're surrounded, teacup!" a random Vampyr grunt insults the tiny Lycan, who is still bigger than all of these Vampyr by a long shot.

Ace continues to defend the defeated Mutant. "Believe me, you do not want this! If you continue this attack, you will be exterminated like the rats you are!" Ace shouts while breaking into an aggressive four-point fighting stance.

"You and what army?" another Vampyr shouts back.

"This one!" the beaten Anarchious says as he begins to get up from the ground, taking his sweet time.

The Vampyr laugh at the stumbling Mutant as he loses his balance and collapses onto the Lycan's back. Anarchious then whispers to Ace, "Take cover!"

The Lycan's eyes grow wide, and he quickly grabs the Mutant as Anarchious shoots the ground with a lightning bolt. A spark travels from the ricochet and lands in a stream of spilled gas from the broken motorcycles. Ace also swiftly grabs Blaine as the spark sets the stream aflame and travels from bike to broken bike, igniting them in a domino effect. As all of the Vampyr scramble to get away from the explosions, Ace escapes, carrying Anarchious over one shoulder and Blaine over the other.

Ace carries them a mile away, deeper into the abandoned industrial side of Drake City. The tiny but strong Lycan brings them to an abandoned junkyard. Ace tosses the passed-out Blaine like a sack of potatoes onto the hood of an old broken-down truck and places the weary Anarchious on his feet. Anarchious stands up, just barely recovered from his exhaustion. He looks over at Blaine's lifeless body on the hood of the truck and quickly stumbles over, legs shaking. He then grasps his jacket collar and slaps Blaine in the face repeatedly until Blaine regains consciousness.

"I am going to ask this only once! Where is Marie?!" he yells while shaking the woozy Vampyr. Blaine slowly regains consciousness and looks up at him bleary-eyed. "Where is she, Blaine?!" Anarchious shouts.

"Who?" Blaine responds to the infuriated Mutant. Anarchious screams at the Vampyr, who is chuckling at the young Mutant's threats. "Do not mess with me. I promise you, I'll have the last fucking laugh!" Anarchious says slapping the Vampyr across the face, and Blaine retaliates by spitting in the Mutant's bruised face.

Enraged, the Mutant grabs the Vampyr by the throat and begins to strangle him. "Son of a bitch, you will tell me where she is!" the infuriated Mutant grumbles to the Vampyr as he tries to choke the life out of him.

Ace hurries over and attempts to break the Vampyr free of Anarchious's death grip. "Anarch, if you kill him, you won't be able to find Marie!" Ace tries to explain to Anarchious as he grabs him, but the Vampyr seems to be losing consciousness.

Blaine begins to black out while Ace tries to pry Blaine from Anarchious's iron grip. The Lycan, pulling on Anarchious, feels the hair on the back of his wolf-mane stand up and energy run through his body. The energy quickly increases and begins to shock him, so he releases Anarchious. The intrigued Lycan stares at Anarchious strangling the Vampyr. His wounds seem to be healing gradually, his eyes are radiating a violent violet hue, and he looks lost in his rage. Ace is mesmerized by what he is witnessing but quickly snaps out of it, remembering what could happen.

"Anarchious! You're going to kill him!" the Lycan roars in a mighty voice. Anarchious doesn't respond. "If you break his neck, you'll never find your family!" Ace tries to use the enraged Mutant's emotional tie to convince him to let go, but it seems as though it has made things worse. Anarchious clutches harder and begins to break Blaine's neck. Hearing the slow pops and cracks of the Vampyr's neck, Ace has to think quickly.

Ace grabs the earth-colored hair on his own head and screams in frustration, "You'll never save her! Never! You have failed Marie!" Anarchious immediately releases the near-dead Vampyr and slowly turns towards Ace. As Anarchious focuses his attention on his associate, Blaine slides down the hood of the truck and onto the dusty junk-covered ground, coughing and gasping for air. Anarchious, with glowing eyes, slowly but aggressively makes his way towards the Lycan. Although he is scared, Ace holds his ground and readies himself.

Anarchious seems to be rejuvenated and to have some of his energy back. Ace has no idea what to do; he just does the first thing that comes to mind as soon as the blacked-out Mutant is close enough. Ace grabs his shoulders, and Anarchious's hands slowly rise towards the Lycan's neck. Ace looks down at the Mutant and utters, "Killing me won't find her!" Anarchious continues to move his hands towards the Lycan's neck but appears to be fighting himself. Ace sees this and continues to try to persuade him. "If we just interrogate him, he will give up what he knows!"

The Mutant grabs the Lycan's throat; however, he still continues to be internaly conflicted, Anarchious's eyes begin to become more normal, but he is still gone. "We will find her together. I just need you to pull through whatever this is!" Ace explains to the Mutant as he continues struggling in and out of consciousness, though continuing to choke Ace. The Lycan digs his nails into Anarchious's shoulders, fearing he will suffer the same fate as Blaine.

"Fight it for Marie!" Ace shouts at the top of his lungs. At that moment, Anarchious snaps out of his episode. He screams at the top of his lungs and drops to his knees, releasing Ace, shaking, not knowing what has come over him. The Lycan bends down in relief and puts his hand on Anarchious's shoulder to comfort him.

Blaine realizes his situation. Panicked, he tries his damndest to crawl off quietly but gives himself away tripping on some debris. He jumps up quickly and tries to hobble away but is quickly confronted by a recovered, more irate Anarchious.

"How'd you get...right there? You were over there; now you're..." Blaine babbles in confusion as the Mutant interrupts him.

"Shut the hell up! You will tell me where Marie is!" Anarchious demands while grabbing the Vampyr's right arm on which the scarf is wrapped. The Vampyr attempts to rip away from him, but the tenacious Mutant trips Blaine up while ripping the scarf from his arm. Anarchious stands over the defeated Blaine dominantly as the Vampyr looks up at him, fearful but stern.

"Where the hell did you get this?!" Anarchious yells at Blaine.

"Do I look like a snitch to you? I'm not telling you shit!" Blaine responds, still holding out on information while trying to crawl away from him. Anarchious advances towards the downed Vampyr. His body begins to surge, with little sparks of electricity pulsing through his clenched fist.

"Anarchious, let him go!" Ace yells from behind the two.

The irate Mutant looks back with a familiar look in his eye and replies, "Not until he tells me where she is!"

"Hello? Are you deaf? I just told you I'm not telling you shit!" the Vampyr says, egging on the Mutant.

"Well, is that so?" Anarchious responds sarcastically. The pissed-off Mutant towers over Blaine. "Well then, I am going to sever each and every limb, slowly, until you do," Anarchious threatens the Vampyr.

Blaine laughs for a moment and then glares at the young man threatening him. "You really think I am scared…of you?! Ha! There are things out there worse than you, more frightening. Let me say quite frankly, you ain't shit!" Blaine replies with a smile on his face.

Hearing this sets the Mutant off. He is ready to kill Blaine, but before he can get a hold of him, Ace bear-hugs the out-of-control Mutant and lifts him off his feet. Blaine sees this and makes his getaway.

A surprised Anarchious watches the Vampyr get away and yells to Ace, "What are you doing?! Let me go! Don't let him get away!"

"Calm down! We don't need him anymore," Ace responds to a struggling Anarchious.

"What the hell do you mean we don't need him?!" the irritated Mutant exclaims.

"Just trust me!" Ace says, struggling to keep his grasp on the aggressive Mutant.

"We don't have shit without him!" Anarchious yells at the top of his lungs.

"We have the scarf!" Ace responds quickly as Anarchious continues to try to break free from the bear hug.

"It's a fucking scarf! It's useless!" the feisty Mutant responds, trying to wiggle his way free.

"I can find her just using that! Just stop flailing and trust me!" Ace replies as Anarchious ceases trying to break free and looks over his shoulder at the Lycan.

The Lycan releases Anarchious and snatches the scarf from him. Ace glares at Anarchious as the Mutant fixes and straightens his attire.

"How much do you know about Lycans?" Ace asks Anarchious while probing his nose into the torn, tattered scarf, smelling it deeply.

"Stop yapping and get to the point, Ace!" Anarchious says to the Lycan, eager and ready to find Marie.

“Did you forget what I told you, or are you just plain stupid? I can track anyone down from miles and miles away using my hyper sense of smell. However, I have to have come in contact with them or something they possessed,” the Lycan explains to the young Mutant.

Anarchious thinks for a moment and grimaces at Ace, then proceeds to speak in a mocking voice, “So you’re telling me you can find her by smelling that piece of cloth!”

Ace replies by grunting, “Yeah,” and continues to smell the scarf deeply.

Anarchious turns in the direction Blaine disappeared and begins to walk in that direction. “No, we need to go find—” And before Anarchious can finish, Ace bolts off in a different direction.

The Mutant turns to watch Ace dart off on all fours towards the busy part of the city. “Not again! Where the hell are you going?!” A confused Anarchious hollers to Ace but receives no response. Soon, Ace disappears around a corner, and the Mutant is all alone. He looks in the direction of junk-filled yard where Blaine disappeared and then looks off into the distance of the bright city of Drake.

Anarchious thinks to himself for a split second. “Damn it!” he mutters out of frustration.

3
Queen Zera

The Lycan hits a dead end on the trail somewhere in the northern part of the city at an old castle under construction with a giant stairway leading up to it. It looks out of place next to the high-rises and skyscrapers. The place makes the hair on the back of Ace's mane stand straight up. It is dark and evil. Marie's smell is masked by the overwhelming odor of blood and death, but he's sure she is somewhere in there. The Lycan thinks to himself for a moment, gawking at the creepy medieval residence.

"Aw, man! This is going to be trouble!" Ace says to himself, stepping back away from the steps. Just then he feels someone grab his shoulder. He quickly turns around, startled. It's Anarchious, tired and weary from following Ace through the entire city.

Breathing heavily, the Mutant signals time out to the Lycan. Anarchious seems almost to have had a heart attack. "Man…you run too fast," he says, still gasping for air.

"I am a Lycan," Ace responds, looking at the Mutant wheezing for air.

"Ima Lycan, Ima Lycan, Ima Ly—shut up! Do me a favor and don't mention that again!" Anarchious mocks the Lycan as he stands up straight, throwing his head back and taking a deep breath. The Lycan turns and looks back at the castle bathing in moonlight yet radiating evil.

"Man, you stirred up all the natives. That was a bad Idea! Running through the main streets like that..." Anarchious begins to try to warn the Lycan but realizes he isn't paying any attention. "Hey, Ace? What are you looking at?" he says to the Lycan as he focuses his sights on the dark castle. "The hell is that?" he asks a confounded Ace.

"I think its Queen Zera's den," Ace mutters to the Mutant, who is now gazing at the castle as well.

"And?" Anarchious mutters back. "And...Marie is here," Ace replies.

"All right, then, let's go get her!" Anarchious says, advancing towards the steps.

Ace grabs his arm, looks the Mutant in the eyes, and says, "Are you naive or just plain stupid? Oh yeah, a gang of Vampyr will just let you waltz into their castle and take their food!"

"I know. That's why you're coming with me...unless you're going to chicken out on me again!" Anarchious replies in a stern tone.

"No, even with me, storming in there would be idiotic. We need a plan!" Ace retorts, aggressively leaning towards Anarchious and tightening his grip on Anarchious'arm.

"The plan is take them by surprise. Let's go!" the Mutant says, ripping his arm away from the Lycan. He continues to walk up the steps.

"They will kill you. You're making a mistake!" Ace says to Anarchious as he continues to walk up the stairs.

"Well, you do it your way, and I'll do it mine," Anarchious replies, continuing to hike up the steps. Ace begins to yell at the eager Anarchious, but before he can finish, the Mutant bolts towards the castle doors. The Lycan looks around and sees no life forms anywhere on the hill or in the castle. Still, all he can smell is blood and death, so he decides instead to use stealth instead of force to search for Marie.

Meanwhile, Anarchious has just forced his way into the castle. It is dark and damp. The altitude has made the air cold. There is no welcoming committee or any sign of life, just a giant hall. It is filled with many medieval decorations, but they all seem to be extremely damaged. The Mutant begins to walk through, carefully gazing upon the artwork of hundreds of years past. The hall is extremely interesting but has been clearly battle scarred. At the end of it is a stairway. He walks slowly through this hall, passing many moonlit doors and observing the uncanny scenery.

Anarchious hears a sound. It is unfamiliar, so he follows it quietly up to a room connected to the end of the hall. He peeks around the corner, curious as to what he might see, and witnesses a Vampyr sucking his victim dry. The occupied Vampyr notices Anarchious but continues to feed on the young female's blood. The sight of the carnage sends the young Mutant into a panic. He almost goes crazy at the thought of this happening to Marie, so he bolts up the nearest steps. They are circular and seem endless, but eventually he reaches the top floor.

Anarchious comes to a giant old door. He slowly creeps towards the door, and as he approaches, he realizes the door is cracked open. He peeks in but sees nothing but darkness. He slowly enters the room and quickly feels nervous about the situation. The room is mostly in shadows, but the center is immersed in moonlight. The moon shines through a gaping hole in the destroyed roof of the castle. He begins to get a familiar feeling in his stomach when he and catches a glimpse of a pair of shining eyes across the room. They seem harmless as they shine, resembling the full moon.

Anarchious remains speechless. He doesn't know what to say. The eyes glare back, and, as they approach, the Mutant sees a silhouette of a short and slender womanly figure. The footsteps of this ominous female figure echo through the room. Just shy of stepping into the moonlight, she stops. All Anarchious can see is her lean, pale legs.

"Wasn't expecting you!" The woman's voice echoes as if she knows the lone Mutant. Anarchious steps forward to try to get a better look at the woman. "This can't be about the arrangement. I held up my side of the bargain no matter how crappy the information was!"

Anarchious, confused, stops just shy of the moonlight and stares at the eyes gazing at him. The feeling in his stomach begins to become stronger.

"Well? Are you going to explain yourself, Abel?" asks the woman.

Hearing a familiar name, Anarchious rushes forward and responds to the woman. "Abel? What do you know about him?" The pair of eyes and the womanly figure fade back into the darkness of the room. The lone Mutant stands in the moonlight looking around. Anarchious begins to become frustrated and unsettled. He yells at the top of his lungs, "Hey! What do you know about my brother?!"

The clones continue to dance and giggle as the voices taunt Anarchious. He slips into another rage. His eyes glow again with that same violent purple light and his body surges with energy as he valiantly rebukes the voices. The clones of the mysterious woman continue to laugh and giggle while prancing around him. Anarchious becomes annoyed. He swings at the first giggly woman near him. This time he actually lands a punch to the gut of a clone, who drops to her knees, laughing, and vanishes.

"One of you has to be real! That means...that's your ass!" Anarchious exclaims as he launches an all-out assault on the mysterious woman and her clones. The furious Mutant batters and destroys every one of the clones until the last one. The woman laughs aloud and cynically as he slips behind her and grabs her. "Found you! Where is Marie? And what do you know about Abel?" The woman looks back at him and continues to laugh. Anarchious lets his anger get the best of him once again, and he bear-hugs her body until he hears her bones beginning break. She drops to her knees and falls flat on her face.

The body lies there lifeless as Anarchious calms down. His eyes return to normal, and he ceases to radiate lightning sparks. Realizing what he has done, he inspects the body. He kneels down and reaches for her hair, but as soon as he comes within an inch of touching the body, it vanishes with a poof into thin air.

Anarchious stands up, startled, and surveys the room once more, looking over his shoulders, worried and wondering what is going on. Then he hears the woman's laughter, which unsettles him once more. In an instant, the many clones reappear taunting and frolicking around him. Realizing what is going on, he yells, "Stop fucking toying with me!" With every bit of energy he has left, Anarchious scatter-shoots every one of the clones with lighting from his fingers.

Anarchious charges all his remaining energy into one shot and blasts the last woman in the head at point-blank range. The woman's head explodes as the lighting crashes through the stone walls, creating another gaping hole in the side of the castle.

Astounded but dead tired, the lone Mutant wipes the blood off his face and looks at his hands. "Shit, I've got to get it together!" he says to himself. He turns to the Lycan, who is still seemingly bleeding out, and staggers over to him, but before he can take more than one step, he hears the woman's laughter once again. "Ah, shit!" the Mutant mutters to himself, dropping his head in disappointment.

The woman swoops down, appearing out of thin air and knocking Anarchious flat on his back. She stands over him and looks down on him with a curious look on her face. She then straddles the helpless Mutant, sits on his lower abdomen, and stares at him closely. She grabs his jaw and rotates his head from side to side as if inspecting him. Anarchious can't move but is itching to choke the woman.

"You look just like him!" she says to the pinned Mutant.

"Abel? Tell me what you know about him, or I'll kill you where you stand!" Anarchious shouts to the woman as she gazes down on him seductively.

"You mean where I sit!" the woman retorts, throwing her head back and laughing for a brief second. Anarchious struggles to move his limbs, but he feels paralyzed. "What grounds do you have threatening...me? Queen Zera?" She looks down and explains to the pinned Mutant, "I could feed on the both of you, drink every last drop of your blood, or I can let my minions, the Blood Pack, get revenge and torture you till you're on the brink of death. But I digress. I am full right now, and I could use someone with your determination around here." She continues to babble at the Mutant as he keeps his eyes locked on her. She leans over and comes face to face with him. "I have a deal for you, young Mutant!" she says, grazing Anarchious's nose flirtatiously against hers.

She then stands up and begins to cat-walk back into the shadows. "Rise," she says nonchalantly, and in an instant, Anarchious is back on his feet but still unable to move. She walks into the shadows and sits down on what seems to be a throne. "Come," she utters, and Anarchious is propelled over to her. He looks into her striking moon-colored eyes and feels nothing but evil.

"The way I see it," Zera says to the captive Mutant, "you have two choices. The first is to die, of course, and we both know we don't want that, cutie. The second is clearly the better of the two. You do me a huge favor, and I do something for you."

Anarchious glares back at her into her eyes and responds, "What's the catch?"

"Catch? No catch! It's life or death! It's your choice!" she answers the Mutant hovering in front of her.

"Why should I trust you?" Anarchious yells at the Vampyr dominatrix.

Queen Zera laughs aloud at the petrified Mutant's question. "What is it you choose?" she asks, her smile with her pearly white teeth and wicked fangs shining in the shadows.

Anarchious, frustrated, looks away from Zera and her evil smile. He doesn't trust her and knows something is up, but he has no choice. "I'll take the second choice," he replies, still looking away from the Vampyr queen.

"Great choice!" Zera replies immediately, as if she is glad about Anarchious's choice. She waves her hand in the darkness, and Anarchious regains control over his body.

He stands for a moment and then collapses on his face at her feet. The Mutant is exhausted from his futile assault on her. He tries to recover and work his way to his elbows and knees, but he is too weak. He continues to struggle to a better position when Zera begins to speak again.

"OK, the deal is you deliver a message for me to the top of White Lion Mountain within seventy-two hours during the harvest moon, and if you even make it on time, I spare Marie's life and give you information about Abel."

The Mutant hears her but is entirely too tired to respond, so he nods. Anarchious, determined, forces himself to his feet quickly and turns towards Ace's beaten body. He takes one step and passes out, falling flat on his face again.

Eight hours later, Anarchious awakens in the forest outside of Drake City's walls near his old campsite. He looks up and sees the morning sky breaking through the trees. He sits up and places his hand on his head. He still has a headache from the night before. The Mutant tries to recall what happened, and as it begins to come back to him, he hears some moaning amongst the chirping of the morning sparrows.

He investigates his surroundings and spots Ace's body. The Lycan is in his human form facedown in the grass. Anarchious gets up and runs over to his body. Ace's body is healing but is still in bad shape with bruised ribs, stab wounds, bite marks, and claw wounds.

"Ace? You awake, man?" Anarchious asks as the Lycan lets out an even louder groan. The curious Mutant picks up a stick and pokes the Lycan on one of his butt cheeks. The Lycan signals to stop with his hand, shooing the stick away. Anarchious drops the stick, grabs the Lycan's tail, and tugs on it. "Get up!" Anarchious says to Ace as the Lycan turns around, looking up at Anarchious.

Ace flips over, sits up, and yawns. Anarchious bends down and looks at the wounds close to Ace's heart. "You OK?" Anarchious asks the Lycan as he dusts off his dirty face.

"Oh, I am great! Freaking ecstatic!" replies the Lycan sarcastically as he looks the young Mutant in the eye.

Anarchious stands up and looks down at the Lycan. "Good. Well, I'm off to White Lion Mountain. Take care!" Anarchious says after turning away and walking towards the forest exit.

"What? Wh...wha...what?" the Lycan stutters, speechless at Anarchious's unflattering farewell. The Mutant continues on his path, raising his arm up and signaling peace and goodbye to an astonished Ace. The Lycan then runs and follows the trekking Mutant.

"Wait! Where are you going?" Ace asks the Mutant.

"Just told you. White Lion Mountain," Anarchious responds, continuing his exit through the forest, not even making eye contact with Ace.

"But why?" Ace asks as they step out of the forest onto hilly plains.

"I have something to do!" Anarchious responds while striding up the first hill.

"Can't I please go with you?" Ace asks while jumping in front of the Mutant, trying to get his attention.

"No," he replies while continuing up the hill.

Ace, astounded, stops and says, "I thought we had a little agreement!"

"We did. For wasting my time in the first place, you helped me by finding Marie in return. Since you did that, you've upheld your part of the deal and don't need to hang around me anymore," Anarchious replies as he continues to stride up the hill.

"Well, the least you can do is let me hang with you until these wounds heal, seeing it's your fault I got them!" Ace exclaims.

Anarchious stops in his tracks and looks Ace dead in the eye. "You decided not to follow me and tried to sneak around people who can see in the dark – and vicious Vampyrs who were expecting us at that. Your fault you got the shit kicked out of you," Anarchious explains to Ace, who glares back at Anarchious.

"How the hell was I supposed to know they can see in the dark?" Ace retorts.

"I don't know. Because you're a Lycan," Anarchious grunts, mocking Ace as he turns away and continues his path up the steep hill.

"What?" the Lycan says as he continues to trail the Mutant.

Anarchious finally gets to the top of the hill. From there they both can see White Lion Mountain in the far distance. "Besides you're too much of a liability." Anarchious continues staring at the mountain shining in the morning sun.

"What?" Ace says to Anarchious, surprised.

"You left me hanging. Twice," the Mutant says, glaring at the Lycan.

"No, I didn't!" the Lycan yells back.

"Yeah, you did!" he replies. "When I needed you to help me the most, you bailed and I got my ass whooped! Then you didn't trust my decision and decided run off, and then we both got our asses whooped." Anarchious resumes his walk down the hill in the direction of the mountain.

"Well, I'll just follow you," Ace says as he follows the Mutant down the hill.

Anarchious turns and gets in the Lycan's face. "Go home!" he yells at the Lycan.

"Yoo-hoo, teenage Lycan with no pack, aka I have no way home! You don't listen very well, do you?!" Ace responds, holding his ground firmly against the Mutant.

The Mutant's eyes fall as he turns around, shaking his head in disappointment, and continues his path towards the mountain. Anarchious walks away as Ace stands by watching, depressed by this desertion. The lone Mutant walks about a hundred yards away, finally stops, and turns back to the saddened Lycan. "You coming or what?"

The Lycan races down the hill and is back in his friend's company in less than five seconds. Anarchious doesn't say another word, continuing his path towards White Lion Mountain as Ace follows.

4
Trail Trials

"OK? So you have about three days to get to the top of the highest mountain on this continent?" Ace asks Anarchious as the two continue to march towards the mountains by way of the golden hills.

"Yeah," the Mutant answers nonchalantly with his eyes on the dirt road surrounded by gold-colored grass.

"Funny, I lose some foot speed and strength when harvest moon ends," the Lycan says to Anarchious, really just babbling as both continue the path.

The two have already been walking for half a day and are still wondering if they can make the deadline. They know walking to the mountain isn't that hard. The hard part will be the hike up the mountain. Suddenly, Ace stops in his tracks and looks at the Mutant, who still seems to be bent on making forward progress.

"Didn't you say you're supposed to be delivering a message?" the curious Lycan asks as Anarchious stops and cringes at hearing the question.

"Shit!" he yells as he looks back towards Drake City, which he can't even see in the distance anymore. Anarchious paces back and forth, trying to think of what to do as Ace watches. "I'm going back," Anarchious says to Ace as he began to take off.

But before the Mutant can start running, Ace stops him and says, "Quick, check your pockets first."

The Mutant stops and feels around in all his pockets, even his vest pocket. He feels nothing until he checks his underwear. "Wait, whoa! What's this?"

It's a white envelope addressed to "Luna" with a smeared lipstick kiss on the back. It's kind of damp and damaged from his sweat but seems to still be in OK condition. "Must have slipped it in after I passed out. Good looking out, Ace."

"No problem, Anarch," Ace replies to the relieved Mutant.

"Anarch?" retorts the Mutant in a surprised tone of voice.

"Yes, figured its way easier to cut your name in half," the Lycan replies, looking at Anarchious. "What idiot is always going to say your entire first name all the time? That's like four syllables. Not me!" He begins to walk back towards the mountain.

Anarchious doesn't reply. He just tucks away the letter in the front of his pants and follows behind the Lycan. He thinks to himself, That name, Anarch. He pictures his mother's beautiful smile and gleaming gray eyes; she called him that. Abel refers to him as that when he is mad at him. "Anarch!" He hears his brother's many angry screams, and they make him happy for a moment. A little grin appears on Anarchious's face as both men continue on their path to the mountain. The Lycan sees this and figures it is the perfect time to spark a conversation.

"So how old are you?" Ace asks the obliviously grinning Mutant. Anarchious doesn't answer and instead continues to stay in his own world. Ace glares back at him and yells, "Anarch!" At that moment, Anarchious snaps out of his daydream and looks at the Lycan, puzzled. "Asked how old you are, man!" Ace says to Anarchious, smiling.

The Mutant throws his hands behind his head to gaze at the sky and begins to speed walk past the Lycan, seemingly ignoring him. "Eighteen," Anarchious sighs.

"Cool! We are the same age," Ace exclaims enthusiastically, but it doesn't seem to draw more conversation.

The Lycan is determined to talk to Anarchious, whom he still finds extremely mysterious. He knows nothing about this kid except how determined he is and how scary he can get when things aren't going his way. He has to think quickly before the door closes to actual conversation again, so he just asks the first thing that comes to mind. "Why are your people nearly extinct?" the Lycan blurts out to Anarchious.

"Heh," Anarchious answers nonchalantly, shrugging his shoulders and continuing to walk faster.

Ace is dumbfounded and quickly becomes irate towards Anarchious's attitude. "What's wrong with you? You must be bipolar!" he yells at the Mutant, trying to catch up with him again.

Anarchious stops, turns, and looks Ace in the face. "Look, this isn't some damn walk in the park! I'm not out here for my own leisure and casual conversation. If you don't like it, you can go back," Anarchious says to Ace, making it clear he is still focused on his task and is not out to make friends.

"You're a dick with serious anger issues!" Ace retorts with a huge smile on his face.

"And you are extremely annoying!" Anarchious replies, quickly standing face to face with an irritated Ace staring back.

The two have a staredown for a moment. Then Ace breaks into a huge laugh and begins to walk towards the mountains. The Mutant watches, baffled by this behavior, as Ace continues down the road.

The duo continue their journey to White Lion Mountain, quickly passing through several tiny towns in a day's time. The duo don't stop to eat or rest at all until they reach the last town at the foot of the mountains that evening. The tiny town called Small Brook is hidden in the thick of the forest at the foot of a mountain that seems to be hugging the heavens. Most of the mountain seems to be hidden by a thin white haze, but you can see the shadow of the peak beyond it.

"This is gonna suck!" Anarchious exclaims to himself while gazing at the snow-laden mountain along with his companion. "Oh well, let's get to it," the fearless Mutant says to himself as he sets out towards the trail separating the town and the mountain.

"Wait!" Ace yells to the Mutant. Anarchious stops and looks back at Ace as the Lycan explains the sudden outburst. "We should definitely get something to eat in that town to prepare ourselves for the hike, Anarch."

"You're right, but I don't know what type of town this is or if they will accept your kind in there…or mine, for that matter," Anarchious replies.

"Well, check that out," Ace says as he points to a tiny symbol on the sign next to the name of the town. The symbol is an eight-pointed star and has a gemlike shape in the middle. Anarchious looks closely at the tiny symbol, confused, then looks back at Ace. "This is a town protected by this weird religious group. They are everybody friendly," Ace explains to the ignorant Mutant.

"'Everybody friendly'?" Anarchious asks.

"Yeah, they are a peaceful organization that feeds the hungry all over Terra Belle, the world, and I know this because, for the most part, they've fed me these last five years," Ace answers as he begins to walk towards the town's gates. Anarchious follows.

The two step into the town and immediately notice that it is lifeless. The buildings are old and run down, the streets have been destroyed, and the atmosphere is depressing. The two don't see a single sign of life until they walk to the farthest side of town, where they find an old barbershop. The barbershop looks as if it's in better shape than the rest of the town. The place has working lights, and the barbershop sign bears the symbol of the "weird religious group" Ace has just mentioned. They walk up to the door intending to knock, but before they can, they are greeted by an older gentleman who seems to be just human.

"Good evening!" the old man greets the duo, who are still kind of shocked the guy answered without a knock. Anarchious and Ace look at each other without saying a word for a moment. "Come on in, boys. My name is Jeb, but you guys can call me Jay," the charismatic old man says while pulling the two into the shop.

The inside of the shop is very well organized but dusty, as though the old man hasn't had any visitors for a long time. Despite this, it is still very warm and cozy on the inside, very homelike. The charismatic old man sits Anarchious and Ace down. He seems very happy to have guests. He offers them both some warm beef stew, and they both accept. The old man leaves the two in the front while he goes to the back. The duo quickly make eye contact with each other. Anarchious jumps up and checks the front door, outwardly frightened. It's locked and barred shut. He goes back over to Ace and looks him in the eye.

"He's gonna kill us!" Anarchious whispers, leaning towards Ace.

"No, no, he's not," Ace replies to the paranoid Anarchious. "I suspect if he was going to kill us, we'd already be chained to a radiator in a basement somewhere."

"Yo, he's way too happy to see us and all the more willing to 'feed' us beef soup. I didn't see any cows on our way here, and if not that, I bet he's poisoning our soup!" Anarchious continues to whisper irately.

"Clearly he's just excited 'cause we are his first victims in a long time," the Lycan sarcastically retorts, laughing at Anarchious's exaggerated paranoia.

Anarchious reaches over, grabs the Lycan's collar, pulls him close, and says, "You'd better be right because I will kill him...if I have to." Ace looks into Anarchious's coffee-colored eyes and for the first time sees fear. He sees Anarchious struggling to be strong, but he isn't. What could make such a strong person cower so quickly at someone so unthreatening?

The young Mutant's eyes are fixed on all the old weapons, which are aged human technology. Firearms of all sorts are scattered in many spots in the shop. Ace notices Anarchious's eyes darting through the obsolete weapons, but that isn't all that is bothering the young Mutant. The old man has guns that remind Anarchious of that dreadful day when his life changed forever. It is as if he can't escape those memories no matter how hard he tries to suppress them.

"Ready for some grub!" Jeb says as he pops out of the back room, jolly as ever. Anarchious still has a hold of Ace's jacket, staring at the weapons and in his own world. Ace looks at the Mutant, wondering what could have brought him to this. He begins pondering why Anarchious is full of so many surprises, and yet Ace knows very little about him.

"Y'all all right?" the old man asks, interrupting the duo and their extremely awkward situation. Ace pops out of it immediately while Anarchious, nervous, stares blankly yet suspiciously at the old man.

"Yeah, we're fine…just a little nervous around the rifle collection," Ace says, pointing out what is bothering Anarchious primarily. The Mutant, hearing this, turns to Ace and raises an eyebrow, slightly astonished that Ace has figured it out.

"Oh, these old things? I got those from my days as a commander in the Rebel Army," the old man replies, placing the bowls of soup in front of both men.

Anarchious, hearing this, fixes his eyes back on the old man. "The Rebel Army?!" he asks, glaring at the old man.

"Yes sir, but about twenty-something years ago, I quit. I didn't and still don't believe in what they're doing. I was all for protecting our people and continents but not the way we were doing it. Shoot, they've gotten so aggressive, I've even heard whispers of revolution against them," the aged man explains as Anarchious lets out a sigh of relief. Even so, he still closely watches the old gentlemen, still not trusting him.

"C'mon now, son, sit down, eat, rest up a bit," Jeb says to Anarchious with a great big smile on his face.

The Mutant reluctantly sits down and looks over at Ace, whose face is buried in his soup bowl. Anarchious looks down at his but can't shake the jitters he is getting. He pushes the bowl away and says, "No thanks. Not hungry right now."

Ace quickly finishes his soup, grabs Anarchious's bowl and dives in it. Making every obnoxious noise he can, Ace slurps, burps, and belches while enjoying his second helping of soup. In no time, he is finished.

"So, where you boys headed? To the cliffs or the monastery on the other side of the mountain?" the old man asks the duo.

Ace, refreshed, answers, "No sir!"

"So why'd you stop here?" the curious old-timer asks, knowing there isn't anywhere else to head from this point.

"Well we saw the mark of the Spirit Church or something like that. We figured it would be smart to get food, supplies, and rest before the trip up the mountain," Ace explains to the old-timer.

"Up the mountain?! Are you young'uns crazy?!" the old man replies to the Lycan. This comment causes both Ace and Anarchious to cast their undivided attention on the old man.

"What do you mean?" Ace asks the old man attentively.

"Well, there's nothing up there but that monster," he responds.

"Monster?!" the duo reply simultaneously, cocking their heads back. The Lycan and Mutant look at each other, reading each other's facial expressions. They don't believe what the old man is saying for a second.

"Oh yeah, and the ghost of a beautiful woman," Jeb continues.

The Lycan and the Mutant look back at each other and snicker a little more. Monsters and ghosts? They definitely don't believe him.

Sensing their disbelief, Jeb gets a little more serious and defends his story. "It's the truth! All the people from this town, including the church, left years ago when they showed up. That's why I keep my firearms loaded and ready."

"Why didn't you leave?" Ace asks the old man.

"Too old to travel," he replies.

"Well, have you ever seen this ghost-monster?" Anarchious asks, almost mockingly.

"It's a monster and a ghost that stays in the cave at the top and sings, very deafening sometime, during the day....And yes, I've seen the monster. He circles the mountaintop, screaming, on some of the clearer nights, and the ghost whistles a tune. Personally, I've never seen her. Before everyone left, several young'uns went up there out of curiosity. They all confirmed they spotted her on the mountain path, and they couldn't touch her at all."

The young duo still don't believe the old man. They both laugh hysterically at his story.

"Don't mean to be rude, sir. It's just...monsters?" Ace says, trying to explain their amusement in the situation. "I know it's far-fetched for an outsider to believe, but it's true," the old man says, staring Ace in the eyes. Immediately, Ace begins to somewhat believe what the old man has told them.

An awkward silence surrounds the shop for a little while until the young Mutant begins reeling with laughter again and mocks the old man. "Ohhhh, monster! Ha-ha-haaaaaaaaaa! It's true!" Anarchious laughs for a while until he realizes Ace isn't laughing with him. The old man and Ace stare at Anarchious sternly so that he will understand the situation is serious, but he fails to notice, and the Mutant continues to think it's ridiculous.

"Look, you guys can stay tonight. Tomorrow I'll gather up whatever you may think you need for that hike." The old man continues ignoring Anarchious's juvenile behavior.

In the morning, the old man has gathers old coats and hiking picks and gear and gives it all to the duo. They both gear up and ready themselves for the trip, then leave the deserted town to begin the two-day hike up the mountain. Some way up, it begins to get cold. It doesn't affect the Lycan much. He just decides to give his coat to Anarchious and transform to his Lycan form to use his mass and body fur to keep himself warm.

"Thanks!" Anarchious says to Ace.

The Lycan nods and replies, "You're welcome!" As they continue walking up the path on the side of the mountain, striding against the winds, Anarchious laughs again. Ace just ignores it and continues to march on. "So what do you think about monster ghost?" Anarchious asks Ace, curious as to what he really thought.

"I don't know," Ace replies, not really caring about the question.

"So do you think they're real?" Anarchious asks, still receiving a nonchalant reply from Ace. "Oh, c'mon, what did you really think about that guy? Crazy or what?" Anarchious continues.

"All I know is it was nice to have a real conversation for once," Ace replies to Anarchious in a passive-aggressive way. Anarchious scoffs, understanding what the irritated Lycan sarcastically suggests.

They continue up the mountain. The higher they hike, the more brisk the air becomes. A calm but chilly wind picks up and begins to blow snow flurries. The frigid breeze doesn't really bother the Lycan or Mutant much, but Anarchious is feeling tired and still refuses to slow down. About halfway up the mountain and halfway through the first night, Anarchious collapses and falls unconscious.

The Mutant's weakened body slumps over and rolls towards the edge of the trail and the long drop over the edge. Ace reacts quickly, grabbing Anarchious's clothing and lifting him like a mother bear does her cubs. The Lycan knows instinctively what's wrong. The weather continues to worsen, so he finds a small cave in the mountain to set up camp and wait for the morning.

Ace huddles in front of the fire as the storm rages on, threatening to blow the fire out. He is lonely again. The caves remind him of his family and immediately bring his mood down. He then directs his thoughts to his mysterious partner, who is still in a fatigue-induce coma. The Lycan has never seen someone so angry and stubborn or someone who reminds him of both his father and himself. He notices Anarchious's subtle body movements. The guy is dreaming and mumbling, but all Ace can smell is fear.

The sun shines brightly, and a beautiful bronze woman holds his hand. It is his mother, with a head full of long, puffy, curly hair, the kindest eyes you could imagine, and the most stunning smile. When the light hits her, it is almost as if she were from the heavens. Her radiance gives her an angel's halo. Anarchious is happy with her and can't stop crying tears of joy. He remembers a panic, gunfire, and bloodshed. His mother teleports him to a safe place close by. He is covered in blood, but it isn't his. Mom is bleeding badly, but she is so strong, it doesn't faze her. She kisses him on his forehead, and in an instant she is gone. Feeling lost and confused, he follows the sound of Mom and Dad yelling and screaming.

"You up?" the Lycan says to Anarchious, who is coming to. The Mutant looks at Ace, confused, with a tear rolling down his cheek.

"What happened? Where am I?!" he asks the Lycan, who seems worried about Anarchious.

"You passed out last night. I had to bring you to this cave in the mountain till the storm broke," Ace responds.

"All right, well, let's get going!" the young Mutant exclaims while jumping up and walking quickly towards the trail.

"No, wait!" Ace tries to stop a tired, weary Anarchious, but it's too late. Anarchious's legs buckle. He loses his balance and is headed over the edge of the trail once again. The Lycan, on all fours, almost in a blur rushes over and grips the Mutant with his fangs before he can tumble over the cliff. The Lycan pulls him back and sits him down.

"When was the last time you ate?" Ace asks the Mutant, already knowing the answer for the most part. Anarchious looks at him and begins to think about it. "You haven't eaten at all since you began searching. Been too worried about your aunt, so you never noticed how hungry you were," Ace obnoxiously explains for him.

"Oh, so you're psychic now?" Anarchious responds and begins to notice his giant headache.

"No, I'm Lycan. I can hear everything...like when your stomach growls but you ignore it, dipshit!" Ace replies, taking a plastic bowl from one of his bags, popping the top off, and handing it to Anarchious. It's some of the soup the old man fixed two nights ago. Anarchious signals no and tries to get up again, but he's too weak.

"Stop being such a tough guy and eat the damn soup!" Ace snarls at Anarchious, his voice booming off the mountain and echoing. An extremely stubborn Anarchious refuses. This angers Ace, so he goes back to drastic measures. "Fine. You won't make your deadline, and Marie will die!" the smart-aleck Lycan says to the persistent Mutant.

In a burst of energy, Anarchious hops back up, quickly charges a lightning punch, and swings at the Lycan. Ace avoids it with a simple and very cocky slow sidestep. The Mutant stumbles over and faints, collapsing once again from overexertion.

While Anarchious is passed out, Ace picks up all their equipment, grabs the Mutant, and ties him to his back along with all the other equipment and hoofs it up the mountain. As the morning passes, the sun gets hotter, and the air gets thinner. The Lycan continues to stride up the mountain with the Mutant still limp and lifeless on his back. Ace knows he could just scale the mountain the easy way and it would be effortless, but he can't run the risk of dropping Anarchious and the supplies.

As nightfall approaches, Ace feels movement on his back. Figuring he will have to force-feed the Mutant, the Lycan calms himself and gets ready to deal with Anarchious's stubbornness. As soon as Ace mentally prepares himself, he looks back, and before he can open his mouth, he is surprised to see the stubborn Mutant has taken it upon himself to indulge in the soup he had spitefully rejected earlier that day.

The day is quickly coming to an end. The duo are almost at the top of the mountain. Ace is dead tired, and Anarchious, full and rejuvenated, begins to hear something. It is like a light whistling, very elegant, very peaceful. "It's coming from the top," he says. "Sounds as if it's coming from a cave."

Ace informs his now-alert Mutant counterpart, "OK, let's get there, then."

Anarchious is anxious to see for himself, although he already has a pretty good idea what is making the sound. It has to be the person he has journeyed to deliver a message to. He just knows it in his soul. He is only about ten minutes away from freeing Marie.

The anxious duo rushes up the remainder of the trail, passing hardened obstacles with ease. The closer they get to top, the louder the whistling gets. In just minutes, they reach the top of the mountain, both tired and out of breath.

As they get closer, the duo realizes that the whistling has become singing, and it seems to be coming from the cave right in front of them. Anarchious is sure it's the person he's supposed to deliver the letter to, so he darts into the depths of the cave as Ace staggers along, drained. Anarchious rushes in past where the moonlight reaches, almost running into a woman.

He comes to a screeching halt, excited to see her. "Hey, hi! I was sent here to deliver you a message!" Anarchious exclaims to the woman. He notices she is glowing. The glow is almost like a halo, though her aura is cold and gloomy.

She turns to the Mutant and looks him in the eye. She is pretty, short, and petite but busty, with hazel-colored eyes that seem to glimmer as the moonlight gleams off of them. Her skin is pale, so the duo assume she is a Vampyr.

Anarchious, excited, reaches in his pants and pulls out the letter, which was now in even worse condition than when he found it the first time. "Here is the letter, Luna, I guess." The relieved Mutant hands the emotionless woman the letter.

She neither smiles nor shows any care for the letter as she gazes upon it. The woman looks up at Anarchious with Ace standing by and says, "It must be that time of the year again." As she says this, she slips into the shadowy depths of the cave, losing the cold aura that has surrounded her like a halo.

Confused, the Mutant steps towards the shadows, asking, "What? Wait, what does that mean?" But he receives no answer. He continues to walk forward, trying to spot the woman, but there seems to be no sign of her. He looks back at Ace, who is also puzzled but seems a little more attentive than usual.

"Anarch, be careful. That chick was kind of creepy," Ace says to the Mutant, worried that something bad is about to happen.

"Hello, just need to know if we can leave now. Luna?" Anarchious says as he continues to look for her in the pitch dark.

"Ahh!" A womanly shriek echoes through the cave.

"Luna?!" Anarchious yells as he runs deeper towards the sound of the screaming.

"Anarch, don't!" Ace yells, but it's too late. The Lycan, even with his keen eyesight, loses track of the Mutant's whereabouts in the darkness. He darts forward, but something stops him. He smells something, something fierce, and the hair on the back of his neck stands at attention.

Deeper in the cave, Anarchious hears little whimpers and cries but can't see anything. Then he hears something he can't quite make out. It sounds like cracking and crunching. Anarchious continues to walk forward, trying to make out what those sounds are, until he walks face first into a hard but hairy barrier.

The crackling continues as Anarchious tries to figure out what it is. He blindly grasps upward on this fuzzy barrier, caressing it, contacting two rotund objects extruding from the wall. He cups the burgeoning swells, but they are too plump to fit in his bare hands. They feel cold to the touch and soft. It's not the mountain, he thinks to himself. It can't be; it's too soft. Maybe I can get around it. Anarchious feels a big, warm huff, and it immediately dawns on him what it might be. "Oooooh, shit!" Anarchious yells as he is immediately grabbed by this object, but the Mutant tears himself loose and runs back to the entrance of the cave, tripping and stumbling.

At the entrance, Ace stares into the dark of the cave, hair still erect on the back of his neck and almost frozen almost in fear. He hears Anarchious's screams and yelps and becomes more afraid, but he stays to be brave and to prove to the Mutant that he isn't a coward. He hears footsteps getting closer and closer. Someone or something is running towards him, and he readies himself.

Out of the shadows bursts Anarchious with a look of horror in his eyes. "A monster! A monster ate Luna!" Anarchious yells as he scurries toward the frightened Ace. Before Ace can reply, out of the shadows crawls a giant evil-looking creature. It resembles a Vampyr bat but is enormous. It's roaring and snarling as it chases the terrified Mutant down.

"No, the monster is Luna, Anarch!" shouts Ace as Anarchious tries to avoid the beast, but it's too late.

The tenacious beast pounces on Anarchious, pinning him to the ground. The animal then proceeds to pummel the Mutant to the point where it literally knocks his mind back to minutes ago when he thought this thing was a furry wall. Then Anarchious realizes something. "Furry giant monster tits!" he blurts out with a giant perverted smile on his swollen face.

The worried Lycan looks at the battered Mutant, confused and wondering what the hell he's talking about. Even the creature stops battering the Mutant, drawing a blank at his comment. The Mutant, coming out of his forced daydream, looks up at what is allegedly Luna and gets a glimpse of an upshot of her giant, full, furry breasts. He couldn't help staring at them.

Anarchious then realizes the predicament he is in, and his instincts take over. Simultaneously, the beast sees what the Mutant is gawking at. It angers her, so she proceeds to grab his head and tries to squash it like a grape. Anarchious, thinking quickly as the monster tries to squish his head with her giant batlike claws, lightning-blasts her with everything he has.

The cave erupts and seems to shake the entire mountain. It knocks Ace on his knees and nearly blows him out of the cavern, but he digs his claws into the groves of the cave's rough surface and hangs on. There is a rumbling outside, which seems to be simultaneously occurring with the shaking of the mountain. The blast is so spectacular, it causes an avalanche on the east end of the mountain.

Meanwhile, inside the cave, which surprisingly hasn't collapsed or taken much damage, the smoke is clearing. Ace anxiously tries to make out what happened in the blast. In one flap of its wings, the beast blows away the rest of the settling smoke. Anarchious is still pinned under Luna, who has suffered hardly any damage and struggles to get free.

"Yo, are you going to just sit there, or are you going to help a brother out?!" the angry Mutant yells desperately at the Lycan. Ace hesitates for a moment as the bat beast victoriously snarls at the top of her lungs, exerting her dominance.

Ace thinks to himself intensely. He hates violence and fighting and doesn't want to do it, but he remembers Anarchious's words to him a few days ago. "Look, in this world sometimes you have to fight when you don't want to, and other times you shouldn't fight when you want to." The Lycan musters up all the confidence he can, and in a fearless burst of power and speed, he tries to spear the creature off of Anarchious's crushed body.

Ace smashes into her shoulder first but is repelled backwards before he even touches her. For a moment, he sits back, surprised, and admires his courage. He never knew he had that type of power or force in him or, most importantly, such bravery.

"Hello?" Anarchious yells impatiently, waiting for the Lycan's assist as the beast chuckles at the Ace's attempt.

Back to action, Ace thinks to himself. Something has prevented him from making any type of contact with the bat beast. It's like an invisible barrier. "Anarch! There's a barrier preventing me!" Ace informs the Mutant as he continues to try to defend himself from the attempts to end his life.

"No duh! Figure something out!" the Mutant responds as he drops his guard. The bat's onslaught continues. She throws Anarchious up against a cave wall and pummels him some more.

Ace tries to tackle her again, but his attempts are feeble. Every time he fails at striking her, his newly gained confidence begins to crumble more, becoming fear.

"Dude…kill the bitch…before she… kills me!" Anarchious says as he begins to feel his consciousness slip away while the beast continuously slams him on the cold, hard ground.

Ace, feeling hopeless, terrified, and infected with cowardice decides to flee from the cave, leaving Anarchious to fend for himself. The last thing the battered Mutant sees is Ace fleeing into a bright white light out of the cavern before he starts to black out. He knows he is done for. He is weak, numb, and mentally broken at this point. Death, he thinks to himself. It would be so easy. He is going in and out of consciousness as the beating from the bat creature with the huge breasts continues. Death...he's beginning to accept it. It feels right as his lights are seemingly punched out for the last time...

5
History

My mother used to sing to us to keep us at ease when times were hard. As a matter fact, after she…left, Marie tried, but it was never the same. Mom was such a beautiful person, and not just on the outside. There was something about her that was different from anyone else I had ever met. Even as a child I noticed. All children think of their mother as divine when they're young, but this was different—just something about her that was genuinely good.

My father was a lucky man. The whole reason they let us stay after the incident was that she was such an asset to the town before everyone figured out who she was that awful day. Or really, it's what she was that made them act the way they did towards my family afterward.

Regardless of what happened, though, after that, it was Marie who kept us protected for the last fifteen years or so of my life. Every single day she was there. Marie even tried to help me focus my power, though it didn't turn out well. She may have had a…creative way of loving us and raising us, but she always had our back no matter what. I remember one time in the humans' study halls, they tried to sit me away from the other kids in the back, and she came to the place and argued them down and refused to do anymore surgery and medical treatments for the District if they didn't stop segregating me. I hope she's doing well. This journey has been tiring, and she is close. I can feel it.

ous pops up in a rage, ready to fight off the beast. He looks and notices he's not on the mountain anymore. He re mbers his death and thinks to himself, This must be the afterlife...although I thought this place would be a little more clean and holy. The floors and walls seem to be made out of old wood. The afterlife is very log-cabin-like to him. The room is a little messy with loose-leaf paper all over the floor and on the desks. There are two very distinct colorful silk robes hanging on the wall next to the door. He thinks to himself, What the heck? Not every day you get to wear something this rare or loud. He walks over and proceeds to put a robe on when he notices there's a window in the hallway. Through it, he sees the mountain.

Anarchious realizes that he isn't dead, and somehow he has teleported, leaving Ace behind on the mountain. The Mutant becomes worried and takes off down the hallway to what is hopefully an exit. He is determined to make it back to the mountain to help Ace, when suddenly, out of thin air, a blinding light appears in front of him, stopping him in his tracks.

From the light comes a voice. "Calm down! You're safe!" The voice is different. The accent reminds him of the Spanish-speaking humans in the village his mother used to talk to, yet he doesn't trust the voice.

Anarchious quickly becomes irate and screams at the top of his lungs, "Get the fuck out my way!"

"Calm down, amigo. Everything is bueno," the voice coming from the light says, trying to calm the furious Mutant down. But with no hesitation, Anarchious charges a lighting shot and aims it at the light with the intention of firing. In a flash, an old man slaps Anarchious's firing hand upward, directing the lighting to the ceiling, blowing big hole in it.

The old man is short and has a head full of white hair, a handlebar mustache, caramel-colored skin, and a clear taste for wearing very colorful, expensive things. Anarchious completely ignores the fact that the light is gone and the old man came out of thin air. He just knows immediately that the robe he is wearing has to belong to the old man.

"Son, you are safe now!" the old man repeats in his thick Latin accent, trying to put the confused Mutant at ease.

Anarchious, speechless, just looks at the old man, wondering what has happened and what's going on until he hears Ace's voice coming from outside. "Anarch?" The Mutant runs outside, following the Lycan's voice. He sees Ace sitting at a campsite in the middle of the surrounding dense, green forest. The Lycan is in his human form, eating a plate filled with cooked rice and chicken in front of the cabin. Ace glares back and begins to speak. "You're awake? After taking a beating like that?! Shit, you're a tough man. Dumb but definitely tough!"

"What the hell happened?" the Mutant asks the Lycan while grabbing his head, noticing the giant headache he has.

"Here, sit down," the old man says, sitting Anarchious down in one of the seats near Ace.

"What the hell happened?" Anarchious repeats, rubbing his head and looking at Ace, who is stuffing his face. Ace gives him some quick eye contact with a guilty look on his face, then quickly continues eating his food.

"Now that you're both awake, could you explain to me what it is you were doing in Luna's cavern at the top of one of the tallest mountains on this planet?" the old man asks, looking Anarchious in the eye as he hands the Mutant a big plate of food.

Anarchious looks down at the food and begins to consume it. During his meal, Anarchious explains the story about Marie's kidnapping, hunting down who did it, meeting Ace, all the way up to delivering the letter.

"Is that all? So Zera told you she'll return your aunt if you deliver this letter?" the old man asks as he flashes the envelope.

Anarchious glares at the envelope and responds, "Yeah, that's what she said. Instead of that, I almost got killed!" Remembering what happened to him before he blacked out, the Mutant gives Ace an evil glare. "Yo, what the fuck?! You left me to die…again!" Anarchious yells at the Lycan.

"It's not like that at all, Anarch!" the Lycan retorts, afraid the Mutant may go off again. He quickly changes to his Lycan form.

"Then how is it, you piece of shit?" Anarchious says, shoving the Lycan back.

Ace, tired of the Mutant's attitude, shoves him back, forcing Anarchious back twelve feet before skidding to a halt. "I couldn't even hit the bitch! What else was I going to do? What fool do you know will wait around to get his ass kicked by a twenty-foot bat bitch?" Ace yells, snarling back, trying to make peace with Anarchious, but it doesn't seem to work.

The shove pushes Anarchious over the edge. He begins to lose his cool again. His eyes begin to glow, his body surges with electricity, and he even begins to float as a fog starts to creep into the area around him. This time he isn't fighting it.

"He's telling the truth. He had no choice but to run," the old man says, stepping between the infuriated Mutant and the irate Lycan. Anarchious continues to glare at Ace as he continues to slip into his rage.

The old man faces Anarchious and holds up the open letter. The paper is blank except for a familiar swirly symbol on the middle of it. "This is a seal release symbol. It was written and sanctified by a Witch and/or Warlock," the old man explains, face to face with the Mutant. "I'll explain to you the reason for it and why you shouldn't be mad at your friend here, but you have to calm down first, amigo," the old man continues while placing his hand on Anarchious's shoulder, guiding him back to the ground. The Mutant begins to calm down as the old man continues to talk him down. "That's it, son. Everything is bueno."

After five minutes, Anarchious is as calm as he'll ever be, still fuming but hiding it by trying to be attentive. Ace is back in his man form and is sitting down, waiting for the explanation as well.

The old man sits down and looks at Anarchious, handing him the envelope he had delivered to Luna just eighteen or so hours ago. "In order for you to understand why that symbol is important, you have to know Luna's story," he explains. So the old man tells the duo the story of Luna and Zera.

"About five years ago, Drake City and most of Vampyr country were ruled by a feral Vampyr named Drake. He was cruel, like most rulers of our day or in the past. He had many underlings. Two of them were Luna and Zera. He forced himself upon both of them and basically made them slaves, specifically sex slaves. They were tormented and tortured in many sick ways. They got sick of him and wanted to kill him but were not nearly as strong as he was. So they followed the legends about Vampyrs—not only do they grow stronger with age, but they also grow stronger by becoming feral, which is feeding off humans or any living soul. So they both did so.

"They both became feral and very strong but still weren't strong enough to kill Drake. He found out what they were doing, so he beat and violated Zera in front of his entire congregation, but most importantly in front of Luna, knowing they were in love with each other."

"Wait, wait, wait!" Anarchious interrupts the story. "Zera? Luna? Lesbians? Vampyr lesbians?!"

"Yes," the old man answers the Mutant. "Anyway, after all the humiliation and mortification, both women tasted Vampyr blood for the first time, and it made them both enormously strong, another Vampyr legend as well. Both of them gained new mystical such as psychic and transformation abilities. Even with all the new power, they still weren't strong enough.

"Then they came across a new being with dark powers and even darker abilities. They referred to it as a monster, seeing its form was something hideous, I guess. They asked it to join them, and it refused. So Zera seduced it in order to get its participation, and it worked. The three of them killed Drake together with ease. When they did so, Luna fed on dying Drake's three-thousand-year-old blood, and that made her extremely strong…and crazy as well. She lost control, becoming consumed with the thirst, and lashed out against her own kind. She couldn't handle that type of power.

"So Zera and her new colleague found a Wiccan and they magically binded her to that mountain in order to control her feeding to siphon away some of that power she received. Not only that, but they placed a seal on her to stop her from doing harm to anyone or anyone trying to do harm to her. Only one who has been unsealed can be harmed by her. This was also to control her feeding. Every harvest moon, Zera has the Blood Pack bring someone or trick some poor fool to climb up there only for them to killed and fed on by Luna just to keep her alive."

"How do you know all this?" Ace asks the old man.

"Well, because I was there when she was sealed. I hid in the darkness of the cavern. She's also mi amigo. I bring her pigs' blood so that the containment is less harsh on her. I have been stopping fools like you two sent from Zera from time to time. I've been able to stop some but not all. The ones I stop tell me their unfortunate stories, and every time I tell them this story."

The old man explains his involvement in the whole situation. "You two are lucky. During the avalanche, when I went to help Jeb from the town at the foot of the mountain, he told me of you two, and I came immediately. Well, at least you were lucky, Lycan, because that envelope was made only for the messenger to be 'unsealed' in order to be killed and eaten. Your life was spared," the old man explains to the duo.

"So thank you, I guess. I've heard enough. All right, well, I'm going back to Drake City to get my aunt back, then kill that leech!" Anarchious says as he stands up and walks away from the Lycan and the suave old man.

"That's where this last bit comes in. Whatever information you bargained to get from her and whoever it was you were trying to save...forget about it. They're most likely dead. She sent you up there to be killed! So it's best to let her think you're dead. I suggest you don't go or you'll be killed yourself, mi amigo. She is too strong for you," the old man explains to the Mutant, making him angry in the process. The Lycan hops up, walks over to Anarchious, and places his hand on his shoulder for comfort, knowing that what the suave old man just told them would upset the Mutant.

After a few moments of awkward silence, Anarchious takes off towards the mountain in a bright purple electric burst, shocking Ace in the process. With his eyes glowing and tears running down his face, all he knows is he needs to get revenge, and he knows just how to get it. In a bright white flash, the old man appears in front of the speeding Mutant, grabs him with one arm, and hip-tosses him. The Mutant lands on his back and tries to get up, but the old man flashes in front of him and places his foot on his chest, stopping him from getting up or gaining any leverage.

"So what you going to do, hombre? Kill Luna? I'm sorry, but that's not smart," the old man says, trying to talk sense to the emotion-filled Mutant. Anarchious, still out of control, tries to get up, but the old man keeps him down, even with Anarchious giving off copious amount of uncontrollable energy.

"Do not throw your life away, amigo. You're nowhere near as strong as Luna, and forget about Zera. At your level, they'll mop the floor with you, wring you out, and continue to mop the floor with you some more!" The old man continues to try to talk more sense into the Mutant, but it doesn't seem to work at all.

Eventually, he lets the Mutant stand up and speaks face to face with him. "Look, I train on these mountains; I can show you a thing or two." The old man tries to make amends with the Mutant, but as soon as he offers a handshake, Anarchious bolts into the forest.

The distressed Mutant runs until he can't run anymore. The thought of losing Marie is too much to bear. Sitting in the dark of the forest with just enough of the setting sun's light peeking through, Anarchious can't stop thinking about how much of an idiot he has been. He lost Marie and can't do a thing about it. What will he tell her daughters about her certain death? His brother, Abel, is missing, and he can't shake this bad feeling about it all. The situation has gone from bad to worse, and he has no idea what to do.

After a few minutes of thinking, the worried Lycan comes peeking from behind the trees. "Hey, man, are you all right?" Ace attempts conversation with Anarchious, but it doesn't work. After a few minutes of sitting there in the silence of the forest, Ace continues to try to talk to the Mutant. "You know that guy is just like you?"

"What do you mean?" Anarchious responds, confused, still staring at the ground and not really showing any interest.

"He's a Mutant just like you!" the Lycan tells Anarchious. He looks up, makes eye contact with Ace, and asks, "How would you know that?"

"Well, for one thing, he smells just like you, and for another, he mentioned it right before you woke up," Ace informs Anarchious. Hearing this, Anarchious begins to walk out of the forest back to the campsite. Ace follows.

The sun is setting behind the forest, and it was getting dark. The old man is stacking wood in front of his wooden shack. The Mutant walks over to him intending to ask him if what Ace told him was true, but before he opens his mouth, the old man says, "I thought I was the only one left too...until you blew the roof off mi casa," he says, pointing back at his shack while chuckling. Anarchious, stunned, doesn't know what to say. "Mi llamo José, José Destello! Y tu?" the suave old man says in Spanish, introducing himself to Anarchious.

"Oh, I'm Anarchious. Anarchious Athar," Anarchious replies, shaking José's hand.

"That's a very Eden name. Here, have a seat," the old man says to the duo, sitting them back in the same area they sat in earlier.

José snaps his fingers, and flames burst from the wood he has stacked in the middle of the campsite. Surprised, the duo jumps back away from the blazing lumber. "Chill! Chill! That is my elemental gift, the power to control el Sol," José explains to the duo his power.

"The sun?" Anarchious asks the older Mutant.

“No, not really. The power of light, but I’ve become extremely...in tune with my power. I can make the light emanate extreme heat, create the power of a star in my hand, and disperse it the way I need to. This is how I saved your ass. Vampyrs can’t see in the sunlight, and they’re extremely vulnerable in it,” the old man says, explaining his power to his newfound brethren.

They all sit down around the fire and get warm and comfortable. José gazes at Anarchious with a curious look on his aged face and asks, “Amigo, how much do you know about our race?”

“Not much.” Anarchious turns his head, almost ashamed at his lack of knowledge about his people.

“Well, what do you know?” José asks, curious about the extent of his brethren’s knowledge.

“Well, my mother told me that our homeland was plagued by a war. So that’s why she and my dad left,” Anarchious explains to the old-timer.

“Well, that’s definitely a start. Did your parents tell you anything else?” José continues to wonder if Anarchious might be holding something back.

“No, not really, other than the element thing. And of course the bounty thing,” Anarchious answers, sure he didn’t miss anything.

José looks at Anarchious, frowns, and begins to tell the young Mutant and his Lycan partner recent Mutant history.

"For as long as I can remember of my sixty years, our kind have been at war. Our homeland's soils bubble with the blood of our people spilled by our own people. Rumor has been we were engaged in this civil war for hundreds of years and lost sight of the real reason we were fighting. When I was in country, our fight was over land, I believe, but this all came to a screeching halt about twenty years ago.

"There was a raging battle going on between the two sides when the humans' army came with their flying machines. They filled the sky with hundreds of thousands of them. They dropped clusters of bombs that, when detonated, lit up the sky like a thousand suns. The bombs swept our lands, killing our people. If you weren't killed by the blasts, heat, fumes, or the diseases the bombs released, the men in the Cyclops suits hunted you down. By sea they came with their steel ships and swept the islands with terrible weapons. Luckily, like your parents, I left before this show of power and genocide took place."

Angry, Anarchious gets up and turns around with tears in his eyes. He wipes his face and looks up to the clear skies, wondering why anyone would do such a thing. This only worsens his clear distaste of humans. "I mean, was the war endangering other races?" Anarchious asks, continuing to stare at the sky and holding back his tears.

"Not at all. Our war was our war!" José answers the young emotional Mutant, also becoming emotional himself. "It never carried over to the mainlands where the humans or other races resided. That's why I wonder to this day why this happened to our people. We were introverted people. Who would want to go out of their way just to have us exterminated?"

"Well, you guys should try to find out why," Ace says, interrupting and also showing signs he'd been sobbing as well.

"I did a little investigation. To no avail," José answers the curious Lycan. "I used my many connections, but it was stifled due to the price on any Mutant's head issued by the Rebel Army. That made it harder to move around. I mean, I can move at the speed of light, but I'm too old now. One mistake and their technological guns will get me."

Anarchious stands there, just trying to make sense of it all.

"I've got an idea! We can go look for answers to what happened to your people," Ace suggests to the grieving Mutants.

"No, I have this. No reason to get you young men into it. My investigation is still going on. It's just not moving as fast as I want it to. My informants range from human government officials to religious Cadinals. They have to be careful because if they get caught, they will be executed," the suave old Mutant says making a throat-cutting gesture towards Ace.

"And I still have to save Marie and find my brother," Anarchious adds. "The only way to do that, I figure, is to beat Zera. That's all I care about right now!"

"I agree," José says, walking over to the young, angry Anarchious. "Right now I feel the best thing to do is to help pass on our culture and teachings to you, young man. As your elder, I feel a strong obligation to teach you what I know to help preserve our peoples within you. Now, I cannot promise you the power to beat either of those Vampyr women or promise you'll ever see tu familia again!" the older Mutant continues as he places his hands on Anarchious's shoulders. "But I can promise you, if you accept my teachings, you'll learn things about yourself you never knew existed," he continues, trying to spark the young Mutant's interest.

Anarchious turns to the suave old man and says, "Seems I don't really have a choice in this, but if it will help me become stronger, I'll do it." Anarchious smirks while looking the older Mutant in his aged, big brown eyes.

"Bueno! We'll start mañana! Get some rest, boys!" José replies as he retires into his cabin, leaving the duo sitting around the fire.

Ace and Anarchious sit in silence around the cracking fire. Neither one knows what to say to the other. Several seconds of awkward silence later, Anarchious finally speaks. "You could leave at..."

"Nah, I'm good. I want to see this play out," Ace replies, curling into a ball, using his stretched-out leather jacket as a blanket. He is ready to sleep. Anarchious can't fathom sleeping after finding out his history.

The night goes by quickly, with the Mutant never falling asleep. He stays up obsessing over his aunt and the bombings, wishing his brother were here to learn these things as well. As soon as the morning birds begin cooing, José is up and out of his cabin, looking frisky.

The old man rounds up and marches the duo a few miles away from the mountain to a forested area where there trees aren't as thick and there is enough space to move freely. The older Mutant begins to stretch and warm up. The younger Mutant begins doing the same, mimicking his elder.

Ace, feeling left out, approaches José. "Hey, I was wondering a li'l last night—is it possible for me to learn this too?" he asks.

"Well, Mutant-specific things? No, but I thought of this too, and I figured since a lot of these lessons are extensive for Anarchious, in the afternoon I could teach you lucha libre. Is that cool?"

Ace's face expresses confusion for a moment. "I have no clue what you just said, but sure, better than nothing!" Ace replies ecstatic.

The sun beams through the trees as José directs Ace's attention to Anarchious. "OK, so first lesson," he says to the Mutant. "Since you clearly have an issue controlling your anger, we're gonna get down to that first," José says, and Anarchious nods in agreement. "So as you already know, there were seis main elements controlled by Mutants, and over a millennium, seis became something like catorce due to all the mixing among the tribes," José states.

"Fourteen. I didn't know that," Anarchious replies.

"Si. Well, human science says it's simple genetics. You inherit your element from one of your parents, but when opposing elementals intermingled, it created new pools. Most of the time, the secondary element was more dominant than the primary one, so that got passed on. You are a Storm Mutant, a controller of lightning and weather, so most likely you had a parent who was also a storm element as opposed to having an agua parent and wind parent."

"Well, my mother is—was—a Storm Mutant, so you're spot on there," Anarchious replies, intrigued.

"I am a primary being. My element is luz. We call you all secondary. What you also probably do not know is that inherently, we are muy, muy emotional beings. This created issues within our race, so our ancestors developed a five-step training to counteract all the lashing out and emotional problems. Steps one through five are taming your emotion, achieving your element, becoming your element, conservation, and simply peace. After a while, this all became hokey, and our people would do only the first two or three, which probably explains all of our wars."

José sits down, crosses his legs in a lotus position, and motions for the young Mutant to join him. "Now, there are two ways to tame your emotion. One is that you are to be trained the moment you begin using your abilities around the años cinco. Obviously, that has gone out the door. The second way is through a special meditation that can be used only by an elder who has reached stage five with his student. Isn't this your lucky day, hijo? In my years of seclusion, I have reached five. It took twenty years, but I did it. This method, though, is much tougher and will rid you of your element until you learn to tame your emotions. So are you ready?"

"Ready as I'll ever be," the young Mutant answers.

"First, close your eyes and clear your mind of all thoughts and emotions the best you can," José instructs Anarchious.

The young Mutant follows the instructions, shutting his eyes and trying to clear his thoughts. After a few moments, Anarchious huffs as he begins losing patience. He thinks this is stupid and wants to quit. He can't help thinking about killing Zera, saving his aunt, or the fate of his parents, for that matter. It is impossible.

"Stop focusing on the negative," José interjects, perceiving his student's thoughts. "Clear your mind. Focus on the now. You are alive, healthy, and in a beautiful forest. Listen to the chirping of the birds and the whistle of the wind. Focus on that!"

Anarchious huffs once more and reluctantly begins following José's lead. He calms himself down and tries pushing his negative thoughts out of the way. He concentrates on the ambience of the forest, listening to the different types of tweeting birds, listening to the rustle of the leaves on the trees and bushes when the gentle wind pushes them.

Moments later, the Mutant feels calm. There is nothing but the forest, which soon begins to disappear. Anarchious opens his eyes, and there is nothing, just the blue sky and clouds. He gets up and looks around, confused.

"We're inside you," José says as he appears behind Anarchious.

"What?"

"We're in the place where both your emotion and element reside," José states, looking around. "I'm surprised. This usually takes a lot longer, and I did it in an hour. Peculiar. Have you done this before?"

"No," the younger Mutant answers, looking confused.

The older Mutant pauses for a second and surveys the area. "OK, let's get on with this," José continues. "What I need for you to do is simply think of the things you were thinking of earlier."

"Why?" the young Mutant replies.

"I will talk you through it all. Don't worry; you'll understand soon enough," the hermit encourages his student.

Anarchious, skeptical, feels a little anxious as he continues to survey the area, just he and José floating in a cloudy sky. He notices the clouds are beginning to multiply and the sky gray a little.

"Tu comprende?" José asks.

The young Mutant nods. He begins to think of his family and their fates. Instantly, the surrounding area turns into a superstorm.

The sky darkens, the clouds dim to gray, and it begins to rain and hail. Both Mutants are hit with crosswinds while lightning strikes dangerously close. José eyes glow as he reaches out to his student. "Keep up the emotion, Anarchious!" José says, stabilizing his and Anarchious's position. The young Mutant focuses even more deeply on his pain, emotion, and anxiety. The storm picks up even harder, forms into a hurricane-like windstorm as the clouds circle the young mutant overhead like a giant halo. José remains tough and stabilized despite the strength of his student's emotion.

Soon Anarchious is the eye of the hurricane. "OK, now I need you to release all your emotion. Do not hold back, and I'll take it from there," José continues coaching Anarchious, who, with tear-riddled eyes, contemplates the death of his aunt and feels the blood on his hands once again. Anarchious's eyes glow violet as he grits his teeth, tenses his muscles, and yells at the top of his lungs, releasing it all. His teacher can feel the pressure from the power and lassos it all using his own and begins pulling the power away from his student. It is tough but isn't anything he can't handle. He begins to get control of the storm, and Anarchious lets out another scream. This one is different. José gazes at his student and sees a dark figure descend from the eye of the hurricane, which rushes him.

José is shoved back physically into the forest out of his seated lotus position. "What's up, José?" Ace says, gazing at the older Mutant, who looks as if he just saw a ghost.

José doesn't answer. He just gazes at Anarchious, who is on his feet and lost in his emotion, just as he was the day before. But this time is different. Clouds begin to crowd overhead as strong gales blow trees over. Anarchious begins emanating powerful electric pulses that set fire to the surrounding foliage.

“Anarch!” Ace yells, wondering what is going on. José watches the skies once more as the lightning strikes everywhere, hitting Anarchious several times and only making his power grow.

The older Mutant gets a bad feeling. Anarchious’s glow is so strong, neither he nor the Lycan can see the young Mutant. Just then, Anarchious begins to flash on and off. José grabs the Lycan and throws his hand out in front of them, creating a blinding light. A huge lightning bolt strikes Anarchious, causing a colossal explosion.

6
The Queen's Weakness

The night is still and the moon is full, beaming on a lively Drake City. Yet in the northern part of the city, Drake Castle retains its dark, dead aura. Torches light the throne room along with moonlight from the castle's damaged ceiling as Zera sits with two of her Blood Pack generals. The room is riddled with human bodies, some bled dry, others bitten to be turned. They have just finished a feasting when a Blood Pack grunt bursts into the room as if he were unwillingly pushed in.

"Pardon my intrusion, mighty queen!" the Vampyr grunt says, kneeling before her at the foot of the throne.

She looks upon him, face spattered in blood, eyes gleaming a bright orange. "What is it?"

"We've recaptured the…lightning guy's accomplice," he responds quickly, looking the queen in the eye.

Zera smirks wickedly. "Well? Kill him!"

"My queen, we proceeded to, but the werewolf…"

The grunt tries to explain but is interrupted by a frustrated Zera. "But what, fool?" she yells at him.

"Well, he…it…" the young grunt stutters, breaking eye contact with Zera.

"Spit it out!" she yells at the grunt.

"He has asked to be dealt with by you, my queen!" the grunt blurts out.

A wicked smile rolls across the Vampyr queen's face as she sits back and glares at her grunt follower. "Bring him in," she demands.

"Yes, your highness!" the relieved grunt exclaims as he runs out of the throne room as fast as he can.

A few moments later, the doors of the throne room swing open violently. The Lycan Ace, fully transformed, beaten and bleeding, is restrained by several Blood Pack members, who are struggling to keep him under control. They bring him a few feet shy of the throne and force him to kneel before the queen. Ace scolds the queen as she smirks upon the wounded Lycan with a malevolent gaze and giggles.

"How's your Mutant friend?" she asks, smiling at Ace, making him furious.

"He's fucking dead!" the Lycan retorts, letting out a vicious growl and shaking up Zera's followers.

She laughs at the Lycan, belittling his aggression as he stares her down. She stares back into his chocolate eyes, noticing something different about his demeanor, a fire in his gaze that reminds her of Anarchious. It begins to make her angry. "You disrespectful shit! You're lucky I spared your pitiful life!" she yells at the infuriated Lycan.

"And you won't be as lucky!" the Lycan exclaims as he breaks free of the Vampyr grunts, hurling them in every direction and knocking them all unconscious. Ace steps towards the throne as Zera continues to sit unafraid of the seven-foot, three-hundred-pound Lycan, who seems to have inherited Anarchious's anger.

Zera's two generals appear out of thin air and kick Ace in the face so hard, it shakes the castle. Ace is unaffected and unrelenting. He grabs a hold of one of the generals and suplex-slams him on his back and neck, cracking the stone floor and knocking the general out cold. The other general tries to roundhouse the Lycan once more but hits nothing. In a blur, Ace appears behind him and applies a chokehold, breaking his neck with no effort. Both generals' bodies explode into dust and burning cinders.

Zera smiles, then laughs at the werewolf's display of power. "It seems you've finally learned to fight back! No doubt from your friend," she says to the Lycan, making eye contact with him as he continues to advance on her. "It's too little too late, though. Seems you're going to have to learn the hard way like your Mutant friend did," she continues as the irate Lycan lunges at her and grabs for her neck. As soon as Ace touches her cold, dead skin, an awful pain surges through his brain.

The Lycan drops to his knees, writhing in pain and growling. Zera laughs and utters, "I'll let you...endure this for a moment. It would be all too easy to kill you." Soon the growls became whimpers as Zera's psychic power seems to melt the Lycan's brain. "It's funny, really," she says, sitting on the throne as she flicks her wrist in a shooing motion, sending Ace flying back several feet and hitting the cold stone floor hard.

"The Mutant you befriended is dead only because you decided to help him." The Vampyr queen stands up and continues, "Sad, his brother wouldn't have died so easily. Too bad, he was kind of cute," she says as she looms gracefully over the helpless Lycan. "Men...they are such simple creatures. Show them a little sexuality and they'll trust anything you say," she muses out loud as the Lycan continues to shudder with the stabbing pains in the lobes of his brain tormenting him.

"Well, enough of this toying around. I have more important matters to deal with," Zera proclaims while using her kinetic powers to bring the Lycan to eye level. Ace closes his eyes and tries to fight the forces binding him, but it is no use, seeing his energy is drained. She sees the fight the Lycan still possesses and smiles sadistically.

"You know the person you said you were leading him to? The Witch? She was dead for a week before either of you showed up in Drake City," she says in the Lycan's ear, trying to get a reaction out of him. Ace doesn't respond. He just avoids her eyes and struggles harder. Zera becomes irritated at the Lycan's resistance. She wonders why he is able to keep regaining energy while she is draining him. "Ironic. She died protecting him, yet the seal she created was the death of him," she continues, trying to poke at the Lycan's anger.

Ace comes to attention and snaps at her face but is stopped by her kinetic energy. Zera grabs his snout and stares him in his eyes, "That's a good boy!" she retorts as she readies to end the werewolf's life.

At that moment, Ace drops something from his palm. Zera hears the objects as they hit and bounce along the floor. They sound like dice dancing their way along the stone floor, landing in one of the dead human's blood. Curious, she turns her attention to them. Grabbing them kinetically, she frees Ace in the process. With a "come hither" gesture, she brings the two spike-shaped, blood-doused items to her face. As the items float in midair, she blows away the blood from them, trying to identify what they are.

Zera glares at Ace, who is on one knee. "She was strong enough to kill my friend," the tenacious werewolf says as he begins to make it back to his feet, "but she wasn't strong enough to take me!" Ace informs her of her counterpart's demise as she recognizes the items as Luna's canine teeth.

Zera glares at the fangs in disbelief. "You couldn't have! The seal! The barrier we placed around her!" she exclaims to the grinning Lycan.

"The seal that...'witch' created released the protection barrier placed around her permanently the moment Anarchious struck her!" the Lycan retorts, turning the tables and toying with her emotions.

Zera glares at the teeth, then at the Lycan and then back to the teeth as if she is panicking. A great anger builds within her as she clutches the fangs in her palm.

"I ripped those precious puppies from her pretty little mouth before I tore her head from her body!" Ace says to antagonize her.

Zera loses her cool and tries to swoop down to attack. They Lycan catches her arms in midair and digs his vicious claws into them, drawing blood from gashes on her! "Gotcha, bitch!" a growling Ace exclaims as the Vampyr queen hisses at him. With tears in her eyes, still restrained in midair by Ace, Zera stares down into the eyes of the Lycan, giving him another brain-melting psychic attack.

The pain ricochets through his brain, causing his clinch on the queen to become only tighter. Zera screams as she begins to feel the bones of her arms crack. Hearing her screams, the grunts begin to revive. Zera loses her psychic hold over the determined werewolf as her followers stand by, hesitating to help. Ace, ears and nose bleeding, gives the queen a big, bloody, psychotic smile.

"You fools! Stop him!" the queen yells in desperation as her followers stagger to her defense.

Ace laughs and says, "Well, enough toying around. I have more important matters to attend to!"

"Are you mad?!" the Vampyr queen yells at the werewolf, baring her fangs. "You are surrounded! You will not survive this endeavor, Lycan!"

"Oh yeah, I'm so doomed!" the Lycan says sarcastically, taunting the queen.

Suddenly, an enormous rumble shakes the room. The torches placed all around go out, and only the moonlight shines through. The grunts look on in shock, not knowing what just took place.

A piercing pain shoots through the queen's chest. Blood splatters across the Lycan's face. It is the Vampyr queen's blood. Ace laughs as Zera looks down at the right side of her chest in shock. An arm, covered in her blood, is impaled through her breast. She looks over her shoulder and leers into a familiar set of eyes.

"What's up?!" the voice whispers into her ear. "Now, what kind of fucked-up errand was that to send someone on?!" Anarchious grunts angrily as he clenches his fist, cracking his knuckles.

"Bro, wait! Chill!" Ace yells as he tries to let go of Zera, but he is too late. The Lycan is shocked by a vigorous energy and sent flying back, smashing into a decorative steel armor suit. "Anarch! You fucking moron!" Ace yells irately as he unburies himself from the armor.

"My bad!" a grinning Anarchious responds, peeking over Zera's now frizzy and smoking hair.

"What, you couldn't wait to blast the bitch?! You just had to zap me too?!" the Lycan says, shaking himself off on all fours like a wet dog.

"Well, you should have let go!" the Mutant say, the first thing that comes to mind.

“What the hell do you mean? You could have killed us in the process, dipshit!” Ace responds, still trying to shake his fur to normal.

“The plan wasn’t to kill her,” Anarchious retorts, confused.

“The plan wasn’t to shock me either, but you fucking did…you damn…ugh! You know what?! Make that the last time you shock me!” Ace says furiously, glaring at the shocked Blood Pack grunts. At this point, the grunts are so unnerved and frightened of the duo, they take off running.

Ace huffs and angrily walks over to the gaping hole in the ceiling where the moonlight shines through in abundance. As Anarchious stands by, arm still jammed through Zera’s chest, the werewolf basks in the light. Slowly his wounds begin to fade away.

“Thank the Spirit for the full moon being out,” Ace says, continuing to take in the light as he turns to face his partner. “As many wars between my kind and hers as there have been, you’d think she’d figure out why it was so hard to put me down,” he continues to explain to the Mutant, who has gotten back to his feet, still dangling the petite Vampyr queen from his arm.

“Hey, Anarch, about your aunt…” Ace says, making his way back to his partner.

“I already know,” the Mutant says, dropping his eyes in disappointment.

“So did you know your aunt was a Witch?” Ace asks with some frustration in his tone.

“Witch?” Anarchious asks, confused, noticing Ace’s subtle irritation.

“Yeah, the ‘it’ on your arm confirmed that!” the werewolf explains.

Anarchious looks at his Lycan counterpart as he begins to think over his years he lived with Marie. He thinks about her medical profession in the village as well as the weird symbols in the house, the same symbols she wore on her skin, which she used to hide vigorously from everyone but the family. He draws up deeper memories. He has one memory of him as a child. Marie tried to help him control his electricity power so he could go to school. He thinks to himself, It never worked out. She quit after I shot lightning from an angry scream and damn near killed her. She deflected it with a wave of her hand.

"Oh, wow, I guess she was," Anarchious says, confirming the Lycan's claim.

They hear a faint laugh. Anarchious feels a tug on his arm as the evil laugh gets louder. It is Zera. She has regained consciousness. Anarchious clenches his fist as the Vampyr queen holds his arm in place with claws of her own. "And not only was she a Witch, she made that seal to protect you, but I killed her anyway, weaklings!" Zera yells and continues her evil laugh.

"Laugh at this, leech!" the angry Mutant yells at Zera, shocking her once again. He tries to knock her unconscious again, but it backfires. His shock only makes her claws dig deeper into the muscles of his forearm. Anarchious stops. Zera continues to clench down and laugh hysterically. The Mutant tries to push her off with is free hand but can't, so he panics, trying to fling her off his arm, but it is no use.

"Anarch! Her arms!" Ace says, but the Mutant is still too busy flailing about wildly trying to fling her off his limb. The Lycan quickly grabs Zera, restraining her arms and pulling them away from Anarchious's now-gashed arm. The Mutant pulls his arm away violently, stumbling backwards and falling flat on his back from the momentum.

The werewolf lets one the Vampyr's arms free as he steps back and hurls Zera like a rag doll at her throne. The Vampyr queen hits her throne, bending the gold back, making it completely fall apart. Anarchious hops back up quickly but feels a slight weakness.

"Zera must have absorbed some of your Ki, Anarch," the Lycan says, glaring at Zera's body, which is bent out of shape after his devastating toss. "There! Look at her arms," Ace continues, pointing out that Zera's arms have healed significantly.

"Damn it!" Anarchious exclaims while trying to shake off the weak feeling. "Yeah, she got me good. We have to finish this now or she'll drain us both!" Anarchious yells to Ace with urgency as his body begins to glow like lightning striking across the night sky.

"Got it!" The Mutant's counterpart acknowledges his partner's warning as they both charge Zera's body. At that moment, Zera pops up, clutches the castle wall, and hisses at the duo. Anarchious and Ace stop simultaneously, confused, but then resume their charge.

In that instant, Zera's body bursts into thousands of swarming Vampyr bats. They quickly swarm the duo. Soon the bats knick, scratch, and bite the surprised duo up. "What the hell is this?" Anarchious yells while covering his head, ducking and dodging some of the bats.

"I don't know, but I feel her getting stronger!" Ace responds.

"Back to back, bro! I have an idea!" Anarchious says while positioning his back against the Lycan's. "Take cover, Ace!" the Mutant says, raising his hands in a surrender gesture and swiftly clapping them, expelling thousands of tiny lightning bolts in every direction.

The sparks quickly pass through the bats, not hitting or affecting any of them. Anarchious sees this in a glance as the bats continue to swarm the duo. “Ace, plan B!” Anarchious yells as his eyes flicker violet purple.

“Plan B?” Ace asks, confused.

“Yes, plan B!” Anarchious confirms.

“What plan B?!” the Lycan replies, even more confused.

“Plan B! You don’t pay attention for shit!” Anarchious retorts to his counterpart, who is dumbfounded.

“There is no plan B!” Ace replies.

“Just follow my lead!” Anarchious says to the Lycan as the whole area is engulfed by a sudden fog.

In an instant, the fog surrounds the entire throne room, blocking out everything in sight. The fog is so thick, the duo can’t see clearly a foot away. The flapping and beating of the bats’ wings leave the duo’s ears shot as the queen reappears in the middle of the fog, trying to make sense of it all. She stands there, eyes glowing like the moon, searching the thickness of the fog.

“You know Abel battled me like a man,” the queen states out loud, looking to draw Anarchious out. The room stays still and quiet as the queen’s eyes continue to scan the foggy room. Suddenly, her eyes met a dark silhouette, “Oh, so you’re ready to die?!” Zera cockily utters to the still silhouette staring back at her. The silhouette nods at the Vampyr queen, irritating her. Zera angrily yells at the top of her lungs, “Disrespectful!” while trying to use her psychic ocular power on the figure, her eyes glowing like the harvest moon.

Nothing happens. Zera walks forward, trying to get closer, but the figure only backs away from her. "Coward!" she yells as the silhouette continues to avoid her in the thick of the fog. She runs toward the silhouette. "Fight me like a man!" she screams, trying to lunge forward, but before she can step off, she is grabbed from behind and bear-hugged. She feels the bones in her upper body crackle and the wind beneath her feet.

"Eh, no thank you!" Zera's captor utters in her ear as the silhouette flies overhead towards her from the fog. Anarchious emerges, grinning. With great force he drops a vicious elbow to her cranium, knocking her out cold.

7
Blind Truth

"Hello?!" a male voice says in Zera's ear.

The Vampyr queen comes to. Her eyes are open, but it is still dark. She tries to move, but her hands are bound behind her back. She is sitting on the ground, leaning on something that feels scratchy. The hole in her chest is still there, festering but still trying to heal. Her skin feels clammy as she feels an unfamiliar heat kiss it.

"Wake up!" the male voice shouts. The sound of snapping fingers seems to be in front of her face, but she sees nothing.

"What is this?" Zera yells at the man, trying to get to her feet, but she is shoved back down on her rear end.

"You sit!" the male voice demands.

"When I get out of here…" the queen says, irate, but is cut off by the male.

"You'll what? You won't do a damn thing!" he finishes, cutting Zera's arrogance. "Now, sit there and listen. We ask the questions. You answer them. Do not make this harder than it has to be!" the man states to Zera firmly. Zera doesn't respond. She just huffs and stubbornly turns her head.

"Abel. You've seen him and have interacted with him! Where is he?" the voice asks firmly. Zera doesn't answer and continues to ignore the man. "Where is Abel?!" the man asks firmly again, but the queen doesn't respond. The man grabs her by her throat, lifts her off her feet, and slams her back against the sturdy, scratchy surface. "I'm going to enjoy frying you!" the irate man says to Zera as she dangles in midair.

"Stop!" another more gentle male voice says a little further away from them.

Zera then hears some angry whispering and arguing take place as she dangles and gasps for air. The man drops her, and she lands hard on her bottom. He continues his side argument with the other man. Zera wheezes for air as she hears one of the men storm off. She then feels a gentle grasp of her head and a slight pull. Scared, she closes her eyes and feels heat on the pale-brown skin of her face. Her head feels exposed.

"Look at me!" the softer, calmer voice requests, but Zera continues to disobey. The man places his hand on her shoulder. She feels his fingernails sharp against her cold, clammy skin. "Please look at me!" he demands more firmly. Zera still holds her head away and keeps her eyes closed tight. The man pinches her hard on her damp skin and twists. Pain shoots up her arm, forcing her eyes open.

Sunlight glares across the Vampyr's eyes, blinding her for a moment. "Sunlight!" she yells, becoming deathly afraid and beginning to hyperventilate. She shuts her eyes once again and turns away from her captors.

"We are under a tree, within it shadows. It's midday. The sun will not blind you or harm you...much. So I'm going to ask you again to look at me! You're going to open your eyes and look me in the eyes!" the voice orders Zera, ready to pinch her again.

Reluctantly, she opens her Vampyr eyes. They try to adjust to the sunlight. She sees glimpses of her abductors, but they are more like silhouettes because her eyes aren't able to adjust totally to the sunlight.

Sunlight—Zera has never seen or been in contact with it before. Soon her vision improves. She can make out what she is seeing but can see only as far as the shadows of the tree. She is face to face with the Lycan, Ace, currently in his human form. She looks beyond him. Standing in the sunlight just shy of the surrounding shadow is Anarchious. She can hardly make him out, but his profile reminds her so much of his brother.

Zera looks Ace in the eye, still skeptical of the situation at hand. "Tell me everything you know about my partner's aunt and brother," Ace demands.

Sensing she is in control, she gives Ace a very suggestive look and answers, "What exactly is it you want to know?"

In a blur, Anarchious slaps Zera's face, nearly giving her whiplash. "We ask the questions! You answer them!" the Mutant yells angrily.

"Self-control, Anarch! Remember José's teachings!" Ace yells at the infuriated Mutant as he stands up. Ace then kneels back down and looks Zera in the face. "Look, this would go easier for you and save me a migraine if you just talk," the Lycan explains to the Vampyr. Zera remains silent, giving Ace a dead stare and periodically glaring at Anarchious, who is next to him, steaming mad. "Nothing?" Ace asks a silent Zera. "OK, let's try this approach. The 'darkness,' the being that helped you and Luna kill Drake—was that Abel?" Ace asks Zera. He sees an immediate reaction and change of emotion in her.

"Who told you that?" she responds, looking the Lycan in his trusting chocolate eyes.

"Don't worry about that! Answer me or I'll let 'Me Angry' over here slap you up like a slave trafficker!" Ace quickly retorts.

"So what if it was him?!" Zera says, looking up at the irate Mutant.

"Quit the games and tell me about Abel before we drag you into the sun!" Ace replies, yanking on the chains that bind her hands.

"OK! What is it you want to know?" the Vampyr reluctantly says.

"Where is he?!" Anarchious asks immediately.

"I don't know!" Zera replies even more quickly than Anarchious asked the question. Anarchious pushes Ace out the way, grabs the chain, and tries to drag Zera into the sun. "I seriously do not know!" Zera says, trying to fight back. "Last time I saw him was a few months ago on business," the terrified Vampyr says, spilling what she knows.

"Business? What kind of business?" Anarchious asks.

"I don't know. He asked something about a Sage or someone who was close to the Vampyr nation," she replies, looking the infuriated Mutant in the eye. "I knew nothing about whatever he was speaking of. All I knew was he was different, completely different."

"Different how?" Anarchious says, tightening the slack in the chain.

"Just different, when I first met him about four years ago, he was sweet, shy, and completely naïve, but this time around, he had this…wickedness about him," she explains, biting her lip and seemingly turned on by the thought of Abel.

Anarchious yanks her chain, forcing her to her feet. He stands face to face with Zera. "What did you do to my brother?!" he snarls at her.

"I did nothing. Sure, I manipulated him a bit, put a spin on reality for him, but even after helping kill Drake, he wasn't that...cold," she replies with an intrigued look on her face.

Anarchious glares at the Vampyr in her big, dilated eyes, not knowing what to feel.

"Abel for me was like a diamond in the rough," the Vampyr queen explains. "There was something hidden beneath all that innocence, and I harnessed it for a short while. He became my little 'monster,' but he was searching for something else, and that's when he took his leave. It's a shame! I could have really used a hand like his." She lets out a tiny sigh.

Anarchious glares at Ace, not sure if he wants to believe anything the queen has said, but the look on Ace's face lets him know that the woman's statement is true. The Mutant refuses to believe it because he knows his brother didn't have one bad bone in his body, but then again, he hasn't seen his brother in nearly five years, so it all is quite possible. Not to mention, Anarchious can feel in his heart that something is off balance with his brother. Even with all of this uncertainty, he's relieved to know his brother is still alive.

"So do you know what he was searching for the first time around?" Ace asks Zera out of curiosity.

"Well, he mentioned the Mutant old country, and he would always harp about becoming stronger," she replies, easing her way back to the tree.

"And? Is that all?" the Lycan demands, making eye contact with the Vampyr while Anarchious stands by, lost in deep thought.

"I'm not a geographer," she snaps at Ace. "I don't know where the old country is to be found. I'll tell you like I told him—all I know is that the Mutant old country was a large island off the west coast of this continent. Don't even think it's there anymore."

"So he went to the old country, then came back to you four years later, stronger and more evil? Is that it?" Ace asks.

"Maybe, yeah. Well, that place or..." Zera begins to reply hesitantly.

"Or where?!" Anarchious jumps back into the conversation.

"Well, he wanted to get stronger, so I told him," Zera replies.

"Told him what?" Anarchious asks.

"About the God-King," the Vampyr queen responds to the curious Mutant.

Simultaneously, the duo exclaim, "God-King?!"

"What the fuck is a God-King?!" Anarchious exclaims.

"She means the Demon-King, or turd, depending on how you perceive him," Ace replies.

"Only stand-up-straight, squares-for-justice, stiff-backed 'protagonists' like you refer to him as the Demon King!" Zera replies to Ace, shunning his correction.

"Excuse me; your 'Turd-King' burned Pride territories and Pride homes with a snap of his fingers because we refuse to worship him. Demon-King! I stand by the title he has earned!" Ace snaps at the Vampyr, who has a wicked smile across her face.

"What the hell does he have to do with Abel?" Anarchious interjects, trying to get them back on subject.

"He quite possibly could have killed the God-King. This would make him the strongest in the world and perceivably its ruler," Zera explains to Anarchious.

"Impossible," Ace proclaims.

"Oh, really?" Zera continues. "Drake, at three thousand years old, was maybe the third or fourth strongest being in this world. Abel killed him nearly single-handedly and didn't even break a sweat as a teen," she explains to the confused Mutant and dumbfounded Lycan.

"It's impossible. If the Demon-King had been deposed, then the world would have known already. I would have known," Ace says in disbelief.

"You have a point, mutt. This seal of his followers would have dispersed from my skin. You have one too, huh?" Zera asks while showing them the glowing red inverted crescent moon symbol on her hip.

"Yeah," Ace replies, sighing.

Anarchious listens on, still confused and not knowing what to say or what to ask. He begins to feel sick and feels his heart flutter. He knows just one thing. He has to find out if all this is true. He has to find his brother.

"Look, shackle her up. We're going to the District," Anarchious says to Ace.

"So you're just going to chain me up and leave me out here?! I will not survive. The rancid Lycans will smell this disgusting, bloody, festering hole you put through my chest. " Zera snaps angrily at the Mutant.

"No, you're coming with us, leech!" Anarchious snaps back.

"What about the sun, idiot?!" she yells back, trying to keep them from shackling her.

"The worst that could happen is your skin will boil up, and you'll be blind for a few days," the Lycan replies, yanking on her chain and pulling her closer.

"You're lucky that's all we're going to do to you," Anarchious follows up, walking out of the shadow of the tree into the sun beyond Zera's eyesight. "You killed my aunt. Now I have to go tell her daughters. I'm going to let them decide what to do with you."

Zera scowls at Ace as he shackles her neck like a dog and tugs on it to check its tightness. He then tugs on the end of the chain, trying to pull her beyond the shadow. Zera fights back, scared of what may happen.

"Now, be good, and I might put a pillowcase back over your head!" Ace says to the Vampyr, smirking.

"Fuck you, mutt!" Zera yells at the Lycan. "This is embarrassing. You're going to have me walking around on a leash like a one-tit freak."

"It'll grow back! Stop whining!" Ace responds, pulling her into the sunlight.

8
The District's Monster

The Mutant-Lycan duo, dragging the Vampyr queen behind them, walk for two days and two nights before they reach the outer perimeter of the Old District. It is around noon and very humid. Anarchious, who has been mute the entire trip, stops and sighs at the sight of his crater of a village, not really looking forward to what happens next.

Ace, with a blindfolded Zera on an iron leash following him, trails his Mutant ally into the old city's ruins, not really knowing where he is going. The streets are littered with old broken-down vehicles, abandoned bombarded buildings, concrete, old rusted steel beams, and glass. With the street filled with obstacles, it's extremely tiring for the group to get through this place. Ace thinks to himself that this would be the perfect hole to hide in to keep away from the wars and violence this world has to offer. It's literally like walking into a giant hole in the ground.

After walking through jumbled piles of concrete and asphalt, they finally reach a tall, steel-spiked gate. The Lycan gazes beyond the gate at the Old District. The place looks as if it has gone through three world wars, and a nice little community has been rebuilt over the remaining debris. It is a surprisingly clean town considering it's in a crater and surrounded by debris.

Anarchious turns to his Lycan friend and says, "Hey, can you do me a favor?"

"Yeah, no problem," Ace responds, noticing the down look on the Mutant's face.

"Hand me her chain, please," Anarchious asks, holding his hand out for it. The Lycan hands the Mutant the chain, continuing to monitor his friend's emotion. "Could you stay here, please? I don't know how they'll react to a Lycan. It's bad enough we've got Queen Turkey Bacon frying over here," Anarchious says, trying to explain the disposition of the village.

The last time Ace had seen Anarchious this depressed and lifeless was the night he learned the truth about his people's genocide. The Lycan becomes too worried to wait outside the gate, so he thinks of a plan. "I'll tuck my tail in. No one will ever know," Ace says, trying to determine a way into the village so he can learn more about the mysterious Anarchious.

The Mutant looks at the Lycan peering through the gates while tucking his tail into his sweatpants and sighs. "A'ight, OK, then," he says, reluctantly approving of the proposal.

Anarchious knocks on the gate and yells, "Taxation without representation!" In a few moments, the gate opens wide, and they all walk in. The Lycan immediately notices the one long, smashed-up street stretching nearly a half mile up the road. There are decent-looking homes on both sides of the road and half-naked children playing in the street while their parents watch them.

Anarchious places his hood over his head, tugs on Zera's chain, and begins to walk the length of the road. Right away, Ace notices people's reactions to Anarchious. Parents begin to panic, pick up their children, and retreat to their homes with urgency, slamming their doors and windows.

Soon after the group has walked the first block, all activity has died. The residents of the next block are locking up, anticipating the Mutant walking by. With no emotion or real reaction to any of this, Anarchious keeps walking straight towards their destination while Ace follows, astounded by these people's display of fear. The Lycan wonders what Anarchious could have done to make them so frightened of him. It must have been his angry outbursts, but even with his current demeanor, Ace thinks that theory seems far-fetched.

They continue to walk another block over, and again everyone flees from Anarchious's presence. The third block over, some teenagers and older villagers stay outsidc and watch the Mutant like a hawk. Some chuckle, and some scowl at the sight of him.

Anarchious drops his head even lower and puts a little more pep into his step when a group of misfit teenagers who seem like a gang surround him on all sides and walk alongside him. They laugh and giggle, giving each other signals and some even dancing around, taunting him. The older teen signals the others, and they all quickly reach into their pockets and throw rocks and rotten fruit at Anarchious, nailing him from all sides.

The gang opens up an all-out assault and begins a barrage of rocks and rotten fruit and vegetables. Even some of the adults on the sidewalk join in while others laugh and scream insults. "Black monster!" "Demon seed!" "Abomination!" Ace is astounded at this display of disrespect. He's even more shocked at Anarchious's reaction. The Mutant just keeps walking, taking everything the villagers give him. This all begins to anger Ace.

An old hag cuts infront of the teens, points a religious star at Anarchious, and begins to sermonize. "Here he is! The demon seed! The black seed of the black demon! He doesn't deserve to live amongst us. Rebuke him! Rebuke him! Baptize him in stone! Baptize him in his blood! In the name of the Spirit!" She spits right in the Mutant's face.

"Assholes! Leave him alone!" Ace screams at the top of his lungs, ready to hurt the humans for their unwarranted violence. He lets out a frightening growl and unleashes his claws, but before the villagers notice, the Mutant grabs Ace's forearm and pulls him close.

"No, Ace!" Anarchious pleads to his Lycan counterpart, whose arms are growing fur. Anarchious angrily squeezes Ace's forearm harder, teeth gritted with blood and tears in his eyes. "Don't do it! We're almost there," he continues to plead with his partner, who only wants to defend his partner. Ace retracts his claws and his Lycan form, which didn't really get past his human stage, so the villagers are confused about what has just happened.

The Mutant then turns around, tugs on Zera's restraints, and continues up the road. The mob continues their assault. How could Anarchious go from being a badass to a punk ass in a matter of days? Ace thinks to himself, frustrated. This wasn't Anarchious's persona at all. If it had been him or if a Vampyr had tried this, Anarchious would have removed all of his limbs with a wrathful quickness. Not only this, but the mob is so bent on making the Mutant's life hell, they don't even notice the roasting Vampyr he is walking like a dog. The mob continues to assault the Mutant for another block. Then the teenagers run away, and the adults disperse.

Anarchious keeps walking until they hit what seems a deserted part of town. The houses are old, boarded up, and uninhabitable. The street turns dirtier and rockier, with old stone barriers and warning signs nearly every ten feet. Soon they reach a graffiti-riddled house on a corner with a little black fence around it. It is built of brick and has a bright red door and boarded-up windows.

Anarchious chains the Vampyr to the gate, covers her with an old tarp from the yard, and slowly makes his way up the steps to the door and exhales. He rests his forehead on the door and stands there for a moment. Ace just watches, sensing the pain his partner is feeling. Anarchious raises his hand, ready to knock on the door, but before he can, the door opens up wide, and out comes a teenage girl. She jumps into his arms spider-monkey style and hugs him tightly.

"Archie!" the girl cries out with tears in her eyes. Anarchious hugs her back and tears up himself. The girl has honey-brown skin and long brown hair. She unwraps her long legs from around the Mutant and stands on her own two feet, still clutching him tightly. She begins to sob harder. From the street, Ace feels it all. He can tell she knows that her mother is dead. Two slightly older females emerge from the home, one taller and one shorter. The taller female is fair with freckles and short peach-colored hair, and the shorter one is a deep chocolate with long raven-colored hair. They join in on the hug with Anarchious and the sobbing girl.

The family of four stands there crying, mourning the death of the head of their household, Marie. This goes on for a little bit until the younger one pulls Anarchious into the house. The other two follow, inviting Ace along with them. Despite the outside the house looking old and raggedy, the inside is nicely furnished. The house was clearly owned by someone who had a little wealth and great taste. It is like nothing Ace has ever seen before. The floors are hardwood, the walls are painted the color of pink lemonade, the padded chairs have glossy wood frames, and the couches are leather and suede. Every wall has an abstract painting, and the entire house is lit by candles even though there are light fixtures and fancy gold lamps.

Ace sits down on one of the chairs in the living room. Anarchious tells the women everything in detail leading up to the discovery of Marie's death. He recounts meeting Ace and fighting, then being tricked by Zera, taking the message to Luna, meeting with the hermit Mutant José, and finding out the history of his people and information about his runaway brother, Abel. He ends with the confirmation of Marie's death by her murderer.

Anarchious stands and removes his combat vest and hoodie as the three women congregate on the couch. Ace can't take his eyes off the women huddled up on the couch. All three women are extremely attractive, but he can't shake an odd feeling about them. There is something familiar he can't put his finger on.

"Oh my goodness, they stoned you again?" the taller, younger sister exclaims, observing Anarchious's minor lumps, bruises, blood, and scars on his face and arms that are already beginning to heal.

"Nothing new, Tina," Anarchious sighs, wiping the blood off with a towel.

"I'll go get some ice!" the woman with peach-colored hair says, quickly leaving the room.

The chocolate woman with raven hair looks at Anarchious with attitude and disappointment and says, "One of these days…one of these days they'll regret everything they've done."

Anarchious looks at her but drops his head, not really believing that statement. "I still don't see why he puts up with it, Nat," Tina says to her sister, getting up and helping Anarchious wipe off some of the blood from the back of his fuzzy head. Nat shakes her head, crosses her legs, folds her arms, and lets out a tiny grunt, agreeing with her sister.

"Don't talk about me like I'm not here. Y'all know if I fight back, they just have more reason to turn me in," Anarchious replies, explaining his passive behavior towards the mob.

"Well, run home!" Tina yells in a condescending tone and popping him on the back of his head.

"Running isn't an option," Anarchious replies, cleaning the blood from his inner lip. "That'll just bring them to our front door. I'll be damned if I let either of you get hurt or let them try to burn us again."

"That was long ago. You know we can handle ourselves now!" the peach-haired female says, stepping back into the room and handing Anarchious the ice pack.

"Thanks, Lynn," Anarchious says as he places the ice pack on his swollen forehead. "And speaking of knowing something, did y'all know your mother's a Witch?" he asks the trio.

They all look at each other and simultaneously respond, "Yeah!," and begin to giggle.

"When the hell was y'all gonna to tell me?" Anarchious retorts, confused and in the.

"Oh, c'mon, you can't be that stupid," Nat says, laughing.

"What?!" Anarchious responds.

"No, what?! You seriously didn't know?" Nat continues, looking at him as if he's crazy. Anarchious glares back, not really knowing what she is talking about.

"You don't recall the events that took place when our mom was trying to help you control your 'emotions'?" Lynn says, jumping into the conversation. "She survived every one without a shock, burn, or scratch."

"I remember the scream incident but never thought anything of it till two days ago," Anarchious responds, still feeling in the dark about it all.

"So you don't remember that time you were sick in bed, she was feeding you, and you sneezed lightning, setting the sheets ablaze?" Nat asks Anarchious.

"No, not really," he replies.

"What about the time she was teaching you to swim and your water wing fell off? She couldn't stop twitching for a week!" Lynn says, adding to the memories.

"Um..." Anarchious says, nearly speechless.

"What about the time she got you that puppy and you shock-hugged her?" Tina remembers.

"What about when Abel disappeared five years ago?" Lynn asks, giving Anarchious a serious glare. Anarchious drops his eyes to his feet, remembering the event vividly and feeling ashamed again. "No human would have been able to survive such a hit!" Lynn says, refreshing his memory about the details.

"It wasn't a hit; it was a push," Anarchious replies, depressed. "I couldn't control myself. I never left her bedside until she got better after that."

"You were never able to control your emotion or powers, and each time, it put her life on the line," Lynn states, then sits back down on the couch along with Nat.

After that statement, the room becomes awkwardly silent for a few moments. Ace, who has been enjoying the conversation, looks at Anarchious and says, "Hey, show them what the hermit guy taught you."

Anarchious looks at his counterpart for a moment, not really knowing why he would want him to do that, but he eventually catches on from the bright look on Ace's face. Anarchious holds his hand up as his finger begins to light up purple and flash electricity. The trio of women looks on, wondering what this is. Eventually, he creates a tiny ball of electricity and allows it to float in midair.

"The hermit I told y'all about, he taught me to control my power," Anarchious says to the sisters while toying with the ball of electricity. "It's true that before I met him, I didn't really know how to control this curse, so it came out at times of heightened emotion or desperation," Anarchious continues as the sisters follow the ball, astounded at its beauty. "I am sorry it put you guys in so much danger. I wish I could apologize to Marie, but I can't."

Tina stands up, looks Anarchious in the eye, and waves her hand, taking control of his electricity ball. "It's not a curse, Archie. It's a gift," she says as she makes some quick hand gestures, turning the ball of electricity into a purple fish. Anarchious, astounded, looks at the fish as it swims in midair, seemingly dancing around them.

Nat stands up, mumbles in a weird language, waves her hand, and splits the fish into many swimming dancing fish. "Mom loved you. It was something you couldn't control, and we can only imagine if we didn't have Mom to teach us. It's stupid to apologize," Nat says, directing the tiny purple fish to Lynn as she stands up. Lynn snaps her fingers, and the fish returns to electricity. She snaps and waves her hands in opposite directions, turning the ball of electricity into a flat plane, still emanating electricity, and pushes it to Anarchious's face.

There is an image on the ball. It is moving but still too blurry to make out. Soon the image sharpens. Anarchious makes out what it is as he places his hand on it. It's a memory of him and Marie hugging when he was younger. "She would be proud of you!" Lynn says, kissing him on his cheek and then embracing him. A tear drops from his eye as he is still fixated on the moving photograph.

Lynn then snaps her fingers, and an envelope springs up in her hand with Anarchious's name on the front, glowing blue. Lynn hands him the letter and smiles. "She left this letter for you," Lynn says, handing it to him. The memory Lynn conjured disperses and is absorbed back into Anarchious as he opens the letter.

The letter was indeed written by Marie. She had a distinctive handwriting that was neat and sloppy at the same time. It was sort of a cross between cursive and classic print. Anarchious continues to look over the penmanship instead of reading the letter, stalling in fear of what he might read.

"Go on," Lynn says with a smile lighting up her freckled face.

Anarchious gains enough courage and begins to read it. Ace stares at Anarchious, wondering about the letter. While Anarchious reads the letter, Ace notices tiny emotional changes and tweaks in his body language. Then he feels a great pain coming over Anarchious.

After a few moments, Anarchious finishes the letter and gives an insincere smile to the sisters. He then folds the letter up, places it in his pocket, and begins to look around. "Yo, what happened to the electricity?" Anarchious asks the sisters, just noticing the house is being lit mainly by candles.

"Power's been out for about a week in the entire District. Generators ran out of juice again," Lynn replies.

"Well, I'm going to head over to the plant," Anarchious says, swinging his hoodie on and rushing out of the house.

"I'm coming with!" Tina says as she jumps off the couch and follows the Mutant out the door.

"Wait up!" the Lycan says, following right behind them both but is stopped when Tina stops in front of the doorway's threshold.

Ace squeezes by Tina and glares at them, wondering, Why the sudden stop? Anarchious and Tina stand on the porch, staring into the street at a petite woman in a colorful dress. Tina folds her arms and grunts, displeased at the sight, then glares at Anarchious, who really doesn't seem that happy either.

stares at the woman from under the shadow of the really knowing whether to be excited or sad. She reminds his mother with her golden tan skin, her big brown eyes, her distinguished and exotically beautiful face, and her big, crinkly, manelike hair. She is barefooted and wears bracelets on the end of every limb. The woman approaches the group, seemingly cautious, fiddling with her hands nervously.

"Ugh. I'll see you later, Archie," Tina says as she storms back into the house while Anarchious makes his way down the steps, keeping his eyes on the woman.

A few feet away, the woman runs and jumps on Anarchious. "Archie!" she exclaims, happy to see him. Anarchious gives her a half-hug and kiss on the cheek. "I heard you were back, and I came running," she says to Anarchious as he puts her down.

"Yeah, I bet you did," Anarchious replies, looking down.

"Where did you go?" she asks, looking up at him with her big, striking brown eyes.

"Nowhere," he replies, knowing this conversation is heading down a road he doesn't want to travel.

"You don't have to lie to me, Arch!" she snaps.

"I really don't want to talk about it, Sena," Anarchious says, looking away, not able to make any eye contact with her, though that's what she is trying to get him to do.

"But I was worried about you!" she says, grabbing his hands and squeezing, trying to get him to feel her.

"Why?" Anarchious says, dropping his hands from hers and looking up the road.

She grabs his hands and strokes the newer scars. "What do you mean, why? I care. Don't treat me like that," she replies with tears in her eyes. Anarchious sees this and huffs as if it is making him angry. "Don't do this again. Why are you so rough with me?" she says, grasping onto his hoodie collar.

Anarchious removes the hood from his head, exposing his new bruises and scars, and looks her in the eye. "Because you cry for no reason!" he yells.

"I cry because you're being a dick to me when I only try to love you!" she yells back at him.

"Look, my aunt is dead. I can't deal with you right now," Anarchious says, shooing her hands away, then walking due east. Sena stands there and cries, hurt by Anarchious's words.

A few steps away, Anarchious returns his hood to his head, ashamed and guilty at his actions, but he keeps walking.

"Anarchious!" Sena yells, tears rushing from her eyes, her mascara running.

The Mutant reaches halfway up the block. He turns around but continues walking backwards and yells, "And what'd I tell you about coming over here without shoes?! You could hurt yourself!" He then turns around and continues his path while Sena stands in the street, watching him walk away.

Ace, who has witnessed the entire fiasco, runs up to Anarchious, catching up with him around the corner. "Who was that?" Ace asks out of curiosity.

"My girlfriend," Anarchious replies and keeps walking towards their destination.

Ace is confused because the girl is human, and the humans in the town don't seem too fond of him. They all mustn't be that bad, he thinks to himself, following his partner.

The duo walk east for about a mile and come to a gated area where all the electrical and telephone wires in the District seem to be running. They jump the fence and make their way to the dark main building on the power plant site. Anarchious comes upon a door labeled FUSE and enters. The room has big fanlike generator. Anarchious immediately grabs what seem to be exposed wires running from the generator and gives them a big jolt of his power. Immediately, power returns to the building and the entire village.

The room is old and dusty but big and filled with ancient human technology. The Mutant feels at ease in this room. He was here several times as a child and helped the town restore power. He inspects the power towers, and etched on the metal of the door he sees, "Angelica 'heart' Athar 4 ever!" The names of his parents—they both had been here before, but he already knew that. He then lies down in the middle of the floor, relaxing and listening to the loud sound of the large generators as his counterpart watches him.

Hours later, Anarchious and Ace return home to the corner house with the bright red door. The sun has already set, and they immediately notice the Vampyr queen is gone from the yard. They both rush into the house, hoping the Vampyr hasn't gotten to the girls, but it's too late. Zera is in the living room, sitting on the couch with legs crossed, fully regenerated with a smirk on her face. The duo rush her, but before they can grab her, she raises her arms, and they notice her wrists are bound by a weird pink energy. They halt.

"What the hell is this?" Anarchious shouts, still confused about what is going on.

"What the hell are you yelling about?" Nat says, stepping into the room.

"Her!" Anarchious explains, pointing at Zera wide-eyed, not understanding why she is lounging on their couch.

"Yeah? What about her?" Nat replies, looking at Anarchious like he's dumb.

"That bitch! She's the bloodsucker who killed your mother," Anarchious replies, looking back and mimicking Nat's facial expression.

"And?" Nat retorts condescendingly.

"And she's on our couch!" Anarchious responds, thinking Nat is losing her mind.

"OK. You must have a point somewhere in this," Nat responds mockingly. Anarchious quickly grabs Nat's head, yanks her close, and lights up his finger close to her eyes.

"Idiot! That won't work on them!" Zera says to Anarchious, knowing what he was doing. Anarchious continues trying to look into Nat's pupils, but she continues to avoid and fight him. "My ocular powers work only on men," Zera exclaims. Nat breaks free of Anarchious as he turns his attention to Zera.

"Why the hell would I believe you?!" Anarchious says, getting into Zera's face.

"It's true," Zera replies, making eye contact with Anarchious. "Besides, I'm not strong enough to do that at the moment, or you and your puppy wolf over there would be smelling each other's taints right about now."

Anarchious steps back and looks at her, then glares at his counterpart. Ace looks at him, lost, and shrugs, not knowing whether it is truth or lie this time. Anarchious then turns back to Nat. "Why are you being hospitable to the Vampyr who killed your mom?" he asks her.

Just then, Lynn walks in, holding a big bag of some sort. "Simple. Mother would have forgiven her," Lynn says, looking at Anarchious.

"Come again?!" Anarchious snaps at Lynn.

"We're letting her go tonight, Archie," Lynn replies, handing Zera the bag.

The Mutant, aggravated by the sisters' naïve decision, yells, "Are you guys out of your fucking—?!"

Just then, Nat places her index finger on Anarchious's forehead and looks him in the eyes. He can hear her voice in his head. "Calm your nerves, Archie. We can handle this," Nat's voice says, trying to calm him.

The Mutant isn't buying it, though. He thinks to himself, Now Zera knows where my entire family is. If she wants revenge, she can return.

Before he can complete his entire thought process, he is interrupted by Nat's voice in his mind. We worked it all out. In exchange for her life, she and her cronies will leave the District alone forever. And to make sure, I placed a hex on her while I was healing her. If she tries anything—and I mean anything—she will lose her eyes permanently.

Anarchious raises his eyebrow, surprised she can hear his thoughts as well. So he thinks, If that doesn't work?

Nat sends her voice through his mind again. Well, we told her if anyone gets hurt or kidnapped by a Vampyr in this village again, our brother will kill her. She talks a tough game but is completely terrified of that happening, so she'd better control her city.

Brother? You guys have a brother now? Anarchious thinks to himself once more.

You, ya moron! Nat blurts into his mind, frowning and jabbing his head back with her finger, annoyed by his ignorance.

Anarchious steps back and looks at everyone in the room from left to right. Then he looks at Lynn and says, "Only reason I brought the Vampyr is that I figured you guys would want to... 'meet' the piece of shit that killed Marie. Didn't really think you all would let her walk. But if she promised to leave my village alone, then I guess she can live."

Zera smiles and stands up, carrying the bag past Anarchious. "Call it even!" she says, smiling arrogantly while walking towards the door.

Anarchious sighs and looks back at Zera, scowling. "Not even. Except for the missing teeth, your girlfriend's fine," he proclaims as he walks away from them all. He leaves the living room, turns the corner, and heads into the basement. Zera, on the receiving end of evil glares from the entire room, slowly backs her way out of the house.

For the next few hours, the house seems to be plagued by tension. Ace stays upstairs with Nat and Lynn, conversing about the world, trying to help lighten the mood. The Witches are cool and don't seem to treat him differently, knowing he is a Lycan. They even feed him, allow him to bathe, and clothe him. Nat even cornrows his giant frizzy mess of hair. Ace wonders whether this is out of naïveté or just plain ignorance, but it matters less and less as time passes. Soon it is midnight, and both women retire to their upstairs room, sending Ace to the basement with Anarchious.

The basement is big and furnished but cold. Its main light source is a bedside lamp. The basement-turned-bedroom-for-two clearly hasn't been cleaned in weeks. Anarchious has already disrobed, showered, left his clothes lying on the floor, and lain down to sleep. The Lycan, tired himself, curls up on the bed on the opposite side of the room and tries to get some shut-eye.

A few more hours pass, and the Lycan still can't sleep. Although he feels his body shutting down, he's not tired. He can't stop thinking about the day he and Anarchious have had. He then begins thinking about that letter. Ever since he read it, Anarchious has been extremely quiet. The Lycan sits up and notices that Anarchious, scars and bruises completely healed, is up reading the letter again.

"Crazy day, huh?" Ace says, trying to get the Mutant's attention, but his focus is purely on the letter. After a few awkward moments, Anarchious balls the letter up, throws it against the wall, and leaves the basement in a rush. Ace is stuck for a moment and doesn't know what to do until he hears the front door slam. He then glares at the other side of the room and spots the balled-up letter on the floor. He retrieves the letter, smooths it out, and reads it:

Arch, when you receive this memento, you will have become a man. I'm writing this to you because there are some things you deserve to know. I didn't think telling you sooner than you were ready would have done you any good considering your temper and all.

Your mother, before she was killed, teleported to my home and asked me to take care of you and your twin brother. Your mother was such a beautiful soul, as I am sure you remember. The spirit blessed her with the name Angelica because she was truly angelic, and this is what I need to talk to you about.

Your mother was a savior to this village. Before she made her way to this place, it was a dump and overrun with death and corruption. Even in its darkness, your mother saw potential. It was her and your father's persuasion that scared off the old city council, who would secretly sell people into slavery for protection for themselves and their families. It was not the puppet politicians who claimed credit for it twenty years ago, but it was your mother's governing plan that got this settlement built up. It was your mom's defensive plan that kept the constant wars away from this awful town. It was your own mother's Ki that powered this city for a decade, even after she was gone.

This city had a Vampyr problem that disappeared overnight, and that was your mother and father's doing. Your mother helped me on the medical end too. She and your father, before either of you were born, would journey to other cities, towns, and countries to find old medicines and cures for diseases plaguing this city. She helped build schools, homes, and recreation centers, and she cleared a route so that traders and marketers could come to this city. Your mom did all this for the District, and I'm afraid I'm the only one who knows this or cares to really remember because of the incident.

I know that reading this, you will be furious. That is the other reason I am writing to you. After all you and your family have done for this place on top of what the people in the town have done to you, your brother, and your parents' memory, I want to apologize for them. I fear that one day I won't be here physically to ground you as I've done since you were five.

This is why I need you to forgive these people. I know you have hatred for them, but if I know anything about you, I know that you have a lot of love in your heart. Why else would you still help them after the way they've treated you? I know it's going to be hard after knowing the truth, but I have faith in you. You are destined to be great. You are destined to be a king, and by the Spirit you will be someday, but before then I need you to consider forgiving them and continue to be your lovable, silly self. I love you, Anarchious, and I think of you as my son and always will. —Love, Marie

Even the Lycan himself gets upset reading the letter, not really even knowing or understanding it completely. He just knows that his newfound friend must feel worse. So he runs up the stairs and then outside to the porch. Anarchious is sitting on the first step, gazing at the night sky's flickering stars. Ace walks over and sits next to him. Ace's braids are attracted to the energy Anarchious is giving off and start to gravitate towards him.

"I read Marie's letter," Ace says to Anarchious, watching the skies as well. Anarchious doesn't reply; he just continues to watch the sky. Ace knows Anarchious is hurting but doesn't know what to say, and touching him isn't an option. They sit there just gazing at the starry sky.

"You know, I hate them. I hate them all," Anarchious says with an unusual quiver in his voice.

"The humans," Ace replies, knowing exactly what he means.

"I fucking hate them all," Anarchious says, balling his fists tightly. "I've wasted my entire life conforming to them, trying to be like them, trying to prove to them that I'm just like them." Anarchious begins to rant. "The last three years, I openly helped with the Vampyr problem and helped with the power outages. I've proven myself time in and time out, but now I am fucking done with these people. I cannot continue to help these unworthy, selfish, cruel humans after knowing all of this." Anarchious stands up as the clear sky becomes cluttered with dark clouds. "I could destroy them all!" Anarchious says, walking towards the street. "I could summon with all my Ki the biggest storm this village has ever seen and burn it down!" Anarchious continues as the clouds overhead begin to rumble and show signs of a storm.

Ace saw this display before when they were training with the old hermit and begins to panic. He then turns into his Lycan form and makes his way towards his friend. Not a foot away from him, the Lycan reaches out for Anarchious but gets shocked before he even touches him.

"What about your sisters?" Ace yells as the wind becomes more violent.

"They will be fine!" Anarchious yells, staring at his creation spreading over the District.

Ace becomes terrified. He can feel the pain, hatred, and inner conflict afflicting Anarchious. "What about your friend? Your girlfriend, Sena? She will die too!" Ace retorts, trying to talk some sense into the Mutant.

Anarchious turns to Ace. His face and eyes are different, scary. They are the color of his lightning, and his pupils are almost animalistic. His face, half of it ghost-white, cracks up as if it was painted on. The tears pouring from his eyes are blown up and around by the wind, then turn black, painting the curvature, creases, and crevasses of his face with his pain and rage.

"Sena's no different from any of them. I thought she understood me, but she truly doesn't. I'm just some freak charity show for her because at one time, she felt pity for me!" Anarchious rages on as the lightning strikes violently, lighting up the skies. "I don't want her 'charity' anymore. I never wanted sympathy. All I wanted was to be accepted and understood like anyone else. She doesn't know what it's like to be considered a monster, to be treated like a demon, something unholy and detrimental to society. She doesn't know what it's like to be rejected for being different...hated for something I cannot change. She doesn't know what it's like to be stoned and spit on by the very people you've protected!" Anarchious screams at the sky as the rain begins to pour.

He continues to walk up the street towards the populated part of town. "She doesn't know what it's like to consistently blame yourself...blame yourself for your mother's death! If I hadn't given Mom a hard time that day, she and Dad would still be alive! If I hadn't ignored Abel the way I did, he'd still be with me. If I hadn't been so stupid to run away with Sena, I would have been there to stop Zera's gang from taking Marie! Sena always wanted me to get over it, but how fucking can I? No! Not ever, not after all of this, after dedicating my life and attention to these people, ignoring what was truly important all those years. I'm fucking done," Anarchious says, still walking towards the place he had gotten stoned earlier, flickering and flashing more rapidly with each step.

Ace braces himself with all his claws lodged in the ground to keep the strong winds from carrying him away. "You know if you never let anyone in and you remain introverted, no one will ever be able to level with you!" Ace screams at the top of his lungs, trying to get through to Anarchious, who has dropped to his knees a little shy of the populated part of the town and is seemingly pulling his hair out.

"No one will ever feel this kind of pain, this kind of rejection, this kind of guilt!" Anarchious yells back, punching the ground. "It's always fucking there at the back of my mind, Ace, plaguing me! They would be here to help me if I had never betrayed them. The only one who ever understood me was Abel!"

"My mother was killed right in front of me, and I was powerless to stop it," Ace yells to his friend. Anarchious pauses, and the wind suddenly stops. "I was kicked out of my pack for being a runt, for not following my 'nature,'" Ace yells out once more, trying to show his friend he understands his feelings to a certain degree. "I've been alone for nearly ten years. I understand. I don't understand why you're such a douche, but nonetheless, I get it!" Ace says jokingly as the rain stops. Anarchious chuckles at the joke, but soon the chuckles became sobs. "I don't know if you believe in luck or destiny, but I believe we met each other for a reason. Not sure why, but definitely a reason," Ace says, sensing Anarchious's emotion receding.

Anarchious turns to Ace, face back to normal, and tries to smile. The Lycan glares back at the Mutant, looking him in the eye, recognizing the familiar expression on his friend's face. "No! Don't you dare!" Ace says, trying to advance on the Mutant, knowing what he is about to do but is too late.

Anarchious stretches his arms out and curses the heavens as the storm he has created strikes him down with full force, knocking them both out and destroying the surrounding area.

"Archie!" Ace hears a familiar female voice call out. He tries to get up, but he can't move. He is buried under something. "Archie!" The voice continues to call out desperately as the Lycan tries to free himself. "By the Spirit! Archie, get up! Move, please!" the female voice screams in panic. Ace, hearing the panic and feeling the woman's despair, freaks out and struggles harder to free himself from the debris he is buried under.

Ace looks around, half buried. The street has collapsed into an old underground sewer. The lightning has created an even bigger hole in the ground. Ace's lower body is still trapped under concrete and earth when he notices he is in the shallow end of a big crater. He then looks over towards the voice and sees what he had feared. Tina, in pajamas, is embracing Anarchious's mangled body, trying to get a response, but he is limp and unresponsive. Ace finishes digging himself out by the time the other two sisters come running from the house into the street that is now a crater.

"Wake up! You're stronger than this!" Tina screams with tears running down her face while shaking Anarchious's lifeless body. "Nat! Help him, please!" Tina begs as both of her older sisters make it down into the crater.

"Hold on! Let me prepare a revival spell," Nat says, panicking at the sight of Anarchious's body as well. Ace crawls into the crater and joins in trying to call the Mutant back to consciousness.

Soon a crowd of human spectators has gathered around the gaping hole in the ground. Ace is annoyed by their presence, so he lets out a vicious growl. They all flee, fearing the Lycan is chasing them.

"Here goes nothing!" Nat says as she and Lynn utter something in a weird language and simultaneously release a soft healing light from their hands onto Anarchious's limp body.

After a few moments of this, the Witches are drained completely, and Anarchious's wounds and burns are healed, but he still isn't breathing. They drop to their knees, feeling defeated, as Tina holds Anarchious close, weeping.

"No fucking way!" Ace yells. He can't believe it. He refuses to believe that his counterpart could die so easily. He just isn't ready to believe it. Anarchious had struck himself down in training once before, and this lightning bolt wasn't nearly as powerful as it was then. Ace stands over the family of four, grabs Anarchious by his neck, and lets out a terrifying roar.

In an instant, Anarchious's eyes open wide as he gasps for air. Ace drops him and falls back on his bottom as the three sisters embrace Anarchious with hugs. Suddenly, Tina grabs Anarchious's hair, slaps him, and yells, "Don't you ever fucking scare us like that again!" She then pulls him in, hugging him tighter as the rest of the gang chuckles with glossy eyes but relief coming over their wet faces.

9
Destiny

The room is dark and lit by magical flickering torches. At the top of a giant flight of steps sits a flame in the shape of a man, or that's what it appeared to be—a man of black flames, eyes burning hotter than hell. At the foot of steps, there is a man in the shadows, kneeling, seemingly weakened.

"What is it, my son?" a dark malevolent voice says, echoing through the evil, murky room.

"I am not your son," the weakened man answers with the voice of a younger man while grasping at the pain in his chest.

The man of black flames smiles a wicked smile and says, "Apostle, what has made you so...feeble?"

"Feeble is how you describe an old man, something more fitting for yourself!" the young man yells back, angrily standing up on his two feet.

"Good. Good," the man of black flames replies, burning hot at the hardiness of his apprentice. "This pain you feel is weakness leaving your body," the man of black flames explains to the young man.

"Perhaps," the young man replies, not knowing exactly what the pain is. "Why is it that you keep me on this tiny crusade? Why hide me in this castle, in this desert? Why not get on with the plan?" the young man asks the black flame.

"Why? I like death! I like misery! I like this world!" the black flame yells, burning hot again, seemingly shaking the earth beneath his feet.

In a poof, the black flame man is standing next to the young man. He has nearly two feet on him as he looks down on the young man, who isn't at all short. "I'll keep you here until you're ready to fulfill your destiny, until you've harnessed that raw power and completed your training, until you feel no more pain, or until I finally get bored. Then we'll destroy it all!!" The man engulfed in the eternal black flame burns hot once more, walking up the steps back to his throne.

"My king, I am ready to carry out my mission. I am ready to take my revenge," the young man says as his eyes shine like stars on the darkest night.

"Revenge, the sweetest joy next to obtaining absolute power." The black flame continues up the stairs and sits on his throne, seeming to ignore his apprentice's confidence.

The young man clenches his fists, becoming eager. "No, you are not ready," says the man of black flame. "We cannot afford to have one screw-up. So until then, you will report back to me after every recon mission, and you shall continue training in the Red Desert. Do I make myself clear?" he says, seeming to frown down on the young man.

The young man bows, displeased at the black flame's answer, and replies, "Crystal clear!"

Just then, a blue flicker and then a flash appear midway up the steps. Blue flames shoot up from the flash, and appearing in the flames is a magical projection of a fair-skinned man with long, dark hair.

"My lord, intel was passed up to my presence, and my mystics believe they have found one of your marks," the long-haired male says.

"How sure are they?" the black flame responds in a stern tone.

"They haven't yet confirmed the identity, but they have never failed me before. They know the consequences of such a failure." The dark-haired man tries to reassure the black flame, who, however, is cautious and isn't buying it.

"Solomon, once your shaman confirms all those identities, contact me, but until then, be gone from my chambers," the black flame snarls at the man in the projection.

The dark-haired man bows and replies, "Yes, my lord. One more thing before I take my leave, then."

"What is it?" the dark flame asks, becoming aggravated.

"My bride—I was wondering about the progress of her bounty and capture. I fear she has found a way to evade our magic and fly under the radar," the dark-haired projection inquires.

"My...assassins work slowly but efficiently. Their technology will catch up to her. Your wench will be returned to you. Just focus on your mission, or I'll turn your entire kingdom into dead lands," the dark flame threatens the dark-haired man. He waves his hand, and the projection is engulfed in a black flame and burns away.

"Warlocks," the black flame says to himself in disgust as he glares back down at the set of irate eyes glowing from beyond the shadows at the foot of the steps. "Indeed you are strong, but I need you stronger. I need your power to rival mine. Once that is a reality, then nothing will stop us, Abel! We shall judge them all!" the black-flamed man says, sitting back in his throne.

"Yes, God-King," Abel replies as he bows and then turns and leaves the room.

The throne room door shuts, then warps away as if it were never there. The young man marches through the dark, torch-lit halls. His skin reflects the night sky, his hair is black and fluffy like storm clouds, and his eyes are silver-gray, shining more when there is no light. He dons a long black cape attached to what seems like a combat vest, along with black cargo pants tucked into his black boots.

The halls are filled with guards in black armor, who show no more life than a gargoyle. Angry, Abel punches one in the chest, sending him through a stone wall. Immediately, the wall patches itself after being exposed to the moon shining through. The rest of the guards remain lifeless as the young man glances around, looking for a fight, it seems. "Spineless sloths!" Abel yells as he turns his back and leaves the halls, exiting the evil ebony-stoned, tower-like castle that is the color of granite shining in the light of a giant moon.

He walks down the steps, exits the castle, and falls right through nothingness and a cloud. He falls from the heavens, descending towards a desert that stretches nearly ten miles in every direction. He lands like a cat, unharmed by the fall, and glances back up at the castle, which seems even smaller than it actually is from the ground. The castle begins to wave away like a mirage and soon is gone.

Abel then heaves onto the sands. "Damn it!" he exclaims, punching the cold, grainy soil.

"What's wrong with you?!" a voice says, coming from behind him.

"Nothing, Apophis," Abel says, wiping the corners of his mouth.

"Master Abel, that is blood. There must be something more than nothing," Apophis explains as Abel looks at his dark spacelike skin, seeing the crimson of his blood through the light of the stars.

Abel then recovers and rises to his feet. "I'm just worried about my brother," he says to the short man wrapped from head to toe in a deep red cloak and holding a snakelike staff etched deep with ancient symbols.

"Is this going to hinder our mission?" Apophis asks, looking at Abel from the side.

"No, I will complete this bogus mission quickly and prove to the God-King I can rival him," Abel says as he turns and walks the opposite way.

"Good. Good," the man says, following a determined Abel.

The two men set off into the desert until they disappear on the horizon.

10
Glen Haven

"Hold still," Tina says, irritated, to Anarchious. She is trying to help heal his left arm, which is still blistered and burned. They are back in the living room of Anarchious's childhood home with Ace, Nat, and Lynn, all conversing amongst themselves. The mood is light, even though what took place the night before still lingers with them all.

Just then, there is a knock at the door. Lynn walks over to the door and waves her hand. The door immediately becomes transparent from the inside. It's Sena, looking nervous and out of place as usual. "Archie, it's your li'l girlfriend!" Lynn says, waving her hand and returning the door back to its bright red color.

"Shit!" Anarchious exclaims.

Tina slaps him in the back of his head. "Why don't you just get rid of that heffa'?!" she says loud and squeaky, giving Anarchious the evil eye, which he can feel burning a hole into the side of his head.

"Let her in, please, Lynn!" Anarchious says as he stands up and steps towards the door.

Lynn opens the door, and Sena stands there like a deer caught in headlights. "C'mon, Sena," Lynn says, inviting the little woman into the living room. She steps in and looks at everyone, unsure of her decision until she sees Anarchious. She then runs and jumps on him. He hugs her back and places her on the floor.

"What's up?" Anarchious asks, looking at her face and knowing she is concerned about something immediately.

"The hole," she says, stroking the newly healed scars on his left arm.

"Yeah," Anarchious says, rolling his eyes, knowing immediately what she is going to ask.

"You did that?" she asks, looking up at him.

"Yeah," Anarchious responds, confirming her suspicion.

"Why? How, Archie?" she asks.

"Why—long story. How—I conjured up a storm big enough to evaporate the village, and instead of doing that, I struck myself," Anarchious answers, chuckling.

"Why?" she asks, becoming irritated.

"Why what?" he answers, not understanding what she is referring to.

"Why did you strike yourself?" she asks, upset and staring him in the eyes.

"I don't know. Better me being evaporated than everyone else I guess!" he says jokingly but immediately becomes aware that she doesn't like that.

Sena grabs his face. "Why are you trying to kill yourself? Why are you still trying to leave me?" she yells at him, beginning to sob.

Tina scoffs, rolls her eyes, and sits down. Anarchious begins to think of the night he has had and everything he has learned. He quickly becomes furious. "These fucking people! They've betrayed me, betrayed my family!" he yells.

Sena interrupts him. "No! Not this again, Archie! It's the same thing every time. Get over it! The past is the past!"

Anarchious, hearing this, becomes extremely upset but feels conflicted. Tina notices his internal conflict and Sena's ignorance and becomes upset herself. She begins chanting and making subtle hand seals in her seat when Nat grabs her glowing hand and whispers aggressively, "No spells!"

Tina grunts, folds her arms on top of each other, and rolls her eyes. "Don't you know what it would do to me if you actually died, Archie?" she asks him as he is still thinking about it all. "Don't you know how much I will miss you?" she says, stroking his cheek lovingly.

"Well, you're going to miss me anyway!" Anarchious says, pulling his face away and stepping back away from her.

"What do you mean?!" she says, surprised and confused.

"I'm leaving this piece of shit town!" he answers, frowning at her.

"What?!" Sena and Tina both yell simultaneously.

"You can't! You just got back!" Sena yells at him. She steps towards him and grabs his arms tight.

"Yeah, what this idiot just said. You can't leave!" Tina adds, trying to stop Anarchious.

"Even if I wanted to stay, which I don't, I couldn't. That crater is only going to antagonize and scare them more. They'll have more reason to turn me over to the Rebels now. Not only that, I have unfinished business elsewhere and a missing twin brother. Plus, anything's better than getting stoned and treated like shit here," Anarchious says, explaining his disposition.

Archie, it's not that bad! We can move to the—" Sena begins to explain but is cut off by an infuriated Anarchious.

"Not that bad?! Not that bad?! These are the people I protect and 'love'! Your people, who treat me like a monster! No. The simple solution is I'm gone!" he says, ripping his arms away from her.

"Take me with you!" Sena says, trying to get a hold of him again, but he grabs hold of her arms.

He looks deeply into her eyes, then glances down at her naked feet and says, "No! The road is not for you! You cannot even follow simple instructions like putting on fucking shoes."

"I can listen. Please take me with you," she says, ripping her hands loose and getting in his face aggressively.

"No," he responds resolutely, turning his back on her and stepping away towards the couch in the middle of the living room.

"But what about us, Archie?!" she yells, almost in tears.

"What about us?" he responds quickly and nonchalantly, barely glancing back at her.

Sena begins to cry as everyone looks on, feeling guilty, except for Tina, who is yawning. "Boring! Change the channel!"

"You have your choice, Sena. I suggest you move on," Anarchious says, looking into Sena's beautiful brown eyes, turned pink from all the crying and stress.

Sena wipes her face off and races from the house, hurt by her boyfriend's words. The room is awkwardly silent for a few seconds, then Tina asks, "Well, can I go?"

"No!" Anarchious, Nat, and Lynn yell simultaneously at the teenage girl.

Ace, who has been enjoying the conversation, sits indulging in popcorn on the other side of the room. He looks at Anarchious and says, "You have just earned an achievement award. Congratulations, you are the biggest prick on this side of the world!" The Mutant returns his look and grimaces.

The rest of the day seems to move slowly as Anarchious prepares some of his personal clothes and combat gear. He stuffs it all in a book bag, decorated in old, blotchy forest and winter camouflage, which is definitely his style. He even donates some of his old clothing to Ace, who has been wearing next to nothing, including a stretched-out leather jacket taken from a Vampyr grunt and a pair of stretched-out sweatpants.

The evening rolls in, and they all have dinner together. The dinner table is clouded with an awkward silence because everyone knows Anarchious will be leaving in the morning. Ace tries to lighten the mood, but it doesn't work.

Around midnight, everyone is asleep except for Anarchious, who is outside staring at the stars once again. He knows where he is heading but feels that everything has darkened around him in a matter of days, as if the road ahead of him is pitch black and he has no idea where he is going, lost like an orphaned child, which in reality is what he's been for thirteen years. The only thing he knows is that his brother is out there, suffering. He can feel it. He wants to help his brother but also feels obligated to catch up with the hermit, José, and finish his training. He has already come a long way, learning to control his abilities and to use them more efficiently, but he knows that isn't enough to get to Abel.

Soon the morning comes. Anarchious says his goodbyes and walks out of the village with his head held high as Ace follows. They leave the immediate area and find their way to an old highway heading northeast. Anarchious starts down the path, and Ace follows, wondering what exactly is next on their agenda.

"So what are we going to do about Abel?" Ace asks the Mutant.

"So what do you mean 'we'?" Anarchious replies.

"We, as in you and I. What are 'you and I' going to do about Abel?" Ace says, being a smart-ass.

"Well, my brother really respects warriors. I think the more I become one, the more I learn from Master José, I can convince him to come learn with us and help us with the investigation. That is my plan! You know, you can leave anytime you want," the Mutant retorts.

"What the hell's that supposed to mean?" the Lycan says with a smile on his face.

"Just don't want you to feel like you have to help!" Anarchious explains.

"Help? I'm just coming to see you get your ass whooped!" Ace retorts. They both laugh and continue down the path towards Glen Haven.

The duo push through the Northeastern region, continuing their training, coming across many different towns and cities. With each new place came new people. Vampyr, Lycans or Humans, with new people come problems and a potential adventure. Anarchious and Ace, ever the good samaritans, get involved in these adventures often, usually coming out on top and mending the situation. They continued their march and after a month's time, the duo arrive in Glen Haven.

Glen Haven isn't a typical representation of the area. The city is built on a big hill near the eastern seaboard, and it stretches to the surrounding flat grasslands. Like most cities, it is modernized but seems untouched by the war and famine. This city is protected by the Church of the Spirit, which means every race is allowed to live within its walls, but it isn't as peaceful as it seems. There is an odd tension in the atmosphere that is waiting to be cut, and the duo can feel it.

The town is segregated into four sections: Humans, Pride, Witches, and Vampyrs. Each section has been gated off and is guarded. Everyone seems to be watching each other, even the Vampyrs, who have a sentry in full combat uniform in the shadows of their watchtower, even in the middle of the day.

Smack-dab in the middle of the city at the top of the hill stands a giant edifice, stretching to the heavens, built of white bricks, marble, and concrete. It gives off a divine aura that draws the duo right in. They climb the steps and enter the marvelous building.

The curious duo step into a hall full of colorful arched windows and lined with benches, clearly a place of worship. They walk onto a bright red carpet leading to the back of the hall and scope it out. The hall is empty. The perfect hiding place! They decide to start looking for the hermit from here. From a back door, a tall, pale, bearded old man dressed in a silky black and red priest's robe approaches the boys. Both are in the pulpit, curiously fiddling with the instruments.

Ace, in his human form, sniffs the air and turns quickly. "Lycan," he says, informing Anarchious while looking at the old man.

"One of my fellow Pride brethren, welcome to Glen Haven's Church of the Spirit," the old man says, hugging Ace and observing both him and Anarchious, who is toying with the guitars placed on the side of the altar.

"You seem weary from travel," the old man says to Ace.

"No, we're weary from killing giant fire-breathing camel spiders," Ace retorts quickly and sarcastically, looking at the old priest.

The old man laughs and pats the younger, much shorter Lycan on his fuzzy cornrow-covered hair. "Funny little runt," he replies, smiling. "So have you come for refuge with your human slave?" the old man asks Ace.

"Slave?!" Anarchious says, coming to attention.

"You know, once you step one foot into this town, the chains of oppression are broken. There is no slavery here!" the old man announces to the young Lycan as he nods in acknowledgment.

Anarchious walks over, confused, and asks, "Slavery? What are you—?"

Ace interrupts him and slaps his hands over the Mutant's mouth. "Quiet, slave...I mean, Anarch!" he yells at his partner and then glares at the priest. "My counterpart here is free to do what he pleases," Ace says, removing his hand. He glares go away to Anarchious, who is still baffled. Anarchious gets the message, goes back to the instruments, and begins toying with them but still pays close attention to the Lycans.

"Sir, I've been sent here to see a Cardinal Vega," Ace says to the old Lycan priest.

"May I ask the nature of your business with the cardinal?" the old priest inquires.

"I have a message from the town of Small Brook at the foot of White Lion Mountain," the younger Lycan replies, thinking quickly on his feet but not really knowing what to say.

"Really? I thought that town was abandoned," the priest says, seeming to question Ace's message.

Ace stands there dumbfounded for a moment when Anarchious interrupts, thinking quickly on his toes. "It is abandoned, but we were there when an avalanche fell on it. We helped a man by the name of Jeb get out. He needs help and supplies."

"Hmm, well, I did hear of that avalanche, and it's good to hear he survived it," the old man says, looking at Anarchious, who is smiling. "Please excuse me, brethren of the Pride. I had to make sure you were telling the truth. Cardinal Vega is very...important. I cannot allow just anyone to see him," the old man explains as Ace nods, relieved that their search isn't going to become more frustrating than it has to be. "Please excuse me, gentlemen. I'll go summon the cardinal," the old Lycan says as he exits through the door from which he came.

Ace sighs and says, "Thank the Spirit you're good for something, Anarch!"

Anarchious ignores the statement and storms over to Ace. "Aye, runt, who you calling a slave?!" the Mutant aggressively whispers.

"What?!" Ace replies, his yell echoing across the entire hall.

"I'm not your slave!" Anarchious retorts, pointing at the Lycan.

"He said that because he thought you were my human, which my kind happens to enslave, dipshit!" the irritated Lycan whispers back.

"Yo, I'm not your human! I'm not anyone's human! I'm a Mutant!" Anarchious whispers back, offended at the accusation.

"Fucking duh! But you look the fucking part! You forget, there's a fuckin' bounty on any and every Mutant's head, huh?!" Ace replies under his breath, punching his counterpart in the chest.

"Oh yeah...well, shoot...I get it," Anarchious says, realizing why everything happened.

"You're a fucking scholar, you know that?" Ace says to Anarchious while gritting his sharp teeth.

"Thanks, bro!" Anarchious says, smiling.

"On the Spirit, it wasn't a fucking compliment!" Ace says, punching Anarchious in the chest once more.

"Yeah, well, you're the one cursing in a church, genius!" Anarchious says, getting in the Lycan's face.

Ace looks embarrassed and remembers where he is. "We fu...damn it! I mean, darn it!" Ace yells.

Just then the old Lycan in the robe returns to the room. "Right this way!" he says as he opens the door he had exited from moments before. He guides them up a flight of steps to a hall with a door at the end of it labeled Terra Belle: Perfect World. The Lycan priest opens the door for the duo. As they enter, they notice the large windows in the room are all filled with darker, cooler colors, leaving the room with limited light.

"Hello, children of the Spirit," comes a voice from behind a blinder from the opposite side of the room.

Ace immediately says, "Vampyr," alerting Anarchious, who now understands the windows in the room.

"Hit the nail right on the head, Lycan," the man says, coming from behind the blinder. He is a short, middle-aged, porcelain man with blonde hair and Caribbean green eyes that light up his face. The man walks over and shakes the Lycan's hand. "Cardinal Vega!" he says, introducing himself. He turns to Anarchious, shakes his hand as well, does a double take, and stares at the Mutant strangely.

"Umm, nice to meet you, Cardinal Vega," Anarchious says, feeling awkward.

"Hello," the cardinal replies as he unglues his eyes from the Mutant and directs them both to his meeting desk and seats. "So you two need a caravan of supplies sent to Small Brook," the cardinal says, placing his glasses on his face and looking at the duo.

"That would be nice, but that's not all we came to talk to you about," Ace replies, sitting down and engaging Vega, who looks worried for a moment, then sits back, giving Ace a distrustful look.

"Well, what are you here for then, exactly?"

"My friend and I are looking for an old hermit named José, José Destello," Ace replies.

The cardinal thinks for a second and sighs. "You have to be more descriptive. I meet hundreds of people every day looking for refuge from this world."

"You have to know him. He gave us your name and told us to get in contact with you," Ace replies.

"I am afraid not. As I said, I meet hundreds of new people every day," Vega replies, eyeing Ace.

"So you've never been in personal contact with an old guy named José, about average height, with a funny accent, who just happens to be a Mutant?" Ace asks the Cardinal, hoping he'll remember.

The cardinal scoffs. "I'm sorry. I do not know such a person. I don't even think such a person exists anyway. The Mutants were...wiped out over twenty years ago," the cardinal explains to the persistent Lycan.

Ace sighs in disappointment, becoming frustrated. This journey isn't going to continue as easily as he hoped. Anarchious continues to glare at the cardinal, seeming to make him uncomfortable.

"Well, if that is all, young ones, I am a busy man. I have some business to attend to. Maybe I'll see you two at night service sometime," the cardinal says, winking and smiling at the duo as he reaches over the desk to shake their hands.

The cardinal then calls his priest into the room and asks him to escort them back downstairs. After the duo returns to the hall, they exit the church. Ace looks at Anarchious, and Anarchious glares back at the Lycan. "Tonight?" Anarchious says.

"Tonight!" his Lycan counterpart replies.

Dusk falls on Glen Haven. The sky is filled with soft pink and purple clouds. The air is cool and breezy. The city's day patrons begin to recede to their homes as the night citizens begin to hit the streets. Some head to the church; others hang around talking. Even at night, the tension in the city remains. Everyone seems to stay on this or her designated side unless hitting the main street, heading to the church. Soon the sky is pitch black and filled with stars. The church is full and filled with upbeat music and joyful clapping.

From the rear exit of the church comes a short, robed, hooded man. It is the cardinal. The fully transformed Lycan Ace can smell him, watching him from the roof of an adjacent building. The cardinal begins strolling away from the church, away from the main part of the city, heading towards a more vegetated, suburban part of Glen Haven. Ace thinks that he has to be heading to his home as he follows the holy man.

The cardinal is difficult to follow due to the limited visibility, but Ace keeps up, undetected, nonetheless. After stalking the cardinal for about a mile, he comes to a dead-end street that leads into the woods. Ace sees his chance and takes it. With nearly the speed of the wind, the Lycan speeds towards the unaware cardinal and tackles him to the ground.

Immediately, Ace notices that the robe and cloak the cardinal is wearing go flat. There is no one in them. The clothing seems to be possessed by a ghost or something. "What the hell?" Ace exclaims as he hears a soft tap of feet behind him. The stunned Lycan turns as fast as he can, but it is too late. A shadow grabs him, and in a bright pink flash, they both disappear off the street.

Elsewhere, Ace falls from a pink spark out of thin air and hits the cold, wet grass face first. He hops up, immediately dizzy from seemingly being teleported. As soon as the world stops spinning, Ace glares at his surroundings, trying to figure out where he is. He looks to the west and notices the silhouette of the old broken-down bridge he and Anarchious crossed about five miles away, outside of the city of Glen Haven. Then he glares to the east and sees the city itself, the church lit up, stretching towards the heavens.

In a blur, a fist comes from behind, hitting Ace with great force, sending him hurling towards the bridge. The Lycan blacks out for a moment and sees colors, even though the field is dark. The only source of light is the moon, but it's blocked by traveling clouds. The Lycan hears the light, wet pit-pats of the culprit's footsteps getting closer. He struggles to sit up to look around, but he sees no one until his Lycan eyes gradually adjust to the dark a little better.

Ace's vision is faint, and he can barely see his adversary. His attacker is wearing a dark full body suit and combat padding on the knee, shins, and forearms. Everything above his nose is exposed. His skin is dark, and his eyes are a deep, dark amber color. His hair is short and curly. Ace gets up to his feet and stands toe to toe with this person. The Lycan looks down on him, noticing a great difference in height and weight.

The dark being quickly takes another swing at the Lycan. Ace blocks it. The impact makes the moisture from the ground splash up. Ace stares into the dark being's eyes and notices it is trying to measure him. Swiftly and before any of the droplets descend, the being tries a roundhouse kick, which the Lycan ducks. He grabs the back of the being's head forcefully. Ace then cocks his arm back and handles his attacker like a rag doll. He attempts to spike the being's head into the ground, but with swiftness and finesse, the dark attacker flips away like a circus performer midtoss, using the Lycan's momentum against him.

"What kind of ninja shit was that?" Ace asks, surprised at the reversal of what should have been the end of the fight.

The dark being lands several yards away and rushes back at the Lycan, disappearing and reappearing all over the field while closing in on his position. The being's speed is too much for Ace's Lycan eyes to keep up with in the dark. The attacker takes advantage and begins an all-out attack, still moving so fast he single-handedly surrounds the frustrated Lycan.

Ace defends himself vigorously, but for every blocked attack, the dark being lands a vicious combo. For every blow he lands on the being, Ace is struck with an even harder one. It quickly becomes apparent that the being is more experienced and swifter, but the Lycan isn't going to allow that to stop him. Ace still focuses on defending himself.

The Lycan closes his eyes and listens. Time seems to slow. He uses his sense of hearing and his instincts to counter the dark being's speed. He can hear every light tap of feet or whip of clothing against the wind. He feels every sudden jitter in the air. Immediately, he takes the advantage. The shadow being isn't able to land any more blows on the Lycan. The attacker tries to pick up speed, but it's no use. Ace counters everything and eventually catches the being in mid-attack, clotheslining his opponent and sending the being flipping and face-planting in the dirt.

The attacker, hurt, struggles to get back up to his feet, dizzy from the hard blow to his head, but that doesn't stop him. Without delay, he speeds back to the Lycan, who is still voluntarily blind. The attacker tries blindsiding the Lycan but is sent flying by a mean twisting backhand to the jaw. The now aggravated shadow being hits the ground and wastes no time charging back at the Lycan, circling him as he did before. The shadow being tries to drop and ax-kick Ace from overhead. The Lycan blocks it, grabs the shadow being's legs, and brutally power-bombs him into the dirt, leaving a tiny crater in the ground.

The Lycan stumbles back from his own power and momentum. He opens his eyes and sees the shadow being lying in the hole defeated. "That was easy enough," Ace exclaims, dropping to his knees, spent. The Lycan lets out a big sigh and looks to the heavens, relieved that it's over.

The clouds move and unveil half the moon, allowing some light to spill on the field. Ace knows after this altercation that the cardinal knows something about José. What other reason would he have for sending this ninja-like shadow being decoy in his place? There is one thing he doesn't understand, he thinks to himself as he glances back into the hole. His attacker has vanished.

The Lycan immediately hops up and looks around, not spotting anybody. "How the hell did he survive that?" Ace yells, turning around. He spots the shadow being about fifteen feet away. It is still too dark to see him clearly. The shadow being's hands flicker and glow as he conjures something out of nothing. The something looks like a curved stick when finished. The shadow being quickly charges with the darkened item and swings it at the Lycan's throat. Ace yelps loudly and pulls back, stumbling into the crater. The Lycan feels for his throat. It is still intact, but a large chunk of his mane has been sliced off. "Ninja sword?" Ace says, looking back up at the being, standing at the edge of the crater, glaring down at him.

The ninja being leaps high into the air and hurtles down, aiming to end the Lycan's life. Ace tries to scurry away, but the ninja already has the advantage. Ace quickly throws his hands up, hoping to block the attack but knowing he could lose a limb.

In a blinding purple flash, the area erupts. Lightning strikes between them. The force of the lighting shocks the ninja and pushes the Lycan in the opposite direction. He hits the crater and splits it open even wider. Dust, mud, and water circle the area like a tiny twister, limiting Ace's vision. He knows who and what has come to his rescue and is immediately relieved when he spots Anarchious, glowing his usual bright purple, walking out of the crater and dirty whirlwind.

"The hell happened to you, Ace?" Anarchious asks, walking towards the grounded but relieved Lycan.

"I have no clue. I was tailing the cardinal, and I grabbed him. Then he wasn't there..." Ace begins to explain but is interrupted by Anarchious.

"What do you mean he wasn't there?" the Mutant fusses at the Lycan.

“Exactly what I said. He wasn’t there! I grabbed him, and it was just a cloak! Then something grabbed me. Then I was dropped here!” the frustrated Lycan yells while getting a helping hand from his much smaller friend. “Wait, what the hell happened to you?” Ace yells at a guilty-faced Anarchious. “You were supposed to be my big brother in the sky, watching my back,” Ace fusses back at Anarchious.

“Well, I, uhh…” Anarchious starts, but his thought is broken up by Ace’s mocking attitude.

“Well, uhh, I don’t want to hear it! You never stick to the damn plan!” the Lycan yells, agitated.

“Well, why you didn’t signal me sooner?!” Anarchious retorts.

“Well, what the hell was I supposed to do? Shine like you and run around in circles? I don’t glow like a flamboyant ass rave stick when I power up, do I?” the Lycan says, mocking Anarchious’s aura.

“You’re a wolf, right? Howl or bark, dummy!” Anarchious retorts and hovers while coming face to face with Ace.

“I haven’t had any time to ‘howl.’ As soon I got dropped here, that ninja thing began attacking me,” Ace replies, gritting his sharp teeth and standing eye to eye with the Mutant while pointing beyond the dying whirlwind and dust.

“You mean whooping your ass! You probably thought, ‘Oh, I can do this on my own,’ but no! See, that’s why you screamed like a bitch!” Anarchious counters, arching his eyebrow in a suspicious look while crossing his arms.

“It was a yelp!” Ace yells back, becoming irritated.

“It was a scream!” Anarchious quickly replies.

"It was a fucking yelp!" the Lycan yells at the top of his lungs.

"Scream or yelp, it was the high pitched sound of you in distress that signaled me to save lil' ol Lycan you," Anarchious counters, pulling Ace's card.

"You're still an idiot!" the Lycan says, smirking.

Anarchious laughs, then pats his partner on the shoulder, turns, and hovers by the now huge crater while calming down the whirlwind. The air is still filled with the smell of burned grass and dust. When the dust clears, on the other side of the crater kneels the ninja, still feeling the effects of Anarchious's lightning bolt.

"Tell me where the cardinal is and we'll spare your life!" Anarchious yells to the ninja. Hearing this, the ninja struggles back to his feet and readies himself in an aggressive fighting position. "Have it your way!" the Mutant says, returning to the soil while glowing brighter and lighting up the field.

The ninja quickly disappears! Anarchious ducks as the ninja reappears, swiftly swinging to decapitate him with the sword. Three quarters of the swing completed, Anarchious rapidly grabs and underhooks the arm bearing the sword, tiger-claws his opposite hand on the ninja's shoulder, and traps him tight! "Struggle if you like. I'll shock you right on your pressure point and turn you into a vegetable!" the Mutant says, looking the short frustrated ninja in his dark amber–colored eyes.

Anarchious chuckles, then looks again at the ninja clear as day. "Seriously?" Anarchious says while chuckling once more, getting a better all-around look at the ninja in all black. Anarchious then turns the ninja around so Ace can get a better look.

The Lycan's jaw drops as he finally gets a good look at the ninja assassin. He is a she, a short, brown curly–haired, very curvy, coffee-with-cream-toned, voluptuous she.

"Ahh…you got your ass kicked by a chick!" Anarchious begins to laugh once more.

Ace frowns and replies, "Ahh…Zera!"

"Yo, that didn't count!" Anarchious replies as the ninja's eyes begin to glow and change color to fuchsia. "Vampyr?" Anarchious proclaims as two more copies of her peel from around her, surrounding the Mutant.

"Hot ninja Vampyr chick! This has to be original!" Ace replies, readying himself to attack.

"Nah," Anarchious says as he blasts the captive ninja in her ribs, sending her back to the other side of the crater and ducking a roundhouse kick from a copy, then sidestepping a haymaker punch from the other. Full speed, the Lycan hits both copies with a double drop kick, sending them flying beyond their original.

"You always gotta show off!" Anarchious says, glaring at his partner as he returns to his feet.

"Well, if you'd shocked the bitch in the first place, I wouldn't have two extra of them to drop kick, would I?" the Lycan replies, smiling down at his smirking friend. "We should probably end this now!" Ace continues.

"Got it!" Anarchious says as he zips through the air towards the female ninja.

Ace power-jumps and clears the crater, following Anarchious. The female ninja is on her knees, hurt. The copies then pull back into the original, who is favoring her ribs.

"OK, tell us where the cardinal is!" Anarchious says, looking down on her. The ninja doesn't respond. She just stands up and hangs her head in defeat. "Oh, it'll be OK. We won't hurt you; nor will we hurt him. We just need to ask him a few questions!" the Mutant states with a little compassion, walking to the ninja.

Anarchious places his hand on her shoulder to comfort her as she looks the other way and utters, "Promise it will be fine."

"Anarch," the Lycan says, trying to get his attention, but it is too late. The ninja dips low and punches the Mutant square in his nuts!

"You little bitch!" Anarchious yells in a weakened, high-pitched tone as the ninja steps back and ports away in a pink flash.

Ace recedes to his human form as he rolls on his back and laughs at the tops of his lungs. "You're an idiot! Now who screams like a bitch?" Anarchious curls up into a fetal position, aching and breathing heavily.

"I feel like…I deserved that!" the Mutant mutters, gasping for air.

The duo sit in the field for about ten minutes, waiting for Anarchious's testicles to stop aching. Then both laugh about it for a few more minutes until Ace gets an idea. "I can find the cardinal!" the Lycan says to Anarchious, who now knows his partner so well that he reads him immediately.

11
The Spirit, the Sages, and the Darkness

Ace bursts through the steel door, transformed and ready to kick some ass. Across the room sits the cardinal behind a desk shaped like a sarcophagus. He glares at the Lycan, smirking, unafraid of his aggression. Ace throws the cardinal's robe at his face as the Mutant enters the room behind him cautiously.

The duo have spent the last two hours searching for the cardinal all over town, wherever his scent was lingering. Vega removes the robe from his face, gets up, and hangs it next to a fancier, more colorful robe and looks back at the duo. Anarchious begins to laugh, looking at the cardinal's annoyed expression.

"Que pasa? What's all the racket?" The duo hears a familiar voice coming from behind them.

"José!" they both yell simultaneously as their teacher enters behind them. Excited to see the old man, they both rush him and begin to tell him flurries of stories about the last month.

"Hombres, one at a time!" José says, chuckling at the duo, who are bickering almost like little boys.

Ace and Anarchious sit down with José and tell him their adventures since he had taken off in the middle of their training. There are so many tales, they last till dawn. "So you stopped a Vampyr clan war, freed human slaves from a Wiccan city, and liberated a city from giant mutated fire-breathing camel spiders?" José says, repeating what he has heard from the Lycan's stories.

"Oh, and we defeated Zera—quite easily, I might add—and kidnapped her!" Ace replies gleefully.

"Wow, I knew you two had cajones, but not enough to beat Zera," José responds to the Lycan.

"Well we had to double-team her because one on one, she could have killed either of us without lifting a finger," Ace explains.

"True, and almost had us too, but I realized her eyes only have power if she can make eye contact," Anarchious adds to his partner's explanation.

José laughs and claps for his young apprentices. "I am very proud of you two, especially the way I saw you handle Magi," José states, confusing the duo.

"Magi?" they simultaneously ask, wondering who or what he means.

Cardinal Vega stands up and claps, and in a pink flash, a short, coffee-toned, voluptuous woman appears in a tight silk red sleeping gown before him and bows. "Cardinal," she states as he places his hand on her shoulder.

"Rest, child of the Spirit," the cardinal says as she turns to glare at the duo with stunning amber-colored eyes.

"The ninja?!" both Ace and Anarchious exclaim.

"Wait a minute. We knew the ninja was attached to the cardinal, but you said you saw us handle her?" Ace asks José.

"Well, yes and no," José answers the curious but confused Lycan.

"Well, is it a yes or no?" Ace retorts, becoming a bit agitated.

"It's better if she shows you!" Cardinal Vega says, interrupting the conversation. "Magi, please show them!" The cardinal stays sitting down in his chair.

The female then turns and stares at the duo, who are focused back on her. Her eyes dilate and change to a sea blue. She then closes her eyes and forces her hands out. Immediately, the Lycan and Mutant begin to see images of themselves as if through dark sunglasses, from the time they were walking through the town, to watching the church, to Cardinal Vega giving her his robe and orders. Her memories through her eyes and ears are being pushed into their minds. They see and hear the entire fight until she low-blows Anarchious.

The Mutant comes out of the vision laughing his ass off at the final image while Ace has nothing but questions. "Why put us through all that surveillance if you specifically gave us the cardinal's name?" the Lycan asks his master diligently.

"While I waited for you hombres for over a month here, I spoke with several of my contacts a number of times through my messenger crow," the older Mutant explains to the Lycan. "I wanted to share information about this investigation, this resistance, and even a little about you two joining it. About two weeks ago, she came back wounded and with half the intel I sent out. She never made it to her final destination."

"So…?" The confused Lycan tries to draw out a straight answer.

"It's a strong possibility everything is compromised. You know as well as I do that there are people on this planet who can imitate you down to the freckles on your bottom. For all we knew, you two got captured, were executed, and copied. However, to duplicate someone's powers, abilities, and mannerisms altogether perfectly is impossible, amigo," the old hermit explains to the Lycan.

Ace glares at him with his eyebrows down. "So that was a test?! I still don't think unleashing a ninja Vampyr on us was necessary!" the Lycan states.

"Ahh, you're just mad she whooped you!" Anarchious interrupts, chuckling. Ace shakes his head, clearly not in the mood to joke around, so he ignores Anarchious's immature response and glares at the ceiling.

José walks over to Ace and places his hand on his shoulder. "You just need your rest. It's been a rough start for all of us," the old Mutant says to the mentally weary Lycan.

"You think?" Ace responds as he sits back in his chair, glaring at Magi, who is glaring right back at him. The Vampyr in the nightgown then disappears in a pink flash.

"Mis amigos, it has been a long night. Either of you hungry? Want breakfast?" the old Mutant asks the duo.

"I want that and a hot bath and a cold den!" the agitated Lycan responds to his master.

"Well, let me show you to the guest rooms. Anarchious, you want anything?" José asks the younger Mutant, who is sitting on the couch across the room.

"Nope. I'm good for now," Anarchious answers, not really wanting to move as his partner and master get up and exit through the busted reinforced door. Anarchious closes his eyes, tired himself, and tries to catch a nap.

The room is silent but hardly empty. Anarchious opens his eyes and sees Cardinal Vega glaring at him suspiciously from behind his sarcophagus. The Mutant doesn't think anything of it and closes his eyes again, feeling them getting heavier, when he hears a tiny crick of the floorboards. He opens his eyes, and the cardinal is in his face, inspecting him.

The Mutant jumps back a little. "You ain't one of those funny priests are you?" the Mutant yells, creeped out by the cardinal. The cardinal laughs as he pulls up a seat next to the Mutant, still glaring, still inspecting him. "Yo, why do you keep staring at me like that, man?" Anarchious asks the curious cardinal.

"What do you know about the Spirit, young man?" the Cardinal asks.

Anarchious frowns, wondering the purpose of such a question. "Are you trying to, like...recruit me into your religion?" Anarchious asks, looking away from the cardinal, uninterested.

"It's converting, not recruiting, and no, I am just wondering," the cardinal responds.

"Well, I know my aunt followed the Spirit," Anarchious replies.

"What did she teach you of the Spirit?" the Cardinal asks, seemingly excited.

"Well, she tried teaching me this stuff, but I wasn't into it," Anarchious explains to the cardinal, who is still smiling.

"The basics? Would you like to know how this world was created?" the cardinal asks the young Mutant.

"No, but I'm sure you're going tell me anyway," the Mutant responds, not really wanting to engage in that conversation.

As much as the young Mutant wants to resist, he is correct. The cardinal sits there and still tells him the story of the creation of their planet, at least from his religious view. He explains, "The world was created by the Spirit, our God, Zo. Zo created the planet and all its inhabitants. First came man, then everything else. He created the world in front of our alpha ancestors' very eyes so that they knew the work and value of it all.

"The mountains, the trees, the birds, the seas, and the earth were all created before the alphas. The spirit then spoke to them. He told them this land, this planet, this world was perfect, as were they, that they were to value the planet as much as he valued them. He told them he was relying on them heavily and that the direction of this planet was all up to them.

"Zo left the planet, watched over the ancestors for a millennium, and returned. Our peoples flourished and had advanced so much, but most importantly stayed perfect. He was so proud, he blessed us with the power to 'become,' and that's how the many races of our planet were born."

Before the cardinal can finish the history of the planet, Anarchious interrupts him. "And he left and then came back? Uh-oh! The world was overrun with hatred, war, and sin! He then promised to watch over the world and never leave it again till it was all fixed. Uh-oh! The Spirit lied! He leaves once more, and shit gets worse," the Mutant bitterly finishes.

"So you do know history."

"No, I know mumbo jumbo!" Anarchious responds, becoming angry. "I know that there are more Demon-God-King worshippers than Spirit worshippers!" he continues.

"The Demon-King uses fear while the Spirit uses only influence and what's inside your heart. It was his promise to mankind," the cardinal responds, placing his hand on Anarchious's shoulder.

"Bull. This is all superstition. Humans proved it already with their science. Vampyrs, Lycans, Wiccans, Mutants are all mutations of humans and evolved during the millions of years this planet has been here," Anarchious says, shifting his shoulder away from the Vampyr priest.

"The Spirit values us, and that means you too, even if..." The Cardinal tries to convince the young Mutant, but Anarchious stands up and heads for the door.

"If the Spirit values us, why is there so much hatred? Why so much misery? Why did my entire race have to be wiped off the face of the planet for no reason? Why did he allow my parents to be executed in front of me and my brother?! That doesn't sound like value. That sounds like people aimlessly looking for hope in something that doesn't exist!" Anarchious angrily snarls over his shoulder at Cardinal Vega, leaning in the doorway, too upset to face the priest.

There is an uncomfortable wave of silence between the two. Anarchious clenches his fists as he leaves the room. "That's the same thing Abel told me before he left," the cardinal informs the young Mutant, who is already walking down the hall. Anarchious's footsteps stop for a moment, and he reenters the room seconds later.

"What did you say?" Anarchious asks Cardinal Vega with his eyes glossy and pink.

"I said, 'That is the same thing your twin told me before he left,' Anarchious," the cardinal answers the Mutant.

"Before he left?" Anarchious inquires.

"Yes, before he left...the same spot you're standing in now. He stood there and screamed at me what you said word for word," the cardinal replies to the Mutant, who is now at attention.

"You know when I saw your face for the first time, I was stunned. I didn't know Abel had a brother, let alone a twin, until the day he stormed out when I talked to him about the Spirit," the cardinal says, explaining the funny looks he's been giving the young Mutant since he arrived.

"So he was here? I mean, when?" Anarchious asks, not really knowing what exactly to ask Vega.

"A few years back, he was just barely an adolescent. He came here remorseful and reluctant about something he had done and stayed for about two weeks," the priest answers.

"You have any idea where he went?" Anarchious asks swiftly, hoping to get a general direction.

"No idea. I sent some of the best trackers in this city after him, but he disappeared. It was as if he disappeared off of this planet," the cardinal answers a hopeful Anarchious. "Your brother had plenty of good in his heart but was being drawn away by a deep-seated darkness that no priests in our church could identify."

Cardinal Vega is explaining something familiar to Anarchious. The Mutant drops his head, upset and internalizing his thoughts. He heard the same thing about this "darkness" from Zera as well. All he knows is he has to find Abel now and quickly.

"Cardinal Vega, I apologize for disrespecting your beliefs, but I'm not going to apologize for believing what I believe. The Spirit isn't something I can believe in. I believe what I see, and I haven't seen a God or Spirit," Anarchious says as he turns to leave the room once more.

"That's all right, son, because Zo, the Spirit, our God, believes in you, even if don't you know it, see it, or feel it," Cardinal Vega says as Anarchious exits the room. As much as the young Mutant doesn't believe in those religious words, they still manage to give him goose bumps every time.

Upstairs in a tiny dining room lit by the rising sun beaming through the window sits an ecstatic Ace, eating a giant plate of red meat and eggs with the old hermit, José, watching. Ace, mouth full of chewed-up food, notices the old man glaring at him. He knows his master has something on his mind.

"Something troubling you, Master?" the Lycan asks, his words muffled by the mush in his mouth.

José, with worry on his face, asks, "Do you remember the day I freed Anarchious's emotion from his power?"

Ace swallows his food, takes a big breath, and responds, "You mean the day he turned the forest into a clearing and damn near killed us?"

"Si, that day," José says, sitting back in his chair, looking at the ceiling fan and remembering the blast that scorched a good portion of that forest.

"What about it?" Ace asks as he continues his meal, focused on the old man.

José then rocks forward and looks the Lycan deep into his eyes. The glare scares Ace so badly he dribbles mush into his lap. "Has anything odd happened to him since?" the old Mutant asks with a half-worried, half-upset face.

Ace sits and thinks for a minute. Other than the fact that in a matter of a month his best friend has become insanely strong and fast, he can't really think of anything odd. Then Ace remembers the night Anarchious struck himself down in the District, which also reminded him of the day in the forest.

"Well, there was this time when his face changed, when he found out something troubling about his parents. I could feel his pain, his hatred. 'Twas quite scary—" Ace explains but is interrupted by the old man.

"His face was ghost white with coal-black markings around his lightning-purple eyes that pierce your soul?" the old man says, knowing exactly what Ace was about to say.

"Exactly. Kind of," the Lycan responds.

"I've seen it too, amigo, when I freed his Ki that day. I saw it in his consciousness. Every night I dream of that face and the destruction it will cause. I got in entirely too easy. I think I released it from some kind of prison," the old Mutant explains to Ace. "What do you mean 'kind of'?" José then asks the Lycan about his previous statement.

"Well, half of his face is white, and I don't know about his eyes piercing my soul. I mean, it happened two more times since then, but it didn't last long, nor was it destructive," Ace explains to the old Mutant.

In deep thought, José replies, "Really?"

"Yes, I mean it's different," Ace continues to explain. "It seems to be triggered by emotion, like when he used to go off before. But it's like a controlled rage. He knew who exactly to hurt and who not to hurt when he changed into that thing."

"Well, hombre, I'm reconsidering stopping his training. I think it may be too dangerous," José states to the Lycan.

"What? No! Why?!" Ace says, dropping his fork and gripping the table.

"I don't think he'll be able to control it after a while. My dreams have showed me those evils, and I refuse to contribute to them or allow them to transpire," José proclaims.

"What happened to 'I feel the best thing to do is to help pass on our culture and teachings to you, young Anarchious'? What if he never learns to fully control it, and that causes him to be 'evil'?" the Lycan asks, imitating the suave old man's voice.

"This world already has too many evil men. I won't be able to forgive myself if I help create one more. I don't know, hombre," José says, this time standing up and looking down on his young apprentice.

Ace stands up and looks José in the eye, giving him a firm look, and sternly says, "On my mother's grave, I promise you. I'll...take care of him myself if he ever becomes evil. But until then, I beg you to continue being our sensei. He needs the mentoring, and I...well, I've become accustomed to dropping people on their heads."

The old suave hermit thinks for a moment, looking at Ace, then considers his options. "If that's your word, I'll hold you to it, amigo. Truth is, I could use some help with this new informacion just gathered," José says, giving the relieved Lycan a stern look as well.

Just then, Anarchious barges in and notices his master and best friend glaring at each other. "What the hell? Am I in some kind of messed-up nightmare? First the priest, now you two. What is this world coming to?" Anarchious states dramatically.

"Anarch, could you, I don't know, shut up and be serious for two minutes?" the Lycan yells, frowning at the Mutant.

"Uh, OK," Anarchious responds, noticing the seriousness of Ace's response.

"What exactly do you need help with? I'm sure we can handle it," the Lycan says, turning back to their master.

José turns his attention to the young Anarchious. "Well, this is about our people. Turns out there are more than just three of us running around trying not to get captured," José proclaims, surprising the younger Mutant and Lycan.

"What?" they both exclaim.

"Yes, it's surprising to me as well. My contact says there are seis familia left all scattered around the four continents, not including Eden," José explains to the duo.

"Six? Where were they when the Rebel Army bombed Eden?" Anarchious asks the older Mutant.

"Well, that's one of the reasons we are going to go look for them and ask them," José says.

"Are they aware of each other's existence?" the Lycan asks next, equally as interested as his partner.

"Another great question," the old Mutant replies. "I think maybe so because the contact also wrote out about a six-sage council and that they are all protected. Most of it all seemed like unimportant gibberish to me. The most important thing is that the Rebels have located most of them, and they are all going to be hunted down for execution. We have to help, and now."

"Wait, I don't know about this," Anarchious states, worried.

"What's wrong, Anarchious?" the older Mutant asks the younger Mutant.

"Well, I want to help, but I really, really need to catch up with Abel!" Anarchious says, showing much more concern for his brother.

"I know you want to find Abel, but that must wait," José explains. "If we do not help these Mutants before the Rebel Army gets there, they will be wiped out, as will our culture, as will our story."

"That's already a reality, Master. At least with Abel, we will have a better chance of survival," Anarchious states affirmatively.

"Do you have any idea where he is?" José asks the young Mutant. Anarchious immediately drops his head, realizing that he hasn't gotten anywhere in finding Abel.

The Lycan places his hand on his best friend's shoulder to comfort him while their master takes a seat and crosses his legs. "A month ago, I could have helped you find him before all of this, but now I have to save what's left of our people," José states reluctantly.

"Master, are you saying we wasted our time helping those people?" Ace replies.

"No. I respect and admire what you did, but what I am saying is, I have priorities in the way of returning a helping hand," the old suave Mutant says, revealing his conflict.

Anarchious looks up at him with a fire in his eyes. "I may not know exactly where he is, but I will find him with this," the young Mutant states, grabbing his chest and signaling his heart. "At random times, I can feel him, and I think he can feel me too. I think those battles that made me stronger, faster, and even smarter have made this sense stronger as well," Anarchious explains.

"I see. But how long will that take, young brother?" José asks, looking Anarchious in the eye.

"I'm not sure. Maybe you can help me use this somehow to find him," the young Mutant replies.

"Well, I can continue to teach you martial arts, but the rest of the training is really you," the old Mutant states, glancing with concern at his Lycan pupil. Ace immediately knows his concerns and nods at him to let him know he intends to keep his promise.

"Teach me what you can, and I'll be on my way. I will find him," Anarchious replies, eyeing his master.

"OK, bueno, but I need for you to find Abel, and fast," José replies, shaking Anarchious's hand.

After a day of rest, the trio returns to the field where Ace fought Magi outside of the city. They waste no time. The suave old man immediately initiates a sparring match between himself and his young countryman, Anarchious. José is still feeling skeptical about training Anarchious but realizes he doesn't really have a choice. "Show me how much you've progressed. Do not hold back," the old Mutant says as he attacks Anarchious at full light speed.

The two Mutants bounce all over the field, lightning blasts and starbursts everywhere. Anarchious still isn't as fast as José but is tracking him like a bloodhound. The old man, more versed in hand-to-hand combat, uses every style he knows on the young man with all kinds of kicks, strikes, and holds. If Anarchious doesn't dodge it or reverse it, he eats it like a champ and keeps coming. Anarchious has become a bit of a tank in the last month, progressing faster than any other Mutant José has ever seen.

"Good, young Mutant! Now, defend against my specialty—light rapier!" the suave old Mutant shouts with a smile. From his dominant hand comes forth a beam of light forming an old-style sword hilt, guard and all. He holds it as if it is solid but slices the ground between them, burning it. José holds his other arm behind his back, takes a wide stance, and is ready to strike. He steps forward in blinding light and slashes at the young one. Anarchious reacts quickly, stepping back, the rapier just missing him, but he can feel the heat radiating from it.

"Yo, that's sweet! How the hell you do that?" Anarchious asks, baffled by the attack.

"Once you master the 'become your element' stage, something like this is easy, amigo," José replies while coming back at Anarchious with more high-speed slash attacks. The old Mutant slices and slashes, hacks and pokes at the young Mutant.

Anarchious dodges, ducks, weaves, and evades each one awkwardly, just barely escaping. "Ha, old man!" Anarchious shouts, teasing José, feeling accomplished after surviving such an onslaught surprisingly without injury. José drops his guard and laughs at the young, tenacious Mutant.

Anarchious arches his eyebrow in confusion as he smells something burning. He looks around but sees nothing. Then he feels heat steadily climbing up his back and knows he has been hit. Anarchious falls to the ground and rolls around as his best friend, Ace, observes, laughing his ass off in the background. It gets so hot, he takes his combat vest and hoodie off and stomps them until the flames are extinguished. The young Mutant picks up the vest and inspects it. "Z?" Anarchious asks, referring to the etched and burned letter on the back of his vest.

The old man smiles and shrugs. "You see, you cannot contend with my melee, Anarchious. What do you do to counter it?" José says in a teacher-like fashion to his student.

Anarchious slams his vest on the ground, and the sky begins to darken as clouds cover the sun. The wind begins to blow violently; the sound of thunder booms across the plains. A lighting storm brews fiercely overhead, covering the entire field.

José smiles and asks, "Clever but expected. How accurate are you with—?" Lightning strikes all around him, simultaneously creating a tiny donut of a crater, leaving him on an island before he can finish his question.

"Bueno, but can you hit a moving target?" José utters right before he zips towards Anarchious in a blinding burst of light. Once more, lightning bolts strike around him, redirecting his path before he reaches the young Mutant in just an instant. Anarchious doesn't budge an inch as José swings his light rapier, slicing right through the young Mutant. "Lightning?" he says, confused, as he phases right through the younger Mutant stumbling forward from his momentum, feeling the electric current shock his skin.

"Yep," Anarchious says as he solidifies and put his master in a playful headlock.

José begins laughing and says, "It seems you've grasped lesson tres, become your element. Muy buen! OK, index. We're finished or today."

José ends the quick sparring match and turns to his student. "Quick assessment: Good element attacks. I can tell you've been working on accuracy. Also, during hand-to-hand, you need to keep your eyes open for patterns and weaknesses in style. I gave you many openings, but you didn't counter enough of them. When things aren't going your way, you need to either block or slip because, Spirit forbid it, you may run into someone stronger or more versed than you are, and you will get hurt trying to run through everything. Anarchious, when did you learn that?" he asks.

Anarchious thinks for a moment and answers, "I didn't. It just came to me at the last moment. Let you think you got me, then get you from behind."

Surprised, the suave old man looks on as he thinks of an even more important question. "Good. How much Ki did you use on that, though?" José asks his young student. Anarchious feels for it. He knows he is nearly depleted, as does José. "I mean, you haven't mastered it, but you just turned every cell in your body into your element using pretty much all your Ki. You need to be able to do that without using hardly any. Once you accomplish that, you will be able to do a lot more with storms and can move on to the next step. Conservation is 'Ki,' hombre." José laughs at his pun.

"I mean, it takes a lot for me to even conjure a storm or to lightning-boost for speed, but to use little Ki—" Anarchious replies to his master but is interrupted.

"Do you know how long I can stay in my light form?" José asks Anarchious.

"No," the young Mutant replies.

"Neither do I, but when I jump to light form, I barely use any Ki. One time, just to see how long I could do it, I meditated in my light form for a day and didn't use ten percent of my Ki," the old Mutant explains to his student, who is feeling kind of pessimistic about it but is still motivated to learn.

"So how do I learn to master my element and Ki conservation?" Anarchious asks José.

"One step at time," José explains. "This is where it gets tricky. Only you can teach yourself this. It's so difficult that only elite Mutants are able to figure either out. Took me ten years to figure it out and ten more to perfect it." Anarchious becomes even more discouraged. "Before, most Mutants perfected taming emotion and achieving element in about fifteen years. You've skated through those no problemo. You've even popped your cherry at turning your physical being into your element. That is unheard of! Mastering it and conservation are just tough. No need to quit," the old suave Mutant says, trying to pump up the young one.

"Quitting never crossed my mind, and it never will. I'm just feeling a certain way about it all," Anarchious explains to his master.

"Good, well, this training is one you can take on the road while looking for your brother, and if by some miracle you get it, please use it wisely!" José replies to his young student, then glares at Ace. Once again, Ace knows what the old man means

Just then, sirens go off, and many gunshots echo in the distance. They are coming from Glen Haven. "What's that?" José asks as Ace listens closely to the ruckus.

"I hear people yelling, running, fighting—it sounds like a riot," the Lycan informs his team.

"Let's go!" José yells as he rushes to the city in a blinding flash.

Anarchious jumps into the air and begins to fly towards the city as Ace transforms and begins to dart towards it as well. Less than a mile outside the city, Anarchious feels a difference in his Ki. He quickly descends from the sky and crashes into the ground. Ace, who was a few paces behind him, approaches the weakened Mutant. "You all right, man?" the Lycan ask his counterpart.

"Leave me. Just get to the city. Those people need you," Anarchious replies, struggling to push himself out of the dirt. The statement confuses the Lycan for a moment, but he realizes he doesn't have the time, so he puts his partner on his back and tells him to hold on as he sprints on all fours back towards the city.

Moments later, they arrive in the heart of the city not a block away from the church. It is chaotic. Ace has to push through the crowds of people just to make it any further. The Vampyr sentries have barred off their part of the city. They are armed to the teeth and ready for action while the rest of the town is in complete panic, it seems. There are many cries in many different languages from many different races of people trying to keep the peace while there are many more scuffles and skirmishes between different groups all around.

The main standoff is a big group of human citizens who are also armed to the teeth against a group of mostly Pride citizens. In the middle of it are four humans and a young Lycan. One is holding the Lycan at gunpoint, and the others are beating him. The Lycan is barely in his teenage years.

When Ace witnesses this, he puts Anarchious down and make way forward, pushing through the crowds of sobbing people, innocents, and peacekeepers pleading for the child. As soon as the angered Lycan makes it to the front lines, a human just as big as he sticks a double-barreled shotgun in under his mandible. “Move one more step and I’ll blow your flea-ridden head clear off, mutt!” the man shouts.

Ace is always the one up for peace and compromise, but he knows that the young Lycan will die if they don’t do anything immediately. Before he can react, a quick flash appears in front of him. It is none other than José. He has been watching the situation develop the entire time. He quickly grabs the barrel of the shotgun with a glowing hand, heats it up, and melts it shut.

“Now, let’s be reasonable, amigo,” the suave old man says, trying to come to terms with the man who seems to be the leader of this execution. The man drops his now ineffective weapon and reaches for his side rm.

Ace swiftly grabs his attacker’s arm before he can place his hand on his weapon. “Now, we’re trying to keep the peace and negotiate here. Do not make us resort to violence. You won’t survive!” Ace warns the man, staring him in his eyes.

“Oh, really? Would you like to test that?” the man quickly replies.

“Enough! A life is at stake here! What can we do to get you to spare that child?” José asks, trying to negotiate with the man.

“Not a damn thing!” the man replies, looking back at José angrily.

“Why?” Ace asks, quickly tightening his grip on the man and glaring at him harshly.

"He is getting what he deserves." The man stares back with equal fire in his eyes.

"He is innocent!" Anarchious proclaims, still weakened and holding onto Ace's shoulder, trying to keep on his feet. It seems the Mutant has made his way through the crowd as well, running on nothing but will.

"Tell that to my brother lying over there bleeding out!" the man yells, pointing beyond the teenage Lycan, who is still receiving a hell of an ass-kicking.

There is a man on the ground dying, shaking in pain, surrounded by human and Witch medics trying to save him. He is wearing tattered clothes and has had many deep claw-shaped gashes inflicted on his body. The man is going in and out of consciousness, screaming something, but the crowd's cries are too loud to make it out.

"There will be justice today!" the leader yells at the trio.

"I have no time for this," Anarchious grunts as the sky rapidly darkens and becomes filled with storm clouds. The wind begins to blow wildly in every direction as Anarchious lightning-bursts right through the front lines, knocking the leader out of the way and blasting away the three humans who were beating the teenage Lycan.

The gunman focuses his firearm at Anarchious's head. He has a clear shot and enough time. The irate Mutant glares at him with violet eyes. The gunman stares back but freezes up, frightened of what he's seeing. Swiftly, Anarchious grabs the gun and shocks it, shocking the man and sending him flying over the crowds of people to land on the steps of the church.

In an instant, the young Mutant has the teenage Lycan on his feet with his arm draped over his neck and shoulder, supporting the injured young Lycan's weight. Every gunman in the circle now has his weapon focused on Anarchious, yet none of them fire. They are stunned by the sight of him.

José pushes aside a gunman himself and witnesses his nightmare all over again—ghost-white face, coal-black war markings, and violet eyes that make him feel his soul slip into fear. "Someone…fuckin' shoot it!" the leader yells from the ground.

"No!" Ace yells. Anarchious waves his free arm in their direction and sends a violent gust of whirling around them, knocking down every gunman to his rear end and disarming them all. The white-faced now savior picks up, takes off into the skies beyond the storm clouds, and zips back to their little hideout.

Moments later, Ace and José barge back into Cardinal Vega's hideout with the dying man and the medics. Anarchious has passed out on the floor while the young Lycan is unconscious on top of Vega's sarcophagus. They place the dying man back down on the couch so that the medics can continue to work on him. Ace rushes over to the teenage Lycan and checks him. "The kid is OK!" he exclaims as he listens to his weakened heartbeat. José checks on his Mutant brother passed out on the floor. He is fine, just weak. They keep a close eye on all three until dusk. This is when Anarchious wakes up.

"What the hell is going on?!" the young Mutant says, raising his voice as he sits up and grabs his head. The young Lycan Ace rejoices, happy his best friend is awake. Relieved, he grabs Anarchious, helps him up, and pats him on the back. "Don't change the subject! Yo, why all the dead people?" the young Mutant asks once more.

One of the medics looks over and replies, "Quiet, please. We are trying to concentrate!"

"Don't shush me! I'll break all your concentration if I see fit," Anarchious snaps back while Ace pulls him to the side.

The young Lycan looks his best friend in the eye and asks, "You OK?"

Anarchious, knowing that look, replies, "It happened again, huh?"

"Yep," Ace replies, nodding.

"What did I do this time?" the young Mutant asks.

"You saved the kid Lycan in there from a lynch mob and flew back here."

Anarchious makes a not bad face and nods. "Cool. That makes three," Anarchious says, high-fiving his friend.

"It was awesome. It seems you conquered your fear of guns as well," Ace states.

"What?" Anarchious says, confused.

"You conquered your fear of human weaponry," the Lycan replies as Anarchious looks at him as if he were crazy. "You disarmed, like, thirty humans," the Lycan exaggerates as he informs Anarchious of his bravery.

"They had guns?" Anarchious quickly replies. Ace nods in answer to his question. "I think I'm going to need a drink," Anarchious says with a distressed look on his face.

"No, it was cool. You were all like, 'whoosh,' and they were all like, 'Argh,'" the Lycan says, mimicking his friend's movements during the rescue.

Anarchious, still feeling uneasy, turns and sees the injured man placed on the couch. "Who's the corpse?" he asks his partner.

"Oh, he's the reason the humans were beating on the puppy you saved," Ace replies, pointing out the teenage Lycan who is still unconscious. "It was odd. He was screaming something familiar," Ace says, beginning to ponder it. "So I picked him up, and now we're trying to save him. At least he's not dying in the open anymore."

Just then, they hear a knocking. It is coming from Vega's sarcophagus. Ace and José quickly move the teenage Lycan, who is still unconscious, to another table as Vega exits his coffin. "What is going on here?" the cardinal says as he gracefully floats out of the coffin, glaring at the full house of people in his hideout. José looks his friend in the face and signals him, then walks out the door with the cardinal following. The old Mutant brings the Vampyr priest up to speed on the events of the day.

While in the room, one of the medics approaches the duo and informs them of the critical condition of the man. He explains that he and his colleagues have tried to heal the man and patch up his many injuries, but the age of the wounds, the amount of trauma to his body, and his blood loss have made his death inevitable. "Well, can you do me a favor and heal this kid over here? We need to clear this up," Ace asks the Witch medic. The medic nods and goes to work on the teenage Lycan, who is conscious in minutes but still badly injured.

"Sorry, brother, but we have to skip the formalities. We need to know what happened between you and the man on the couch over there," Ace says firmly.

The kid glances over at the man, then looks back up at Ace. "Nothing, brother. I was in the fields playing. He rode past and fell off his horse like that," the teenage Lycan explains to his Pride brethren.

"He's telling the truth," Ace says as he pats the kid on the head.

Ace turns to the other medics, who are still monitoring the man in critical condition. "Please try to keep him alive a little longer. I have an idea," Ace requests from the medics. Ace makes his way down the hall to José and Vega. "Sorry to interrupt, but I need a favor from you," the Lycan says, looking Vega in the eye.

"Magi?" the cardinal responds, astonished and knowing exactly what he intends.

The cardinal summons Magi into the room and directs her to the dying man. The entire room watches as she leans over him and opens his eye. She stares directly into his pupil, which is large and dilated, reflecting her deep blue sea-tinted eyes. His body begins to tense up as Magi begins to get goose bumps.

After a little while, the injured man's body begins to curl up as if he's protecting himself. Magi begins to shiver. Ace can sense great fear pouring from both the man and Magi. Both their hearts are beating a mile a minute. Magi then lets go of the man's face, drops to her knees, and grips the hardwood floor, leaving deep scratches in it. She tries to scream, but nothing comes out.

The cardinal rushes to her and helps her up. The ninja Vampyr, with tears rolling from her eyes, glances at everyone in the room, trembling in fear. "I apologize for my servant's appearance," the cardinal states to the room. "A side effect of absorbing memories is that you also receive the unwanted emotions from them."

"It's not a problem. We need to see what she saw ASAP," the curious Lycan replies. Magi shakes her head no, still frightened and crying. "Please, I have to clear this kid's name." Ace tries being nice, but Magi nuzzles her head against the cardinal, hiding and still afflicted by the memory.

Anarchious walks up, places his hand on her shoulder, and looks into her peeking amber eye. "Look, show me if you're worried about it," he asks her, comforting her by smiling. Without hesitation, she grabs his neck and forces his head closer, glares into his eyes, and begins pushing the dying man's memories into Anarchious's mind.

It was dusk. An old man came to the city and began screaming and preaching for the God-King. He demanded they kneel or suffer the great king's wrath. The townspeople submitted, frightened, and bowed to the old man sermonizing in the middle of their city. The old man laughed as he waved his walking cane and faded into thin air. A sudden darkness came over the city like a tidal wave.

The man tried to scream, but he couldn't, and neither could anyone one else. There was no noise, just thoughts and emotions as hundreds of shadow hounds began attacking the townspeople, ripping them to shreds. With smoldering red eyes and pitch-black bodies, they ate women and children as the tidal wave of darkness began to destroy the city.

It made him feel hopeless. All the men and soldiers present tried to fight back but were slaughtered even though they heavily outnumbered the shadow hounds, which seemed to be multiplying by the minute. The man thought only of his wife and child and fought his way to his home. It was too late. The shadow hounds had gotten to them first. His pregnant wife's head was missing, and so was her baby.

The man ran screaming into the crowd, but there was no sound, only blood and fear. The man was surrounded by three shadow hounds and dragged onto a side road. While continuously being clawed and bitten like a piece of meat, he saw a horse from a caravan carriage flailing about, trying to defend itself.

He freed one of his hands, grabbed for his six-shooter, and shot and killed his and the horse's attackers. Quickly, he jumped on its back and made his escape out of the city. He thought he was home free until he was chased by shadow hounds once more. Out of the alley they came at full speed behind pairs of silver eyes.

For a half mile the hounds pursued him, but eventually they disappeared as he exited the shadow-engulfed town. All he could think of was his family, the image of his headless pregnant wife and her entrails stretched and splattered all over the room.

Anarchious's stomach drops as his eyes open wide. He backs up, shocked, holding his stomach and heart.

"What? What did you see, Anarch?" Ace asks his speechless partner. The Lycan walks over and shakes him. "What's up, bro?" Ace asks.

"It was, like, hellhounds, and bats that killed that guy. Very evil," the Mutant explains.

"The Demon-King!" Cardinal Vega exclaims.

"Something spread. It let them loose. It was—" Anarchious squeezes his chest tighter while explaining but is interrupted by a scream.

"Darkness! The darkness is spreading!" It is the injured man screaming as he spasms, slumps over, coughs up blood, and then expires.

Anarchious leaves the room as Ace follows and grabs his arm, stopping him. "What are you doing?" the concerned Lycan asks.

"None of this is coincidence," Anarchious says with tears in his eyes. "You brought him in here because you had a feeling. I saw something very familiar."

"Abel?" Ace replies with big eyes.

"I don't know. I don't know what to believe. We have to go to that city," Anarchious says, ripping his arm from his friend.

"How do we know where it is?" the Lycan asks, following after him.

"It's three days northwest of here. We'll get there in one and a half! Let's go!" Anarchious replies, continuing his stride as Ace follows down the hall.

Just then, José comes running into the hall. "Amigos, meet me in the Asbury Dunes when you're done, and do not forget to train!" he yells, reminding his students of the mission.

Both students signal peace to their master and run up the stairs and out of the secured building. Following José out of the room is the cardinal, carrying his now-weakened servant. "I need you to show me, brother," the cardinal says to José.

"What, amigo?" José replies, not knowing what he's speaking of.

"I need you to show me what you saw…the Ghost-face," the cardinal replies to José.

12
Death Incarnate

The tenacious duo travel northwest, trying to find the city of North Torious, sometimes with Anarchious flying while carrying Ace in human form, other times Ace in Lycan form carrying the Mutant on his back. It is noon two days later when they finally reach the outer limits of the city. North Torious is a wreck. It looks like an earthquake hit it, and to make matters worse, the Rebel Army is already there.

"Shit!" Anarchious grunts, casing the city's gates, which are surrounded by Rebel Army guards.

"There has to be a way in," Ace replies, doing the same.

They creep around the city's borders, trying to find an opening, but the guards have a complete 360-degree security on it. The Mutant and Lycan think of flying in quickly, but the guards have machines with spinning blades at the top constantly circling the area. This show of defense reminds Anarchious of the day his parents were murdered by people in the same olive and tan uniforms.

"Hey, I got it! You still have those hooded cloaks the Shiva-Clan gave us as gifts?" the Lycan asks the Mutant, who is deep in thought.

"Yeah, they're in my bag," Anarchious answers, not really paying attention to Ace.

"We can wear them up there and walk right into the front gate," Ace says while digging through Anarchious's gear bag.

Anarchious doesn't answer. He can still remember his mother's blood on his hands and face. He remembers the screaming, loud gunshots, and Abel crying. Even though Abel was the physically stronger twin, he was still the baby of the two.

"Anarchious!...Anarch!" Ace yells, waking him from his daydream.

"Huh?" the Mutant replies.

"What do you think of the plan?" the curious Lycan asks, handing him the cloak.

"What plan?" Anarchious replies, arching his eyebrow.

"You weren't listening, were you?" the Lycan says, glaring at his best friend.

"Nope," Anarchious replies nonchalantly, turning his head and glaring back at the gate.

Ace slaps Anarchious on the back of the head and shouts, "Put this on and follow me, moron!" He storms off onto the road leading to the main gate.

As they approach, Ace practices his story, but as soon as they get within fifty meters, the soldiers rack and draw their weapons on the duo. Ace's plan goes right out the window. "Stop walking or you will be shot!" a man with a megaphone says from a tower behind the front gate.

Both frightened, the Lycan and Mutant throw their hands up. Quickly they are surrounded by five soldiers. "Do either of you have valid NRA identification?" the leader of the soldiers asks with his raspy voice. The duo simultaneously shake their heads no. "What is your business here?" the leader yells, adding more bass to his already deep voice.

Ace had his story down pat, but the weapons in his face make him forget it, so he begins to stutter excessively. The image of the decapitated pregnant woman flashes before Anarchious's eyes, and he begins to sob hysterically.

"A close family member was killed here during the attack. I've come to collect her remains," the sobbing young Mutant informs them.

"Really? What was her name?" the leader asks, suspicious of Anarchious's story.

The Mutant can still hear the man's thoughts of his wife. "Her name was Nisa Cromwell. She was pregnant," Anarchious cries out even harder.

Ace is watching him, trembling, knowing this is a bad acting job, knowing they are going to get attacked. But to his surprise, all the soldiers lower their weapons and look at each other with despair, shaken by the thought of the massacre. It seems they knew who Anarchious is talking about immediately.

"OK, you two, we have to search you for safety reasons, but it will be quick. Condolences to you and your family. I'm sorry for your loss," the leader says, signaling his men to search them.

The soldiers are patting them down when suddenly one of the younger grunts raises his weapon back on Ace. "Sergeant, this one's a Lycan! He has a tail!" the younger soldier informs the leader.

Every soldier places his weapon back on Ace, who stands there petrified now. "What are you doing trying to enter Rebel Army territory?! This town is human only!" the sergeant yells at the Lycan, placing the barrel of his weapon to Ace's head.

"No, please, stop! That is my slave," Anarchious intervenes, stepping in front of their barrels.

All the soldiers look around, confused by the statement. "On what planet does a human ever own a Lycan?" the sergeant asks Anarchious, becoming slightly suspicious of him again.

"This is an exiled Lycan. Not only that, I saved him from cave goblins south of here, so he is indebted to me," Anarchious explains quickly as if the lie were true.

The sergeant holds his weapons on them for a little longer while he thinks. "OK, but we'll be watching you two! Keep the mutt on a leash!" he replies, then orders his men back to the gate and orders an escort for the duo.

The soldiers drop the men off at an empty clearing in the city where the deceased bodies are being kept out of public view. Everybody has already been body-bagged, and corpses freshly dug up from under debris are being brought in what seems like every minute.

Anarchious gets that butterfly flutter feeling in his stomach once more. Were those Abel's eyes? Was he really here? he thinks to himself. The better question, though, is, Is Abel really capable of this type of evil?

"Slave, Anarch...really?" Ace grumbles at his partner.

"Doesn't feel too good being called a slave, huh?" the young Mutant replies with a slight smirk on his face.

"You don't let anything go, do you?" Ace replies, chuckling.

"Only my brother, it seems," Anarchious replies glumly, ready to find some kind of clue or something that will lead him to his twin. He can feel it in his bones.

"Know what's crazy? You have conquered your fear of guns, Anarch, and you didn't even notice," Ace says, bringing attention to the fact Anarchious jumped in front of the barrel of a gun in order to save his companion.

"Nope, I was 'turtling'! Surprised you didn't smell it!" Anarchious says, making his way back to the main streets.

"Oh, thought that was the dead bodies," Ace replies, following him.

The duo reach the main part of town. The place reminds them of the city limits of the District. Buildings have collapsed; debris is everywhere, and grieving people fill the streets. Some people are praying, others crying and lighting candles for memorials for their lost loved ones.

"Where do we start? It's still too early to ask questions," Ace says, putting his hood back over his head.

"I don't know. I'm going with my senses on this one," his partner states.

"Now what are your senses telling you?" Ace asks.

“We should listen for information. I saw an old man in that man’s memories. I also saw these shadow hounds and a pair of silver eyes like Abel’s. Let’s just walk around and listen,” Anarchious answers, placing his hood back on his head as well. “Let’s go!” he says to his partner as they begin their search.

The duo walk around the heavily guarded city for hours, listening in on people’s stories and hearing people trying to find lost loved ones. Nothing comes up until they walk into a pub. It is still intact except the glass windows have been destroyed, and there are is other minor damage. The pub, named BIG, looks very modern. It is huge and has a happy atmosphere. Despite the tragedy that took place, many people are still in the pub drinking and socializing. The duo walk in and sit down at the bar, listening in on the drunken conversations.

“That void thing came out of nowhere! I saw one of those things swallow a man whole and spit out his lifeless carcass,” one man grunts after taking a shot of alcohol.

“Yep,” respond several of the bar patrons.

“I heard some the soldiers talking about the camera systems all over the city. Those incompetent asses even confirmed the black beasts did come from thin air,” another man adds to the conversation.

“Soon as that old man began yelling about worshipping the God-King, I hightailed it out of there and locked my family in the cellar,” the bartender says, taking a drink himself.

“Psh, the piece of shit Demon-King! If I had the power, give me one round with him! I’d kill him myself,” the first man grunts once more.

"We do have the power. The Rebel Army does! All they have to do is do what they did to the Isle of Eden twenty years ago," the bartender states, then makes a flying gesture, swooping his hand in the air while whistling, "Boom!" He then chuckles to his drunken customer.

"That'll never happen," the second says. "For one, no one knows exactly where he is, just that he pops up all over at random times and demands worship. For two, the stakes are too great. If they fail, we'll be just like the people of Eden—extinct!" He chuckles.

Anarchious angrily slams his fist onto the counter after hearing that. The entire bar directs their attention to the Mutant, who is almost in tears under his hood.

"Fuck the Demon-King!" the Lycan screams to draw the attention from his friend.

The entire bar echoes back, "Yeah, fuck the Demon-King!" The bar erupts into a continuous chant as Ace grabs Anarchious and drags him out and back on the street.

"Yo, who the hell laughs at something like that?!" Anarchious yells at his best friend as he is surrounded with a violet aura.

"Ixnay on the neon nightlight. Hey, we're out in the open! Besides, we got a clue from them. Cool it, prince," Ace says, putting his hand on the angry Mutant's shoulder, comforting him. The aura recedes as Anarchious calms down. "We have to get those surveillance tapes, and I think I know where to find them," the Lycan informs his partner. "Let's go!" he says, waving on the Mutant, leading him back in the direction of the main gate.

The duo walk for about a mile when they notice a tall person in a dark blue cloak is following them. The cloak is hooded, so they can't see a face. Last thing the duo needs is another Magi incident to happen in the middle of North Torious, so they walk faster. The person following them speeds up as well.

Soon they come to an alley and run down it; the stalker follows. Halfway down the alley, the follower stops and notices it is a dead end blocked by fallen concrete and debris. Most important, the duo has disappeared. The stalker hears a faint crackling sound from above and looks up. It's Ace in full Lycan form, growling, stuck to the wall like a spider and looking down on him with evil intent. The stalker turns and tries to retreat, but before he can run, another figure drops down and slaps his hand over his mouth. It is Anarchious.

"I promise I can kill you before you even think of screaming!" the young Mutant says, looking the stalker in the eye. "Why are you following us?!" Anarchious mumbles angrily as Ace jumps down behind them. The stalker doesn't respond, just glares at Anarchious oddly. "Well?" the Mutant says, wanting an answer promptly.

"Anarch," Ace says to the Mutant.

"What?" the Mutant replies, agitated.

"Your hand," Ace says, reminding the Mutant that his hand is still over the stalker's mouth, thus his silence.

"Oh, my bad!" Anarchious says, removing his hand.

"Well, why are you following us?" the Lycan asks.

"He looks familiar," comes a womanly voice comes from the hooded cloak. She removes her covering, exposing her pretty face, short black shoulder-length hair, red skin tone, thick lips in glossy black lipstick, button nose, and striking eyes highlighted with black eyeliner.

"Witch?" Ace says, drawing from her features.

"Wiccan!" she snaps at the Lycan.

"No fucking difference, Witch!" Ace replies, getting smart with her.

"Cut that out! What do you mean, I look familiar?" Anarchious says, putting an end to what was about to become a shouting match.

"Familiar, like the sibling of Abel," the Wiccan responds, glaring at Anarchious with her striking eyes.

"Abel? How do you know him?" Anarchious demands, glaring back at her.

"The question is, how well do I know him?" the woman responds, lighting up a cigarette.

The duo glance at each other, knowing exactly what the Wiccan means as she takes a long drag of the cigarette and blows the smoke in the air. "Let's talk about this in my breeze home. This is hardly the place," she says, walking past the duo and out of the alley.

"'He looks familiar.' Are you fucking dumb?...Wait, do not answer that! Don't trust her, Anarch!" the Lycan whispers while turning back to his human form.

"Ace, this was no coincidence," the young Mutant responds. "This is the third person I've run into who knows Abel. Maybe she could point us in the right direction."

"No! No! No! That bitch is evil! Eeeeeeevil!" the Lycan screeches, trying to turn his friend away from the Wiccan stalker.

"How would you know that?" Anarchious replies, giving Ace his trademark rising eyebrow look of confusion.

"Never trust a Witch in black lipstick!" Ace mumbles, giving Anarchious a wide-eyed stare. The Mutant laughs and begins to turn around. Ace grabs him. "No, seriously, trust me on this. Look at your brother's track record. She's evil." Ace tries to reason with Anarchious with no evidence other than his gut feeling.

"Zera and Cardinal Vega? That leaves the score one for one, man," Anarchious replies.

"No!" the Lycan replies. "Zera and Luna! And unless Abel has one those funny fetishes for priests, and I don't think he does, that makes the count zero to two!"

"Yo, that's ridiculous. He never slept with Luna," Anarchious says, grinning.

Ace glares at him. Anarchious looks back, ready to reply, but Ace changes his posture, placing his hands on his hips, turning his head, and giving Anarchious a side glare.

"OK, one win and two losses. Let's just hope this is a win because we have no choice at the moment," Anarchious says, turning his back on his partner. He proceeds out of the alley.

"Telling you this is a mistake. Every female we've met on the search has been bad news," Ace replies, placing his cloak and hood back on and following his friend.

"Magi wasn't bad," Anarchious replies.

"Magi punched you in the dick!" Ace retorts, catching back up.

"You have to stop hanging around me. I'm rubbing off on you too much," Anarchious says as the duo leaves the alley to follow the Wiccan home.

On the south side of the city stands the Wiccan's home, undamaged, unlike the rest of the block, which is wrecked, buried in concrete, wood, and debris. Every home, street, and building is severely damaged in some way. The Wiccan's home is small and looks tidy, but inside the home is filthy. There is trash everywhere—on the end tables, on the couch—along with half-eaten plates of food, dust, and the smell of cat plaguing the air.

"Ugh, disgusting!" Ace says as a pair of cats stroll into the room and hiss at the sight of him.

"Sorry for the mess. Had a spell go wrong in here earlier," the Wiccan replies.

"Yeah, I'm sorry as well. I haven't had my spring grooming either," Ace retorts, knowing that she is lying and that the home hasn't been cleaned in a really long time.

The Wiccan grunts and removes all the papers and debris from the couch cushion. She then snaps her fingers, and her cloak disappears, revealing her thin model-like frame and her medium-size bust fitted in her tight black clothes. "Sit," she says, offering the duo a seat as she takes one herself.

The Lycan and Mutant look at each other, then back at her, and reply, "I think we'll stand."

"Suit yourselves. Anyway, Abel left just a few days ago," the Wiccan says, lighting up another cigarette.

"Where to?" Anarchious asks, ecstatic at the news.

"Not sure. Probably to continue his search for absolute power," she replies, rolling her eyes and blowing out the foul-smelling smoke.

"Why was he here?" Ace asks, covering his nose.

"To get himself a piece of Mystie," she answers, smiling suggestively.

"So you're Mystie?" Anarchious asks.

"Not the smart twins are you?" the Wiccan temptress replies, insulting Anarchious as Ace shakes his head, grinning at the Wiccan as if approving her statement.

Anarchious huffs and squats down at eye level, looks Mystie in her eyes, and says, "So he was here during that attack?"

"I know what you're thinking," the Wiccan says as she takes another long drag of the cigarette. "Abby may be dark, but he doesn't have the power or nowhere near the heart to kill that many people for no reason. He may not be fond of them, but he isn't a murderer by any counts. He really came to warn me of the God-King and left."

Anarchious stops and processes the information. The Lycan sighs heavily, tired of the conversation. "If Abel didn't do this, then why is your home still intact?" Anarchious asks. The Lycan huffs and begins to mumble to himself.

"I'm a fucking Witch...protection spell," she replies to the Mutant.

Anarchious stands back up and thinks once more. Fighting the images he saw in the memories of the dying man, he is starting to believe Mystie's statements. "So I am guessing you two are after the security footage," she states as both men look stunned. "I was in the bar too. My intentions were to get drunk and find a man, but those idiots wouldn't shut up about the attack. I want to forget any of this happened, but then you had that outburst. I saw your face, and I thought you were Abel, so I followed you out, wanting answers, but to my surprise, you weren't him. I figured that out when you started glowing."

Ace huffs once more, then turns to Anarchious and asks, "OK, then, so why are we still here? If Abel didn't do it, then the cameras are pointless. This is pointless, and so is she! Let's go!"

"If you calm down and stop being such a smart-ass, I'll explain," the Wiccan snaps at the Lycan. Ace looks at the woman as if she's crazy. "If I know him as well as I know him, he is on foot. This city's cameras don't just cover the city. They circle the perimeter ten miles out, something they do to keep the Vampyr grunts and Lycans at bay," Mystie begins to explain, but she is interrupted by Ace.

"How the hell do you know all of this?" he asks irately.

"I've had my 'fun' in the surveillance room...several times," she replies.

"Whore," Ace grunts, shaking his head.

"Flea-ridden beast," she retorts.

"Fucking hag-raven!" Ace snaps back.

"Yo, chill out!" Anarchious stops the shouting match. Ace steps back, laughing.

"Look, I brought you here to tell you that the room you seek with all the footage is impossible to break into," the Wiccan explains to the duo. "You two may be strong, but you will be shot and killed by the guards if you're spotted. So since I have a little pull with the human soldiers, I propose that I get you the footage of him leaving and in what direction. I even have some of their technology to play it here."

"Why are you trying to help us?" Anarchious asks.

"Well, if it weren't for baby brother, I'd probably be dead, wouldn't I?" she replies, putting out her cigarette and making her way to Anarchious. The Mutant stares her in her striking eyes as she stares back. "Don't worry. I'll be back within the hour. Make yourselves comfortable," Mystie says while snapping her fingers and magically changing into tighter, more alluring clothing.

She is now dressed in sexy black-leather knee boots, black leggings hugging her long toned legs, a tiny silver tank top that her nipples peek through, a studded leather collar, and silver-studded Wiccan bracelets. Anarchious is amazed. Ace is unimpressed. The Lycan can pay attention only to the many intricate tattoos plaguing her arms. The Wiccan woman winks at the duo, then walks between them and leaves the house.

"Do not trust her! She's a Witch!" Ace states as soon as the door slams behind her.

"My cousins are Witches!" Anarchious responds with his attention still on how good-looking the Wiccan is.

"Your cousins aren't anything like her! Did you see her tattoos?!" Ace asks rashly.

"Yeah, I guess," Anarchious replies, not really caring.

"Look, those are the markings of the Black Mamba Coven," Ace states while looking at his friend with great worry in his eyes.

"So?" the Mutant replies, not knowing why Ace seems so shaken.

"So?!" the Lycan retorts. "They are the most dangerous group of Witches, the most evil and most murderous. Black Mambas killed my momma!" Ace yells at his unaware friend. "I am leaving! If you continue to trust her, I am leaving and doing this myself!" Ace says, glaring at the Mutant.

"Ace..." the Mutant tries to start to explain to his brother at arms.

"You coming, Anarch?" the Lycan says as he goes to the door, ready to exit.

"This again?" Anarchious replies.

"Bye!" Ace says as he leaves swiftly, leaving his best friend in the house.

The Mutant stays. He wants to chase after his partner, but he knows he'll be back. Too much is at stake, and he knows his brother is close. He can feel it in his heart.

A half hour passes, and Anarchious becomes restless. He starts snooping around the house. He notices some picture frames are missing by the color differences on the wall. He walks over to a bookshelf in what looked like the kitchen, which is riddled with empty alcohol bottles.

Several framed pictures are facedown. He picks one up and looks at it. This one is a picture of a bald-headed, pale-skinned man with blue eyes who is smiling. It reminds Anarchious of the high school pictures Marie tried to get him to take when he graduated. He places the picture down again and picks up another. It's the same man in a Rebel soldier uniform. He places that one down and picks up a third. It is a picture of the man and the Wiccan hugging, smiling, and looking blissful together. Just then he hears some familiar yelping sounds coming from outside. They are faint, but he can hear them clearly as they give him goose bumps.

Bang! A loud explosion sound comes from the front door. Anarchious peeks around the corner to see what it is. "Shit!" he utters, irritated. He sees fully geared Rebel soldiers with big-barreled weapons. Anarchious is frightened. He's seen those before. There's no way around them.

He runs to another room as quietly and quickly as possible, looking for another way out. He bolts to the laundry room and looks out the window. There are many soldiers standing guard, waiting for action. "There he is," one soldier says, spotting him through the window. Crash! Broken glass flies past his face, cutting him, as a weird canister drops onto the floor and begins to spurt white gas.

Anarchious tries not to inhale the gas, but it's too late. He gets a whiff of it and covers his mouth but immediately begins to choke, becoming extremely dizzy. He then stumbles to the back of the house and looks out the window. The house seems completely surrounded. Crash! A few more canisters fly through the window, spurting more of the white gas.

Anarchious's eyes begin to water and burn. It is just like that horrible day the Mutant can't forget. He tries to fly and burst his way out of the ceiling, but the smoke has negated his power. The Rebel soldiers' footsteps become louder as their blue lasers wave over the area, searching for Anarchious. He runs back into the kitchen, slips on a liquor bottle, and falls to the ground, choking. The soldiers spot him. "Take him!" Those familiar words. His mother flashes before his eyes. He has no choice but to fight them.

Anarchious quickly spins, conjuring a gust that blows away the smoke and knocks down most of the soldiers blocking his way, but not before one of them fires on him and hits his hand. He stops and looks at it with tears escaping his eyes. It is that same sticky green substance. He remembers it like yesterday. He can already feel his Ki being drained and the substance hardening.

The Mutant gets hit three more times in the legs and lower back. Anarchious can feel the vertigo taking over. He begins to panic and lightning-bursts his way out the front door, knocking down the soldiers still standing in his way and rolling into the street. There are more of them waiting to shoot him again. The Mutant rolls laterally, avoiding most of the muk and zapping all of the soldiers with a twisting lightning beam. He is almost home free and begins to teeter his way into an alley but runs into an invisible barrier. He glares to the side with what little vision he has left and sees Mystie!

"Why?!" Anarchious yells, stumbling to the woman whose arms are held out, conjuring the barrier that is preventing his escape.

"He took the only person I truly care for!" she yells, glaring at him from the other side of the barrier. "His brother for my lover!" she yells as Anarchious charges up lightning in his weakened hand, then punches through, breaking the barrier and blasting Mystie right in the jaw, sending her flying up to the fifth floor of an abandoned apartment building across the street.

The Mutant then stumbles, trying to make it to a place to hide, but he is shot a few more times with the green goo. His power is nearly depleted when he stumbles in front of a few innocent bystanders. He is now seeing double and can hardly walk. He is numb and can't feel anymore. The crippled Mutant looks up and sees a familiar face. "Sena?!" Anarchious exclaims as a Rebel soldier walks up and butt-stocks him, knocking him out cold.

A block down, Ace watches from the roof of a tilted high-rise apartment building as they drag away his partner. He wants to save him but sees no tactically safe way around the Rebels' goo guns. The Lycan decides to bide his time and wait for the perfect moment, but first he has some unfinished business.

Ace jumps from building to building until he comes to another destroyed apartment building. He jumps into a fifth-floor window and spots Mystie still trying to regain her equilibrium. Classic Anarchious stun attack. He knew I was here, Ace thinks to himself as he aggressively approaches the grounded Witch.

She glares at Ace as he begins to transform, looking into his eyes, which reveal nothing but hatred for her. She hops back up on her feet rapidly, chants a quick spell, and forms a barrier. Ace speed-bursts and crashes right through it, grabbing the Witch by the throat and slamming her back into the concrete wall, creating a depression in the shape of her body in it. The entire building shakes and leans more from his power.

"I think I cracked your spine, maybe even broke a rib, Black Mamba!" Ace says, grinning and staring her in her terrified eyes. His eyes change from their normal deep chocolate color to fiery crimson. "Kanji-Spartan!" the Wiccan gasps, becoming even more frightened as she recalls the look of his eyes.

“I heard everything you said to my idiot friend! So no more lies! Where is Abel?” the Lycan yells.

“I don’t—” she tries to reply, but Ace tightens his grip, puncturing her neck with his sharp claws. “I really don’t know!” Mystie yells out in agony.

“If you don’t know where he is, you know where he’s been,” the irate Lycan states while loosening his grip.

“Yes. He spoke of a Red Desert,” she says, choking.

“Now, did Abel attack the town?!” Ace asks. She pauses and thinks to herself, crying. She is speechless. “So you don’t know really if he was the killer during the Attack, huh? You just set my partner up on a hunch, tramp!” Ace yells, squeezing tighter.

“It doesn’t fucking matter anyway!” she yells back, gasping for air. “Abel is clearly in league with the God-King, which would still make him responsible for the death of all those people and for the death of my husband.”

Ace grunts and tosses her aside like a rag doll. “That’s all I needed to know. Now, go crawl back into the hole you came from, hog wart!” Ace says as he makes his way out of the window and climbs back to the roof.

13
Crash the Party

"This is unbelievable! Look at his vital signs! Look at the SHEAG intake! He has enough energy to power a city for centuries!" the voice of an old man states, clearly fascinated with what he's seeing.

"He is a Storm Mutant. I saw the lightning myself. Maybe it's the 'lectricity throwing off the SHEAG meter, doctor," an odd deep-voiced accent responds.

"No, we've perfected the Super-Human Energy Absorption Gel," the old voice explains to what seems to be an assistant. "It is the perfect measure when connected to this machine. Not only that, in my forty years of researching Mutants, I've never seen the SHEAG absorb so much energy from one Mutant without causing a fatality. This one just keeps recharging somehow. No...no, he is special."

"Well, too bad. This one's time is probably coming soon. So, doctor, make the best of it," the assistant responds.

"Yes, too bad. I wonder if I can delay it further. He could be the answer I've been seeking for so long," the doctor replies in a depressed tone.

"Ahh...what is this?" Anarchious groans, opening his eyes, seeing the blurry silhouette of the two figures in front of what seem to be television monitors.

"I'll handle it, doctor," the assistant says, walking off.

The Mutant tries to move his limbs but realizes he is restrained by chains and the green goo crystalized all over his body. He tries to break free but is still extremely weak. Anarchious tries to yell but doesn't have the energy.

The assistant walks back into the room carrying a black box in his hand, walks up to the hanging Mutant, and shocks him on his neck. "That should knock him back out!" the man says, amused. Anarchious feels a bit of energy and begins to yell. The assistant shocks him again in his neck, confused.

Anarchious gets an even bigger rush of Ki to his body and struggles, causing cracks in the hardened gel keeping him stable. "No, Yuri!" the doctor says, walking over and sticking a needle into the neck of the struggling Mutant. A loud buzz rings in Anarchious's head. "You must sedate him. He absorbed the electricity from that obsolete toy and could have escaped," the doctor says irately.

"Sorry, doctor!" the assistant apologizes, scratching his head as the doctor turns around to tend to the constant buzzing.

"Overload? Power nodes? Astounding!" the doctor exclaims while turning back to glare at the Mutant as he passes out once more.

Outside, it is dusk as Ace cases the building where his best f being held. It is big and like an old-style prison facility about a mile away from the city of North Torious, surrounded by three three-story-tall barbed-wire fences equipped with motion detectors. The doors are reinforced steel, and there are no windows. There are nearly one hundred guards armed with green goo weapons with beefed-up security protecting the head honcho on the top floor. The floors are made of concrete, and on each floor are stun gas canisters. The building has at least two elevators able to reach every floor. Wherever Anarchious is being held has to be underground on a basement level. The Lycan can smell and hear it all from the top of a ruined building towering over the facility. He has made his plan, but it is still much too light to make his move, so he waits patiently.

"Mom?" Anarchious can see his mom in their backyard. It was fenced off and away from most of the populace in the District. It was hot and humid; summertime was afoot. This was thirteen years ago, and the Mutant remembers it vividly. They were having a cookout. Lynn and Nat were playing in the flowerbeds. Dad was meditating in the middle of the yard. Mom and Marie were by the grill, conversing and laughing.

"Apoc," his mother called out to his father, who was in a deep trance. "Apoc!" she yelled out to him once more. He ignored her. Mom held her finger in his direction and zapped him.

Dad hopped up and screamed, "Damn it, Angie!" as Marie and Mom laughed at him.

Sploosh! The Mutant turned around. It was Abel. He had the water hose and was spraying Anarchious. "No, Abel!" the young Mutant yelled in his baby voice, trying to get away, but he tripped. "No!" Anarchious yelled, but his brother wouldn't stop spraying him in the face. Anarchious began to gasp for air, feeling as if he were drowning.

"Wake up, Mutant!" he hears as he comes to, still restrained on a table. A white, bearded man is holding a bucket of water, splashing Anarchious with it. "Good, doctor, the subject is up!" the man says in his funny accent.

"Thank you, Yuri," the doctor says, walking over to Anarchious and looking down on him. He is a very old, pale man with a head full of cloud-white hair and a curly mustache. He is wearing glasses that shine with an overhead light, so it is hard to see his eyes. "Welcome, young Mutant. I am Doctor Dexter Stinent, and you are in my observation lab," the old man says, introducing himself. Anarchious just gawks at him with his eyes still blurry from the effects of the SHEAG, remembering he has been captured.

"Look, I have gathered copious amounts of data on you, but there are still things I need to know to complete my database. The only way I can get these things is if you answer the questions truthfully," the doctor explains, revealing the reason for waking him abruptly. Anarchious glares at the doctor, trying to focus his eyes. "You are about nineteen, no?" the old man asks.

Anarchious turns his head, trying to get a better idea of his surroundings. He sees he is in fact inside a lab. It reminds him of Marie's surgery room in the hospital with the observation glass so that pre-med students could learn or family members of the sick could watch the operations.

"Please, I have little time to spare!" the old man pleads. Anarchious glares back and nods to the eager old man. "Yes, so you were born after the Eden incident. How did your parents survive?" the old man asks. The Mutant looks at the old man curiously for a moment, then makes a puzzled face. "OK, where did you grow up?" the old man asks.

Anarchious thinks of his sisters and of the District and says, "I never had a home."

"Where are your parents?" the doctor asks, writing in his notes.

The Mutant glares at him hard, not wanting to answer that question. The old man looks down, glaring back at the Mutant, noticing his heightened emotion. "Well?" the doctor persists, wanting an answer.

"They were killed by soldiers when I was five," Anarchious answers regrettably.

"That is impossible. Their DNA would be in the database. Are you sure they are deceased?" the old man inquires, looking over his glasses into the Mutant's angry eyes.

"Yes!" Anarchious yells as he thinks back and remembers what he witnessed that day as a child, the void his fatally wounded father opened at the end.

The doctor stares at him, not sure whether to believe him or not. "OK, last question. What is your name?" the doctor asks, looking the Mutant in the eyes once more. Anarchious looks away. "At least give me your name so I can tag your data properly and not have to mark you as John Doe like the others," the doctor says, agitated, but Anarchious refuses to answer.

Just then, three soldiers burst into the room, knocking Yuri out of the way. "Doctor, why hasn't the prisoner been prepped?" the head soldier yells.

"Staff sergeant, I'm not done with him."

"Doctor, did you get your DNA samples?" the staff sergeant asks.

"Yes," the doctor answers, nodding rapidly.

"Did you get his chakra data?" the irate staff sergeant asks.

"Well, yes," the doctor says, saddened.

"Well, then, you've completed your tasks! End of discussion!" the sergeant yells at the doctor.

"But...but I haven't gotten his name yet," the doctor replies.

"Too bad. Enter him as John Doe," the staff sergeant retorts.

"Privates, melt the SHEAG and take the prisoner to Echo Foxtrot!" the staff sergeant orders his subordinates.

"Yes, sergeant!" the two younger subordinates say as they proceed to melt the SHEAG, imprisoning Anarchious with a small boxlike contraption.

The doctor watches helplessly. The privates melt the goo back down to its original form, unchain him, grab the weakened Mutant, and begin to drag him out of the room.

"Please, staff sergeant! Assign him to me! Look, he can give us all the answers about that lost culture of people....Please, I can make it worth your while, son," the old man pleads with the soldier.

"Did you just try to bribe me?!" the staff sergeant yells at the old man. "This is just another dead Mau. He means nothing! Need I remind you that what we are doing is necessary to protect human life, especially seeing we are on threat level alpha right now with that superstorm brewing and the Demon-King's attacks becoming more frequent? If that's a problem, talk to my commanding officer, but I'm sure he won't give a flying fuck because he is the one who sent us down here!" the staff sergeant yells at the doctor. He then follows after his subordinates and the weakened Anarchious.

"I'm sorry, young Mutant," the old man says with tears glazing his eyes, catching Anarchious's eye beyond the observation glass before they completely turn the corner in the hall.

The soldiers drag Anarchious down the hall and into an elevator and hit the bottom button labeled EF. The ride doesn't take long. Soon the soldiers drag the weak Mutant out of the elevator and into a massive room made of concrete that is heavily bloodstained and reeks of death.

Anarchious sees it but is still too weak to do anything. The soldiers remove the Mutant's vest and hoodie, exposing his muscular upper body and midsection, and they chain his hands together over his head in the middle of the floor. One of the soldiers slaps a red paint brush over the left side of his chest, marking his heart. He then runs off to the side and stands with his back straight, feet shoulder-width apart, hands behind his back, and eyes forward, along with eight other soldiers who are all geared up for battle, holding their rifles while standing in the same manner.

The staff sergeant stands in front of Anarchious, smiling. "It's a sad day in hell for you. It looks like your ticket is getting punched at any moment, mau-mau." The staff sergeant grins at the Mutant as the elevator dings and opens. "Atten-tion!" the staff sergeant yells as everyone's posture changes in the room. They are all now standing at attention as their commander walks among them.

The high-ranking soldier, a white, plump, bald-headed, clean-shaven man, walks over to Anarchious and the staff sergeant and speaks to him. "At ease, sergeant. Let's get this over with. We still have the Lima Threat to neutralize," the commander states.

"Yes sir!" the sergeant replies, then steps back, does a crisp about face, takes ten paces away, and stops. "Fire squad, fall in!" the staff sergeant yells as the eight soldiers with assault weapons line up in front of him at attention. The sergeant then walks off to the side of his soldiers and stands with them. He executes another about face, facing back towards the commander, who is now facing Anarchious as well.

"By Order Sixty-Six issued by General Dimps, the high commander of the United Rebel Alliance Army, you are to be executed by firing squad for the crime of evasion and endangering human existence. Do you have any last words, Mutant?!" the commander asks, looking the Mutant in his chocolate-colored eyes.

Anarchious looks over the commander soldier and glares at the soldiers with the weapons, the same assault rifles that wounded his parents after the goo slowed them both down. Emotional, the Mutant looks back into the bald-headed commander's big blue eyes and spits in his face. "That's for Angelica, Apoc, and every Mutant you people have ever murdered, you fat son of a bitch!"

The commander calmly pulls a rag from his pocket, smirks, wipes his face, and walks away from the Mutant, clearing the soldiers' firing lane. The alarm rings as they all can hear faint sounds of gunshots coming from floors above.

"Let's hurry. Lima Threat may be coming to save him!" the commander says as he walks to the side and nods at the staff sergeant. The staff sergeant does a left face staring down the line of his firing squad. "Ready!" the staff sergeant yells as the firing squad readies themselves. "Aim!" he yells once more as the firing squad members fix their sites on the Mutant's heart. The staff sergeant turns his head, grins once more at the helpless Mutant, and screams, "Fire!"

The floor quakes as all weapons fire simultaneously, and the lights go out on the floor. Echo Foxtrot is pitch black as a plethora of gunfire echoes on the floors above. "Shit! Privates, put on your night goggles!" the sergeant yells at the guards and firing squad. Boom! There is a horrendous-sounding crash that echoes throughout the room, shaking it once more. It seems to have come from the elevators. "Focus on the elevators!" the staff sergeant shouts.

By now, all the soldiers have on their night vision goggles, focusing on the elevator. They then hear erratic banging on the elevator door, as if something is trying to force its way through. "Fire!" the staff sergeant yells as every soldier empties his magazines on the door. The muzzle flashes light the floor up for a brief moment before every weapon is emptied on the door. The banging stops. The soldiers remain cautious for a moment, listening for anything else, but they can't hear anything. "We got two in one day! Out-fucking-standing!" the sergeant says, putting his sidearm away as everyone seems to relax.

BANG! Something or someone breaks through the elevator doors. The soldiers search the room with their goggles. Scared, they try to spot it but see nothing. "Empty?" comes a deep, rough voice from above.

Everyone with goggles looks up and spots a pissed-off Ace stuck to the ceiling and glaring down with his crimson eyes. "Too bad!" Ace growls as he drops down and begins taking out the humans one by one as they all try to reload their weapons. Ace can now see them all in the dark, and his senses have increased exponentially. He can feel all the soldiers' movements. He can feel, hear, and even taste their fear prowling in the dark. The commander screams and rushes to a corner to cower while everyone else tries to reload in the dark. The Lycan uses his newly upgraded senses to locate his partner, but something isn't right. He feels nothing else is in this room except death.

The Lycan has no time to waste. It is time for an all-out assault on the URA's Execution Squad. Ace winds up and double-clotheslines two soldiers, sending them flying through the darkness. The Lycan then backhands the staff sergeant, sending him flying and thumping against the concrete wall. Ace then uppercuts one soldier so hard, he collides with the ceiling and falls back down. Ace catches him by his leg before he hits the floor, uses his body to knock out three more soldiers, and then flings the soldier into the wall, pummeling the staff sergeant once more.

The furious Lycan grabs two more by their faces and slams them into the wall, cracking it and crushing their goggles and Kevlar helmets. The Lycan then zooms across the room on all fours and spears another soldier. He can feel the last threat has reloaded and is ready to fire upon him.

Ace races across the room, on the walls, and onto the ceiling, seeming to defy gravity as the soldier blazes rounds in his direction. The Lycan is too quick as the rounds bounce all around him, not having a chance to hit him. The lights come back on, flaring the goggles and blinding the soldier. He quickly removes the goggles, and before he can focus, Ace boots him in the back, sending him flying, knocking the staff sergeant back down again.

The Lycan roars victoriously, then glares at all his victims. Everyone is out except for the head honcho. He is still cowering in the corner. Ace then turns and looks for his partner in crime. There is no one else there but a big tree stump of a vine in the middle of the room.

It has several bullet holes on the north side of it. It also has a chain extruding from it that is connected to the ceiling. Ace smells it, and a familiar musk comes to his nose. "Anarch!" he exclaims. "Hold on, buddy!" Ace breaks away the vines and bark, trying to free Anarchious. "Hey, is this a new power or something? If so, it's really dumb but handy!" Ace says as he breaks through to the hollow part of the stump. It is completely empty but reeks of the Mutant's scent.

"What the hell!" the confused Lycan yells. He then notices a gaping hole in the bottom of the stump. It looks like someone has burrowed under it. He climbs in to investigate. There is a dark tunnel under the big stump. It smells as if it was recently dug. It is also laced with treelike vines. He begins to smell the vines, not knowing what could dig this deep into the ground. It has a familiar smell. He can't put his finger on it just yet, but he knows immediately Anarchious has been there.

As Ace proceeds into the tunnel, both his partner's and the familiar smell got stronger. He walks deeper into the burrow and steps in something warm. He places his fingers in it and takes a big whiff. It is Anarchious's blood. He then remembers the bullet holes in the stump. "He could be bleeding to death!" Ace says. He quickly takes another big whiff of the air to locate his buddy. Anarchious is a few miles away and wounded. The Lycan takes off in a flash, refusing to waste any more time in pursuit of the Mutant, praying to the Spirit that he'll make it in time.

Elsewhere, Anarchious lies in an abandoned home on the outskirts of North Torious. He can't remember how he got there or why he is paralyzed. All he can remember is the taste of blood and two people, one huge guy and the other a tiny woman who smelled of fresh daffodils.

His eyesight still weak from the SHEAG, he tries to survey the home as a wild-haired woman enters and patches the wounds over his heart. The Mutant regains his full consciousness but still seems paralyzed. "What happened to the other woman?" Anarchious grumbles to the woman, remembering a different face.

"What woman?" the wild-haired woman responds with a sweet tone.

"The woman…the short one who smelled liked...smelled like daffodils," the Mutant responds. The woman grumbles, shakes her head, smiling, and continues his bandaging.

Anarchious stares at her and keeps seeing a familiar face. "I know you're not her, but how can you look just like Sena?" he asks, still trying to get his eyes to focus on her face, but they are still too weak.

"Sena? Who's that?" the woman responds.

"Old girlfriend," the Mutant replies.

"I get that a lot," the woman says, rolling her eyes.

"What happened?" Anarchious asks, trying to move once more, but he's still paralyzed.

"My partner, Jasen, and I saved you from that firing squad," the woman responds.

"Jasen? Is that the flower lady who was healing me?" Anarchious responds, still having that blurry beautiful face stuck in his head.

"No! That was a hallucination, idiot, a downside to the drug formula I used," the woman snaps, looking away from the Mutant. Anarchious raises his eyebrows in confusion.

"You know you were shot in the heart? I healed it," the woman giggles.

"Heart?! Shouldn't I be dead from a wound like that?" Anarchious responds.

"Well, yeah, but not with someone this awesome healing you. I also gave you blood bug daffodillian sedative. You should be in a considerable amount of pain right now, but you're not. It explains the paralysis, the smell, and the 'flower lady,'" she replies, patting him on the chest and getting up to leave the room.

Anarchious thinks for a moment. "Wait a minute. Yo, why'd you save me?" he asks the wild-haired woman before she can leave. She turns and looks back down at him curiously and gently rubs his face while sitting down. She stares into his eyes, and he knows immediately. "Abel," he mumbles. Her eyes widen. She is shocked, but before she can say anything, the Mutant says sadly, "He's my twin brother."

The woman is speechless, but Anarchious is now scared for his life. Another one of these crazy bitches from Abel's endeavors. He regrets not listening to Ace. So he conjures what little Ki he has regained and sends electricity through his body, killing the sedative and thus destroying the paralysis.

The Mutant hops up and falls immediately to his knees. He isn't in any shape to walk yet and feels a horrible pain in his heart shoot throughout his limbs.

"What are you doing? Lie back down!" the woman yells at the Mutant, but Anarchious, being his stubborn self, fights his way back to his feet and tries to stumble out the door while gripping his chest in severe pain. "If you do not lie back down, I'll force you!" she says, trailing behind him.

"Fucking Abel! Fuck you, crazy bitch! All of y'all!" Anarchious grunts in pain, creeping along the wall for support.

"Bitch?!" the wild-haired woman yells. She snaps her fingers. Something bursts from the floor, grabs the Mutant by all four limbs, pulls him back to the bed, and restrains him. "One, do not ever call me a bitch, or I'll cut your beads off and play hacky-sack with them while you watch and cry, ironically like a 'bitch'! Two, if you do not rest, you will die, so stay still!" the woman yells in Anarchious's face. They both hear a big crash. "What the hell?" the woman yells.

Something crashes through the wall right into the room. From the dust and debris comes Ace. "Witch!" he yells, pointing at the wild-haired woman.

"Lycan?!" she yells back, somewhat confused.

He glares over at the table and sees his buddy restrained by vines like the ones he saw in the execution room. "Death incarnate!" Ace yells as he backhands the woman, sending her flying out a window. The Lycan then picks up his friend and places him on his back, then makes his escape from North Torious.

The duo make their way beyond the forest surrounding North Torious and come to an eerie lake several miles down the road. The water is still and reflects the full moon and stars, making the lake radiate a soft turquoise color that lights the shore. Ace stops running, feeling they are home free. He quickly tends to his friend's wounds.

He then notices Anarchious is patched up already, noting the weird bullet wounds over his heart. Ace stares at them for a moment and begins to connect the dots, realizing, "The prophets..." But before he can finish, Ace is hit hard and sent flying to the banks of the lake. In midskid, Ace quickly rolls up back to his feet, regaining his balance, and shakes off the hard blow.

Ace glares over to Anarchious's body and spots the Witch from the home about to perform magic on the Mutant. Ace quickly gets on all fours and tries to zoom back to his partner to save him, but the Lycan catches another hard blow to the side of the neck, sending him flying into the lake this time.

The Lycan is now pissed off. He's never been struck that hard before in his Lycan form. He leaps out of the water and onto the banks once more. A man, a really big one, is standing between him and Anarchious.

The man is muscular and rugged with a peach complexion and is nearly as tall as Ace in his Lycan form. The man's eyes are big, blue, and menacing. He is wearing soldier's attire and combat camouflage similar to the Rebel Army's.

Ace, unsure of this man's presence, quickly becomes annoyed by the staredown, so he rushes the man. The man rushes back. They grapple, testing each other's strength. Ace begins to gain the upper hand and slides the man back several yards, but the man starts pushing him back. The Lycan glares into the man's eyes. His face is stoic. He looks as if this has been too easy for him. The Lycan gets angrier and lowers himself. The man gets lower too.

The Lycan uses all his strength and gets the upper hand once more, but it's short lived as the man uses his full strength in return. They both try their hardest to gain the advantage, circling each other, maintaining the grapple hold. After a few moments, Ace realizes they are evenly matched. He grows tired of the man, so he breaks the grip and isolates the man's arm in an overhead arm bar, trying to bring his opponent to his knees, but that doesn't work. The man gives Ace a hard right hook to the ribs, forcing him to loosen his grip. The man then snatches his left arm away and uppercuts Ace, sending him hurling through the air and landing stiffly on his back.

The now extremely agitated Lycan sits up, angrily spits blood, and glares at the man, who is shaking his arm from the pain of the arm bar and possibly the mean left uppercut. Ace knows immediately this guy can't be a regular human. Whatever he is, though, it doesn't matter to the Lycan. This man is blocking him from helping his friend, and that means war!

14
Hope

Back in Glen Haven, Cardinal Vega and a travel-packed José emerge from the hideout. The streets of this part of town are unusually empty, especially considering it's the middle of the night. The men think nothing of it and walk towards the front gates of the town. As they get closer, they hear music and see festive lighting coming from the town square. They glare at each other curiously and begin running towards the festivities. The closer they get to the source of the music and lights, the more people there are entering the streets, making their way there too. The music is loud and upbeat, and tons of spring-colored confetti dances in the wind while fireworks whistle overhead.

After minutes of pushing through the crowds of partying people, the cardinal and José find themselves in the middle of the merriment. The music plays loudly as everyone but the older men is dancing and having a good time in front of a stage just a block away from the grand church, which normally is used for springtime sermons. There is a band of several different races playing on stage.

This cannot be the same town, the cardinal thinks to himself. Just a few days ago, another race riot was a drop of blood away from manifesting! He glares at José, who is bobbing his head to the beat and grinning. The cardinal grins back.

Neither of these men has ever seen anything this beautiful before. The entire town, it seems, plus some outsiders have come to this party and are all enjoying each other's company. To the old duo, it really doesn't matter why this is happening. It just seems that true peace and happiness have begun.

One of the performing guitarists begins singing. "We live in a world hailin' war and lust. We were lost 'n' stuck like chain on rust. Till he swooped down, waved round, saved all of us! There's a white-faced warrior in all of us! There's a ghost-faced warrior in all of us!"

The crowd sings along in sync, "There's a ghost-faced warrior in all of us!"

The two old men are astounded! They know exactly what the band is singing about and make a move to stop it, even though the backlash could be a catastrophe. They push and shove their way to the stage, but it proves to be futile. People grab, hug, shove back, and become stationary. After a few more seconds of chanting, the lead singer signals the band to cut the music. The two old men continue to push their way to the stage. The song ends. The crowd goes nuts and begins to cheer at full volume. Over the microphone, the man asks the crowd to calm down.

After a few minutes of uninterrupted applause, the old men are still trying to get to the stage. The singer waves to someone behind the stage, and in moment, a teenage Lycan in his human form emerges from the back wearing a shirt with a familiar face on it. The old men's eyes widen as they recognize the face.

The crowd cheers for the Lycan as the lead singer hugs him and brings him to the front of the stage. The tenacious lead singer waves his arm towards the crowd repeatedly, quieting them down. "We all know this little hero, right?!" she singer yells as the crowd roars in excitement and applauds. The singer waves his hand, and the crowd quiets down once more.

The two old men continue trying to push forward. "Most people on the web know this little man's story now!" the singer yells as the crowd comes to life once more. He places his arm around the teenager's shoulder, pulls him close, and "noogies" him with the mic. "This little Lycan carried one of my fellow humans back to the village and tried his hardest to save him. Then a douchebag of a man and his friends misinterpreted that and tried to hurt him!" the singer exclaims as the crowd boos loudly. "But he remained strong! Then, like a storm approaching, the white face swiftly gave the men what they deserved and saved him." The crowd loudly cheers once more. The singer then takes off his shirt and puts on a shirt similar to the one the teenager is wearing. Then the bandmates do the same.

The two old men panic at the sight this. Vega and José both are jammed up by several drunken patrons of the party but continue trying to free themselves from the crowd.

Suddenly, a loud crackle overhead trembles in the skies. Startled, everyone directs their attention upward. There are no clouds, but the skies seemed disturbed. The wind begins to blow violently. Another blinding flash of light soars across the sky like a shooting star and downwards towards the crowd like a meteor. The light strikes the stage, blinding everyone who is watching it.

"Like a plague, a true power came descending from the Heavens and crushed our pathetic hopes and dreams!" a powerful, booming voice echoes throughout Glen Haven. The earth quakes momentarily, and a crisp coldness quickly fills the atmosphere. Soon the temporary blindness subsides. The two men, the crowd, the band, and everyone on stage immediately focus their sights on the new addition.

A short, pale, liver-spot-riddled old man wrapped in a blood-colored shawl from head to toe and wielding a long wooden staff stands there glimmering. "That will be the last thought of you pathetic beings," he says, waving his staff over the crowd staring in shock. "Did you really believe you all would get away with this blasphemy? Hmm? Worshipping a mere mortal?" the old man asks with a smug look on his face. "No matter. Soon you all shall feel the wrath of a true God!" he booms once more over the crowd as most of the people drop to their knees and begin reciting the "God-King's Prayer" in horror. The old man laughs and slams his staff on the thick wood of the stage. The people pray louder in unison.

"God-King the Almighty, no matter how dark, we give you praise and accept you in our heart. Although I may die as you cause me to bleed, I pray on my knees and accept your creed!"
The ground beneath the praying patrons quakes and shifts a little, terrifying all of the citizens. They pray harder and louder, hoping for the God-King to spare their lives.

The old man's appearance is brief. He laughs and fades away into thin air. Most people continue the prayer, hoping what they have experienced won't happen again, but Cardinal Vega and José have other plans.

"People, get up and out of the streets now! Leave this town! Find somewhere safe to hide!" the cardinal yells at the crowd, but no one listens. Vega glares at José, terrified but ready for the hell to come. "We cannot lose you! The world will be lost!" Vega proclaims.

José looks Vega in the eye as he feels the darkness growing. He's no coward, but they both know what is at stake. José runs up to Vega and shakes his hand firmly. He says, "The Spirit is watching you, brother!"

"Brother, the Spirit is with us! Do not forget that!" says the cardinal.

José backs up slowly, shaking his head, and instantly flashes away as the night sky is devoured by a pure darkness.

Soon the church is devoured by the blackness and crumbles, yet most of the citizens continue to pray, hoping for mercy, while others are too petrified to try to escape. Vega, seeing everything he has built being crushed, becomes angry. He snaps his fingers, and Magi is instantly summoned to him in her ninja gear. He approaches her, opens her mouth, and lifts her tongue. He gazes upon a Wiccan seal labeled Silence and Obedience.

Vega hears familiar howls and screams. He knows what is coming, so he hurries as many structures and people around him are being devoured. Some people even choose to fight back, but it is futile. The hellhounds and hell bats are too much. The cardinal performs a quick incantation in a Wiccan language and breaks the seal placed on Magi.

Immediately she speaks. "What's going on, Master?! Why aren't we running? What's going on? Who...?"

"Shush, my child, and listen!" He looks into her eyes. "I need you to port as many people as you can to my safe house and outside the city now!" he continues.

"But—"

"If you don't do this immediately, many people will die!" he yells at her.

Magi looks around at the carnage taking place and all the praying people ignoring it and gets scared. Vega glares into her eyes once more as his eyes change to a dark plum color and then a crimson red, changing hers to the same colors in the process.

"I am bestowing you with these last gifts! Take them and use them when the time is right!" he exclaims, hugging his fellow frightened Vampyr.

"But—"

"This is the end of the road for us! Your training is over! After you save as many people as you can, do not come back here! Your mission starts now!" Vegas says as he hugs her lovingly, pushes her away gently, quickly turns his back on her, and begins fighting off the hellhounds, ignoring the tears they both were shedding.

Magi begins teleporting people by the masses as the cardinal does his best to protect people using his Vampyric ocular power of telekinesis. The monsters are very strong but still no match for him. Soon the entire city is engulfed in darkness, overrun with hellhounds and hell bats. The streets are riddled with lifeless bodies and blood.

Eventually the cardinal is the last living being in the town. He is surrounded by the hounds. They all approach him, stalking, with their eyes fiery red. Vega is dead tired and beat up but is still standing tall. A deep, dark voice speaks out. "You done yet?"

The Cardinal grins. "Your evil tactics don't scare me. I have the power of the Spirit protecting me."

A dark, ominous voice laughs. "Call him then. Call your God!" the voice howls at the fearless cardinal.

The old man just gazes at his surroundings and calmly sits down. "The Spirit has better things to do right now," Vega proclaims, relaxing his shoulders. He begins to meditate, still grinning.

A black, ominous flame quickly phases its way through the anxious hellhounds, and from it, an agitated voice speaks once more. "It's useless to continue your pathetic charade. Your God is nonexistent. There is but one true—"

"You shall not take my hope! You cannot break my faith!" The flame is interrupted by the cardinal's calm proclamation. "So just do your worst, demon!"

All the surrounding dark entities immediately become livid and unstable. The hellhounds rush to attack and rabidly begin devouring the cardinal. Vega doesn't make a sound, knowing his demise is imminent. He remains in a meditative state as if he feels no pain. The cardinal is completely overtaken and being ripped apart by these monsters, yet the last glimpse of his face displays a smile. He is at total peace.

15
Death at the Front Door

Not far away, two battles are being waged on the banks of the moonlit lake and surrounding forest. The Lycan fights to re-rescue his buddy, still on the shore of the lake and battling for his life against a Witch.

Ace rushes the tall man as he catches his breath, stooping on one knee. Both men are heavily battle scarred, but neither will yield. At the last moment, the man sweeps the Lycan's leg. Ace hits the ground hard. The blue-eyed man quickly raises his leg and prepares for an axe kick. His leg comes down swiftly and forcefully. "Damn!" Ace exclaims as he is too tired to dodge it even with the moon being out. As the kick makes impact, it quakes the ground, filling the immediate area with dust. The man jumps back several yards and coughs, trying to catch his breath.

"You kick like a bitch!" Ace proclaims as he walks through the dust, his eyes glowing crimson.

"Kanji-Spartan!" the blue-eyed man exclaims.

Ace nods as he speeds towards the man at double the velocity he has been attacking with. The blue-eyed brute waits for the perfect moment and hurdles over the advancing Lycan. He turns in midair, trying to keep track of Ace, but Ace vanishes. The man turns back, and before he can blink, Ace clotheslines him, sending him flipping uncontrollably forward. The brute hits the ground hard. Ace twists in midair and lands on all fours, skidding to a stop.

The Lycan peers over at the Witch. She is still casting magic on his partner, whom, through his new power, he can feel slipping away. The Witch chants and waves hand signs. Grass begins to grow all around her and Anarchious's bodies. Soon flowers and bushes grow as well. In an instant, the entire surrounding area except for the lakeshore looks like a springtime meadow. The Witch then opens Anarchious's mouth and blows a dustlike substance into it. Anarchious begins choking vigorously. The Lycan has seen this type of magic before and knows if he doesn't finish the brute off, Anarchious will be a corpse in minutes.

Ace pushes forward once more, rushing on all fours towards the brute, who has just gotten back to his feet. Ace goes to tackle the brute. The man, proving to be a tank and a worthy opponent, stops Ace's momentum for the most part, sliding back a couple of yards to the cold, wet shore of the lake. Thinking quickly, the brute wraps his arms around Ace's waist and quickly rolls him into the air to perform a power-bomb. The Lycan is stunned. With all his might, the brute tightens his grip and prepares for the slam, but Ace isn't accepting it. The Lycan tightens his legs around the neck of the brute and uses his own core strength and momentum to flip the tank, teetering him onto his head with the force of an explosive, once again quaking and cratering the area. The shake even displaces the lake's water, causing a giant tidal wave to crash the opposite end of the body of water, severely damaging some of the forest.

"Hurricaranna!" Ace exclaims over the man's defeated body. He then turns towards the Witch, who is still focusing on Anarchious. He walks up close but decides not to step on the newly grown meadow. He has to be cautious; the grass could be a trap. "If you leave now, I will consider not ripping your head off!" the Lycan shouts at the Witch. She continues working on the Mutant, who Ace can feel is hanging on for dear life.

The Witch replies, "A threat? Give me a break!," irritating the Lycan.

"I know your kind, so I'll give you one more chance. Let him be or prepare for this wreck, Black Mamba!" Ace yells once more, letting out a vicious snarl.

The Witch sighs, gets up, and begins to walk towards the Lycan. The persistent woman begins to speak kindly after reaching the halfway point between Anarchious and the Lycan. "I do not wish to fight, but clearly you—"

Ace shoots forward at blinding speed and full strength and clotheslines the woman, decapitating her. Her body and amputated head hit the ground and explode, splattering blood everywhere, showering the Lycan. "I'll never trust a hag-raven!" Ace proclaims as he spits on the site and turns his attention to his partner, who is gasping for air. She's killing him! the Lycan says to himself as he rushes to aid Anarchious.

Something grabs his feet. He glances down at the grass and realizes immediately his suspicions were correct. "Damn it!" the Lycan curses, disappointed in himself.

The blades of grass have wrapped around and bound his legs tightly. He begins trying to push forward, ripping some of the grass, but eventually he is trapped. He unsheaths his claws and begins scraping some of the grass away, but before he can do much, he notices the Witch's blood changing to a muddy brown color and spreading all over his body.

Ace wildly attempts to shake the blood off, but it's really sticky, and moving only speeds up the process. Soon the sap encases his entire body. The molasses-like substance soon hardens, leaving only his face unscathed. Ace begins to grow tree bark and branches. From one of the branches on the back side of Ace's shoulder, a stalk begins to grow, and many flowers start to bud and bloom from it. One bud grows bigger than the others, and from it blossoms the Witch, smirking as if she is unimpressed.

She drops down onto what would be the Lycan's back, steps down, and sits on his shoulder. She strokes his long, pointy ears. Ace is furious at the Witch's display of power and arrogance. He tries to break free, but it's no use.

"As I was saying before you interrupted me, I do not wish to fight, but since you're clearly an idiot, I have to resort to less civil means such as this," the Witch explains as she jumps down and makes her way back to Anarchious.

"Don't you touch him!" the Lycan yells.

"Or what? You're encased in that amber. Just shut up and let me do this." She continues her path to the Mutant.

Ace has seen this magic before. He sees his mother and sisters in the den, the memory of their lifeless and cold bodies. He can't watch his best friend be destroyed like this. He refuses to watch Anarchious perish the same way. The Lycan's rage takes over as he struggles with all his might. The tree bark and Amber begin to crackle.

"I won't let you suck the life out of him!" the Lycan screams at the top of his lungs, snarling wildly.

"You're not very bright, are you?" the Witch replies, continuing her stride to the Mutant, not even turning to view Ace.

This is the last straw for Ace. The Lycan's eyes burn a hotter red, the ground begins to shake, and in that instant, Ace's rage breaks him free. He immediately jumps back off the grass.

"Impressive!" the Witch says, clapping her hands. "But what's your plan now?" she continues, picking at his nerves.

"Way ahead of you!" the Lycan blurts out as he speeds towards her. The grass blades are too slow to grab him at these speeds. Ace goes for another clothesline, but the Witch ducks it while the Lycan skids to a stop.

He turns and readies to punch her. She huffs and blows thick, black soot in the Lycan's face, blinding him and shrouding the surrounding area. She leaps out of the smoke screen and onto a nearby tree branch like a cat and begins to chant in a foreign language.

"Didn't think you would get away that easy!" Ace screams, leaping after the Witch and ready to pummel her, but she immediately retreats, jumping backwards, surprised at his quick emergence. Ace quickly jumps off the branch and launches himself at her, grabbing her by the foot. "Gotcha!" he yells as he begins to pull her in. Suddenly he feels an abrupt tug at his foot. "What?!" The Lycan exclaims as he looks down and sees the tree has a hold of his foot!

"No! Got you!" the Witch says as she twists away from his grip, flipping and landing on the grass once again.

The tree seems to have a life of its own as it whips Ace backwards, slamming his back hard against its trunk. The tree then grabs hold of his upper body, constricting his arms tightly to his side, rendering him helpless once more. The Lycan continues to struggle, but the more he does, the tighter the tree grips the Lycan.

"You keep on struggling. I am going make the Dahomey tree here grow nine-inch rose thorns!" the Witch says as she watches from the ground.

"Damn hag-raven! When I get out of this one, I will kill you!" Ace screams at the Witch, who turns her back on him once more and makes her way back to Anarchious's body.

"Blah, blah, blah! Shut up!" she responds as she kneels down once again by the Mutant.

"Get away from him now!" the Lycan snarls at the Witch from the height of the tree. She ignores him and continues monitoring the Mutant.

"How long do you think you can hold him like that?" a smooth voice asks from beside her.

"As long as I want, Jasen!" the Witch answers, knowing she is speaking to her companion.

"He's really strong. Those branches won't hold him long!" Jasen says, rubbing his aching head and rocking his neck back and forth, trying to loosen it up.

"I blew a bit of 'shroom dust in his face," the Witch says. "Any moment now it should be kicking in and sedating him!" Hearing this with his super ears, the Lycan gets scared and begins struggling more.

"How is this shrimp?" Jasen asks his partner, shaking some of the mud off his arms.

"I'm not sure," she responds, continuing her incantations and casting her magic on him.

"Will he survive?" the big brute asks her, concerned because the Mutant's skin has become slightly blue, cold, and clammy. Anarchious is looking very pale, especially for his rich chocolate skin tone.

"I have no idea. He was shot in the heart," the Witch explains to her partner. "Those bullets must have been special because that stump skin I protected him with is too dense to be penetrated by their copper-lead rounds. My stump prevented a lot of damage, but they ripped his arteries up. Just give me enough time to force his healing factor to speed up again and to use my spells to keep him alive while it happens."

"Why even try? He's clearly done for!" Jasen responds, crossing his arms, seeming to lose his patience.

"Last thing I want to be is responsible for the death of Abel's twin," she exclaims. "If we had not been delayed, his survivability would be almost one hundred!" the Witch continues while working on Anarchious.

Ace stops struggling when he hears this, surprised by the Black Mamba's words, but before he can ask a question, the world around him begins to warp. His reality flips as if he has dropped into a dream world saturated with the colors of the rainbow. The illusions are beautiful and calm him with peaceful images of his sisters and mother. There is no more loneliness, no pressure to be something he isn't, no fighting, only love. Freedom is a reality, and he can feel it as he is dropped into the old golden-grained fields he grew up in. He can't help but frolic amongst the butterflies and sunflowers.

In the real world, Ace is babbling like an idiot while still stuck in the tree, howling a joyful tune.

"What the hell's wrong with that character?" Jasen asks.

"The dust has taken effect! He is no longer a threat!" the Witch says as she continues working on the Mutant, who seems to be fading by the moment.

"I think you're wasting your time. Leave him, and let's go!" the blue-eyed brute says to the Witch, who is starting to become frustrated herself.

"No. I can save him, and once I do, he'll lead us to Abel!" the Witch yells at her partner.

"No! He'll die, and we'll lose our trail," Jasen replies, walking towards the shores again.

"Shut up! Just do your job and protect me," the Witch snaps back.

Jasen grunts as he continues his path to the shining waters of the lake. Once he reaches it, he begins rinsing the mud off himself in the cool, refreshing water.

"C'mon, you son of a bitch!" the Witch mumbles to herself as she struggles to keep up her incantations on the near-dead Mutant. Her arms are getting heavy and begin shaking. Her voice cracks with every chant.

"What is this?!" a voice yells out.

Both the Witch and her companion direct their attention behind them. It's the Lycan, screaming at the top of his lungs, terrified. "Phoenix!" he yells, still struggling and flailing about, trying to break free.

"What's wrong with him?" Jasen asks.

"I don't know," the Witch replies as the Lycan continues letting out bloodcurdling screams.

"It's like he's having a bad trip," the blue-eyed brute says, covering his ears as he approaches the tree where the Lycan is still trying to wiggle his way free.

"Uh-oh," the Witch says, letting out a little grin as she recalls something.

"What?" the brute asks.

"Yeah, that spell was said to have a bad side effect with a small population, but I've never seen it in action before now," she replies, covering her ears as she approaches the tree as well.

The Lycan's yelling quickly becomes screeching and yelping like an injured puppy as he continues flailing. "Please kill me!" he yelps, still haunted by the Witch's illusions.

"Can you stop him? Now?! This is going to make my ears bleed!" Jasen yells to the Witch over the continued yelping of the terrified Ace.

"If I could I would. I'm totally out of energy," she yells back.

"Let him go." A faint voice comes from behind the Witch and the tank. They both turn around and witness the nearly dead Mutant staggering back to his feet.

The Witch turns to her partner, overjoyed, and exclaims, "True power of the Wiccan!" She smiles wildly at her partner, but he gives no response.

His eyes are fixed on the Mutant, who is now on his feet. She glares back at the Mutant and witnesses something frightening. "I think you've raised some kind of zombie mime with your 'true power,' magic girl!" the brute says, describing the weary Mutant's face.

"No, this is all him!" she responds, gazing at the shining violet eyes of the Mutant.

"Let him go now!" the Mutant screams wrathfully as the winds begin to pick up and storm clouds gather overhead, rumbling with the sound of thunder.

"Jasen, I'm going to need you to hold him off for a while I gather life force," the Witch whispers to her partner.

"Why not just let his friend go?" Jasen whispers back, surprised at her strategy.

"Look at his eyes," she replies. Jasen directs his eyes to the Mutant's. The tank sees fury like never before. It is so powerful, his hair stands at attention, and his skin is covered with goose bumps. "Those are the eyes of a man lost in his rage, and he's already painted us as the enemy. If we let his buddy go, then chances are we'll be fighting two incredibly strong individuals. I don't like those odds when I am pretty much wiped out!" the Witch explains. She begins her incantation, waving her arms and body about elegantly.

"All right, mascara! Let's see how tough you are!" the tank says as he charges forward towards the Mutant, who doesn't even budge. The tank opens up with a whole barrage of his best flurries, kicking and punching combos that even the best fighter would find impossible to dodge, high and low, feints and fakes made to confuse the mind and eyes. None of them hit the Mutant. He dodges them all without changing the expression on his face. This doesn't faze the tank; he just picks up the speed on all his strikes. This causes the Mutant to pick up his speed as well and even parry some of the strikes.

Jasen gets frustrated at the Mutant's lackadaisical approach to the battle, so he tests his opponent and fakes Anarchious out with a double-spinning hook kick. It creates an opening in the Mutant's midsection, and immediately Jasen strikes with his hardest, fastest left hook. The Mutant reacts but isn't fast enough to block it. The punch rocks his body so hard, the ground quakes, cracks, and knocks the Mutant a little off balance.

Jasen stares wide eyed, his jaw dropped, surprised the injured Mutant is able to take a blow that hard and survive. Anarchious glares at Jasen's fist and grabs it, then looks quickly at the tank, giving him a wicked frown. Instantly a massive lightning bolt strikes the dueling men, blasting the entire area and adding one more crater to the several others on the shoreline.

The ground quakes as the Witch continues her ritual. She doesn't lose a beat. As dirt fills the air, she continues dancing around at the edge of the forest. The trees, bushes, and grass all seem to be reacting to her movements, swaying to her graceful ballet while slowly withering. A few feet away, up in the tree, Ace seems to be shaking off his horrible dream and coming to. He witnesses the Witch dancing around, his vision still slightly blurry and colors still saturated. He directs his attention to the ominous figure in the settling dust cloud.

The silhouette of a man stands tall in the crater. The white-faced Mutant leaps out of the hole and lands on the shore. He directs his attention towards the dancing Witch and walks in her direction. She notices him and speeds up her ritual. The Mutant walks faster. The Witch finishes her last step and twirls into a new spell, posing elegantly. The Mutant grimaces as he quickly advances. The Witch directs her hands in his direction as they begin glowing.

“Hell you think you’re going?!” a voice comes from beside the Mutant. The tank leaps from the hole and makes a move to grab Anarchious. The Mutant swiftly grabs the blue-eyed brute’s head and hops over him with ease. Midair, Anarchious turns and double-drop-kicks the tank in the back, sending him hurling toward the shoreline. The tank flips, turns, and skids, grabbing the ground. He runs at full speed back to the Mutant, who has an eyebrow pointed in curiously.

The tank strikes at the white-faced Mutant, surprised at his own speed and precision, which have seemingly increased, and his combos are forcing the Mutant to block now. His rapid assault is putting pressure on the Mutant, and it begins to show on his face. Anarchious ducks the tank’s fierce left hook and hastily jabs him on the front of his left shoulder with a knife-hand. It has no effect.

The tank grins at the plain-faced Mutant and advances for his assault. He tries to throw another straight left, but his arm just flops. His left arm is now heavy, and he can hardly move it. The blue-eyed brute sighs as he realizes what the Mutant has done.

“Pressure point attacks?” Jasen asks, looking the Mutant in his ferocious eyes. Irritated, Jasen advances anyway with a right. The Mutant ducks it and jabs the tank in his right shoulder the same way. Jasen now has no feeling in his right arm. The brute, irate, swiftly head-butts Anarchious, knocking him back. The Mutant stumbles back and looks at the blue-eyed man. A fire erupts in his violet eyes. He shoots forward in a blur and strikes at the brute’s sternum.

"Jasen!" "Anarch!" the Witch and Lycan both scream for their respective parties. The Witch is shocked at the sight of Anarchious's arm jammed in the brute's chest.

Ace feels his heart drop as he hears his promise to his mentor race through his head. The Mutant has finally crossed the line their mentor was so fearful of. This is the first time white-faced Anarchious has gone for the kill. Ace knows what he is going to have to do and can't bear it. He yells out for his partner while trying to muscle his way out of the tree, which now seems to have lost its strength. He keeps his eyes on his enraged partner as he wiggles and flexes, creating a bit more space. He then notices something odd about what the Mutant is doing.

Anarchious backs up and removes his arm from the tank's chest. There is no blood, only a soft blue light attached to the menacing Mutant's arm as he continues pulling away from the shell-shocked brute. The light has been stretched thin a few feet away from the brute. Anarchious snaps his hand back and breaks the light. As it whips back and is absorbed into the Mutant's being, the tanks loses the little life he has in his eyes and passes out, falling face first.

"Jase!" the Witch screams as she whips her arms forward. Vines lash from the soil like spears.

"Anarch! Watch out!" Ace warns his partner as he continues trying to escape the tree's grasp.

The Mutant turns quickly, lightning charges his hands, and he chops, slices, and burns the Witch's feeble attacks. She continues lashing vines in all direction at the Mutant, but he continues to make her attempts look weak with his electrically charged grips. As much as Ace hates this Witch, he knows what is coming will be his fault. He can't live with that either, so he becomes desperate, trying to free himself, plotting a way to stop Anarchious.

The Mutant glares at the Witch and grins wickedly. She grits her teeth and continues to attack, frustrated but unafraid of Anarchious. The Mutant shoots forward as the Witch tries to hit him dead with her vine attack, but he is too quick and blocks the attack. She quickly tries to inhale, an effort to blow some more 'shroom dust, but it's too late; he is already upon her. She shuts her eyes and braces herself for her fate.

A large crackle shoots from storm clouds above, continuously rumbling. The lake shakes from the impact as the sound echoes through the forest. "Anarchious?" the Witch hears as she opens her eyes.

"Ace?" the Mutant responds in a confused tone.

"I knew you were in there, Anarch," the Lycan responds with a grin.

"It happened again, didn't it?" the Mutant asks with disappointment resonating from his voice.

"Yeah, but this time, I happened to pay the price, bro!" the Lycan replies, face to face with his best friend.

Anarchious's face is still white with the usual black tear markings, his irises still as purple as his electric aura, but his pupils now resemble a four-pointed star. Anarchious looks between the two and sees his arm lodged in Ace's midsection. The Lycan has protected the Witch from being victimized by his enraged partner. The Mutant's eyes widen as he begins to tear up.

"I'm sorry, man!" he says, apologizing to the Lycan.

The Lycan smiles, trying to keep upright, while feeling his energy draining. "If I survive this, maybe you will listen to my advice more!" the Lycan replies, grinning. Anarchious slowly removes his hand, pulling a soft blue light from the body of his friend. He snatches his arm away, absorbing the light as Ace passes out, falling aside.

The Mutant, confused about what has taken place, sees the Witch. Anarchious squints and proclaims, "Sena?"

"Not Sena, you murderer," the Witch screams as she begins to swing her arm towards Anarchious. The Mutant, seeing flashes of this attack in his head, quickly shoots forward and chops the Witch across her jugular, knocking her out cold.

16
URA's Most Wanted

Anarchious sits in the corner of an old room on the top floor of a two-story cabin. It's the middle of the night as he attentively watches over the still, near-lifeless human form of his partner, Ace. His body is cold, but every once in a while, a slight sigh will come from the comatose Lycan.

Ace lies on a perfect-fitting bed. It's been nearly three days since the incident that Anarchious holds himself personally responsible for. He doesn't understand how he could have let himself get out of control like that. The Mutant has searched his feelings looking for an answer and has constantly found nothing. He has even struggled to recollect the events that led him up to that point. All he understands is that the power that saved his life was also the power that could be the end of his best friend.

Anarchious remembers his capture and, slightly, the scientist. He remembers the loud boom of the rifles ringing in his ears, causing a familiar white noise and hearing distortion. He remembers the taste of his own blood and being carried through a tunnel. He remembers the pain and the weakness taking over. He remembers being flown on a feather while a brisk wind kissed his neck and back. He remembers the face of the woman patching him up and the tiny scar over her left eye. She was beautiful!

The Mutant remembers the blue eyes of the black-haired man and the Witch who looked so much like Sena. He remembers defying her. He remembers Ace protecting him and carrying him off. Then he remembers Ace's screams and yelps, which echo in his mind. He couldn't allow his friend to be killed. Then he remembers his Lycan friend's eyes going from crimson back to normal then to blank.

The Mutant can still feel the power from the energy gained from the attack hidden amongst other things. He closes his eyes, tries to relax, and clears his mind of negative thoughts and feelings. He reaches deep into himself with the meditation his master taught him.

He clears his mind of the pain, guilt, sorrow, and everything else he is feeling and focuses on this hidden power. He sees a face, his own. It is there as clear as a crystal on a sunny day, the face José unleashed in their training, the one Ace has described to him so many times. But Anarchious has never recalled or felt it, the face painted white as snow, elaborate black patterns and lines around the eyes hugging the crevasses and curves of the face, bringing out the glowing violet irises and their starlike form, the face he dons whenever he loses control of his temper and blacks out.

The Mutant reaches for it, but the closer he gets, it repels him, rejecting his presence. He focuses harder and forces his way towards it. The face frowns and rejects him once more. "What the hell are you?!" he screams at the Ghost-face. It laughs as the Mutant pushes towards it, fighting the repulsion. The face laughs harder, ominously, as the repulsion of the Mutant stops.

Anarchious continues to reach out, and it begins to get dark. The Mutant feels his consciousness slip the closer he comes to the face, so he retreats. The face grins. Anarchious slightly raises his hand towards the Ghost-face, and his view begins to darken and distort. He rests his hands and stares the face in its purple eyes as it glares at him, shaking its head in disappointment. It rolls its eyes and glares at him, annoyed. Anarchious then hears Ace's screams for help, the screams of Marie's daughters as their house burned, and then his mother's and father's voices as they were shot to death.

Anarchious feels the rage taking over his state of meditation. He knows the face is causing all this, and he wants to lash out. He wants to destroy the humans who tortured him and his family for so long. He wants to destroy the URA for murdering his mother and father. He wants to punish the Vampyr who killed Marie. It soon becomes apparent he has the desire for revenge. He wants to destroy them all but thinks of his aunt and all she taught him. Anarchious knows such revenge won't fix anything but rather just turn him to the villain the URA and the humans make his kind out to be. So instead of continuing to fight the Ghost-face, he drops to his knees and smiles. "I forgive them. I forgive myself," he exclaims, looking the Ghost-face in the eye.

The face smiles back and then shoots forward and onto the Mutant's face. He awakes from his meditation in the cabin, full powered and glowing a deep purple aura that is emanating electricity. His power is amazing. It feels as if it has tripled. He looks at his reflection in the window. He is the Ghost-face now.

Anarchious can feel weird energies all around him. He can feel his buddy's energy. It is weak but stable. He can feel the fish in that eerie lake that is near, and he can feel the sorrow of the people in North Torious many miles away, although it was very faint. He can feel so many other anonymous energies. It is as if he can feel life forces. He looks towards Ace and can see his Ki as clear as day. It is like a tiny blue fire. He can see something but can't make out what it was. Nevertheless, it speaks to his conscience. It gives off a noble feeling, a feeling of pureness. His power continues to stretch.

Whatever this power is, Anarchious knows it will be of great use, especially whatever the faint touch is that discombobulated the Lycan. He can still feel that energy he pulled from Ace lingering within himself. It reminds him of his power before he could control it, so he begins working on that. He directs it, cycling it through his body and pushing the power into his hand. From his hand bursts a bright white light, almost blinding himself. It is stronger than he thought it would be.

Anarchious tries a few more times and fails, but he doesn't give up. He has always been a quick learner and even more so in this form. He knows he will have this down within the hour. He eventually contains the brightness and pushes on. The power begins to form a Ki-like energy ball. He forces it out, and the ball energy pops up and begins hovering over his hand. This energy was specifically stolen and developed from the Lycan. It looks like a carbon copy of the moon. It glows just as bright and just as blue.

Anarchious plays with and controls it like those old human yo-yo toys, throwing it around and tossing it like a football. He masters this new power easily. In minutes, he has free range and control. Anarchious can control this Ki without even looking at it. Even though this Ki didn't originate with him, he feels the same energy regenerating within his gut. This is confusing, but he has to try generating the energy again, so he forms another moon ball in his free hand. He is controlling two moons in his hands.

At that moment, the Lycan grunts. The Mutant directs his attention to Ace. His energy seems to be sluggishly recovering. He can feel it and also see the flames flicker. He approaches the comatose Lycan, and his Ki begins to grow more rapidly. The closer he gets, the stronger the Lycan's heartbeats become. "Mmm," Ace moans as the Mutant stands over his friend's body, thinking. The Lycan is progressing but still relatively slowly, and Anarchious thinks it is because of the moon balls.

He quickly comes to a conclusion. "Well, here goes nothing!" he says as he forces the balls of energy into his friend's chest. The Lycan twitches and quickly absorbs the energy. His body convulses and begins transforming into Lycan form.

The Lycan groans and growls as he regains consciousness. Ace completes his transformation, breaking the bed in the process. He surveys the room, muddled, and spots his friend. "Um, hi," the Mutant greets the confused Lycan, not really knowing what else to say. The Lycan turns and faces him, getting off the now too-tiny bed and recalling the entire situation.

"Oh yeah, because an apology would be entirely too much," the Lycan says, stretching and cracking his neck.

"Don't give me that! I revived you!" Anarchious replies, breaking a tiny smirk.

"You killed me, you ass!" Ace shouts as he continues stretching his back.

"Yo, shh....Quiet it down, man. A lot of things have changed since you're...uh, coma," Anarchious says, approaching his angered friend.

"Not until you apologize, you dick—to the same guy who tried saving your ass numerous times after he warned you that Witch wasn't trustworthy!" Ace yells, raising his voice even louder. He stands up and aggressively approaches Anarchious.

"All right, my bad! Now, shh....Shit!" the Mutant says, shushing his counterpart.

"Damn right it's your fault," Ace responds, sitting back down. "Good to see you got a hold of that white-face thing," the Lycan continues, relieved, thinking of his dreadful promise to their master.

"Yeah, I'm a lot stronger in this form too. It's amazing. It's like I can feel life. I can see energies of living beings."

"And take them," the Lycan quickly proclaims, interrupting the Mutant.

"Yeah." Anarchious looks aside, smirking.

"Great!" the Lycan says sarcastically, wide eyed.

"Yeah, well, check this out!" the Mutant says as he holds out his hand, conjuring a moon ball once more. The ball is big and bright and nourishes the Lycan.

"The moon?" the Lycan asks, reaching out to the ball. The Mutant nods. "You produced that from my energy, didn't you?" Ace inquires, pretty much already knowing the answer.

"Yeah, but it's not just that. It keeps replenishing, like my own regular Ki does. It's a part of me now. Kinda cool, huh?" the grinning Mutant says, admiring his own work.

"I've got a new power of my own," the Lycan says, grinning, as his eyes glow crimson.

Anarchious glares at his friend and waits for a moment. "Doesn't seem like much,'" he says, raising his eyebrow at his partner as if he's disappointed.

"Oh, because my eyes don't turn the color of a flimsy boy's panties, and I don't run around here glowing looking like a sad ass-clown who was born in a nuclear power plant, you think that this isn't anything! I'll have you know, although it is in its juvenile stages, this ability enhances my senses tenfold, my strength is doubled, and my speed and agility are now greater than yours," the Lycan states pompously.

"Not like this," the Mutant replies, referring to his Ghost-face form.

"We can test that!" the confident Ace responds, smiling widely.

"Most definitely...but what is the power?" Anarchious asks Ace regarding the nature of his power.

"Well, it seems as though I inherited the spirits of the Kanji-Spartan," the Lycan answers.

"Umm?" Anarchious mumbles, confused.

"It's a special ability that only the warrior bloodline of the Lycan inherits. We allegedly can tap into the strength of our ancestors," Ace explains.

"Yeah, but aren't you all warriors?" the Mutant asks.

"You know better than that. When you first met me, I wasn't a fighter at all," the Lycan explains. "My father is a warrior, but my mother wasn't a warrior; she was a scholar, most notably a history fanatic. That is whom I assumed I inherited my gentleness from," the Lycan continues.

"Well, that's cool. Least you know what that is. This I still don't get it," the Ghost-faced Mutant responds.

Ace looks at the Mutant in his purple eyes with his smoky crimson lookers and proclaims, "Well, this is a curse…a useful one but a curse nonetheless."

"Since this 'curse' is inherited, why haven't you been using it all along?" the Mutant asks, curious.

"I couldn't. The Pride elders usually screen the pups. Needless to say, I failed," the Lycan replies. "By the Spirit, I wish I could have had it years ago. It could have saved my mother. But it's something that has to be earned. I was a coward then." Ace drops his head.

The Mutant looks at his partner, knowing his past and sympathizing with him. He thinks to himself, If I could, I'd have saved his mother too, but I was weak and knew nothing as a child.

The Mutant returns his face back to its normal rich chocolate hue and sighs, remembering Marie and his parents' faces. "Yo, so I guess this worked out for the better. We both unraveled hidden parts of ourselves, and now we're stronger. Our parents would be proud," the Mutant states, trying to lighten the mood back up. Ace shakes his head and huffs, not really agreeing with that statement.

The Lycan then looks around the room curiously. "Anarch?" Ace says to the Mutant.

"Yeah?" Anarchious answers.

"Where exactly are we?" Ace asks with his nose in the air.

"Long story. Just do me a favor and turn back to your midget self. Our hostess might not like the fleas," the Mutant replies, chuckling as he walks out the door.

"Screw you, buddy!" the Lycan shouts, chuckling at his partner as well.

The duo creep down the steps of the nicely furnished cabin. The lights are dim, and they can hear the wind swaying the trees outside the cabin. The duo hit the bottom of the stairs and creep around the corner into what seems to be the living room. There sits a woman, the Witch, and the tank from the lake. The Witch seems to be mediating while the tank is lying on a sofa that was entirely too small for him just as lifeless as Ace was minutes ago.

The woman stands up and smiles at Ace and Anarchious. She is a middle-aged woman of average height and has blue eyes. She is a porcelain-skinned beauty of a woman, wearing a robe and slippers. "And the two mystery men finally emerge?" she says, smiling widely at the duo. Anarchious grins and looks at the tank laid out on the couch, feeling his weak vital signs. Ace pretty much ignores her glaring at the windows, which are all boarded up.

"I know you guys are hungry," the woman says. "Been up there for some days now. I'm gonna go make you some breakfast since it's almost four." The woman walks past them and into another room.

"Who is she?" the Lycan whispers to his counterpart.

The Mutant looks at the Lycan and prepares to answer, but the Witch quickly interrupts, still meditating. "She goes by the name of Joyce, and she is the angel who kept us hidden in her cabin while you were upstairs sleeping like a newborn pup."

"No one asked you, hag!" Ace snaps at the Witch.

"Just letting you know since it's your fault we've been stuck in here for the better part of three days," she calmly replies. Ace glares at his partner, whose eyebrow is raised in confusion. "Yes, that's right, fleabag. This is your fault," the Witch says, blatantly blaming the Lycan for this situation. "If you hadn't openly attacked the URA, run through their streets like a mad dog, and then attacked my bodyguard and me, the URA wouldn't be surveying this entire area every thirty minutes with soldiers and those damn flying machines," the wild-haired Witch, still in her meditative position, continues calmly, taking her frustrations out on the Lycan. Ace is dumbfound and doesn't know what to say. "And because of our little scuffle, they now know there are four of us, and they know our descriptions and our races. Thank you so very much," the Witch says sarcastically.

"The hell you expect? A Witch kidnapped my partner," Ace argues. "Think I'm gonna just let you waltz away with him that easily? You must be out of your tree-hugging mind!"

"I saved him and was healing him!" The Witch peeks her eye at the Lycan, gritting her teeth. "Now, because of you, my bodyguard over there is comatose. Thank you once again," she continues.

"The asshole attacked me!" Ace retorts quickly.

"I wonder why? It might be because you slapped me out of a damn window!" The Witch glares at the Lycan evilly.

"You were practically tentacle-raping Anarch!" the Lycan replies, giggling. Anarchious laughs and playfully punches Ace on the arm.

"Idiots," the Witch scoffs. "I was trying to save his life. He needed to be restrained," she explains, becoming irritated.

"Yeah, how'd that work for you? What did you do to her, Anarch?" Ace chuckles some more and turns to his partner.

"I think I chopped her in a pressure point, and she passed out!" Anarchious replies, mocking her as he and his friend laugh in unison.

The Witch breaks her meditation state and stands up, faces the duo, and speaks firmly. "If it weren't for my masking our presence, we'd all be dust right now from the URA's heat signature searchers. So respect me or—"

"Or what?" Ace interrupts, stepping towards her. "You threaten me, and I'll show you why your kind fear the Kanji-Spartan!" he threatens the Witch.

Boldly she steps forward and says, "You try, and I'll show you how the Black Mamba scrubbed out the Kanji!"

The Witch and the Lycan are face to face, ready to rumble. The Mutant is trying to step between them, but the Lycan has begun his transformation, growling at the Witch, whose palms are glowing.

"If you people wake up my babies, I swear by the Spirit you'll be the ones putting them back to sleep! Got it?!" Joyce says aggressively, sticking her head back in the room, eyeing the arguing trio. The Lycan, Witch, and Mutant stop their bickering and calm down. The middle-aged woman leaves the room, and they all glare at each other.

After a long, awkward silence, Ace finally speaks to his partner. "Let's go find your brother, Anarch! Well, after we eat."

"Sounds like a plan," Anarchious replies.

"Whoa! What about my partner?" the Witch asks with concern.

"Not our problem," Ace replies, smirking. Anarchious shrugs and begins walking back up the stairs.

"Is this how you treat your own?" The Witch raises her voice, almost pleading.

"He's not one of mine. Think I would know," Ace says, turning about as well.

"Not yours, idiot. I was talking to Abel's brother," she replies.

The footsteps stop. Anarchious comes back down and glares at the Witch. "What do you mean?"

"So you don't remember what happened in your brawl with my bodyguard?" she asks, glaring back.

"Not really," he replies, remembering mostly darkness.

"This guy took a full-on lightning bolt that should have killed him. Instead, he came out swinging, stronger than he was before," the Witch explains.

Ace and the curious Mutant look at each other, confused. "Well, I did think he is way too strong to be human," the Lycan states.

"Still doesn't prove anything," Anarchious says, crossing his arms.

"You go and ask him, then," the Witch replies, gesturing towards his comatose body.

The Mutant looks at him and turns Ghost-face. The Witch startles at the purple flash and jumps back. The Mutant looks at the body and sees its energies are low. It also begins to speak to his intuition and gives the Mutant an angry and lost feeling. "Still don't know what to do," the Mutant states.

"Give him his spirit back!" she replies.

"His what?" the confused Mutant replies.

"Just shock him or something," she rapidly retorts.

"All right," the Mutant exclaims as he sticks his finger out. He gives the tank a tiny jolt, and in seconds, the man is sitting up in his seat, surveying the room.

The Mutant eyes the tank. The tank eyes him back and asks, "Got a problem, zombie?"

"You're a Mutant?" Anarchious cuts straight to the chase.

"What's it to ya?" the blue-eyed tank asks the Mutant, trying to antagonize him.

Anarchious isn't at all convinced. "Where's your element if you're a Mutant?" he asks.

The tank just frowns and stares at Anarchious. "You don't have to have an element to be a Mutant," the Witch says. "The fact he can absorb your energy and pop up like that is proof enough."

"As much as I don't like the hag-raven, she's right," Ace intervenes. "He has a faint smell that reminds me a little of you and our master."

"If he's such a Mutant, then why is he in the Rebel Army?" Anarchious says, pointing at the tank's belt buckle, which was an R for rebel on it.

"Yes, he is in the Rebel Army, but he's taking a break to help me find your brother," the Witch explains.

"Yes, so he can try to kill him!" the Mutant grunts, eyeing the blue-eyed brute.

"No, so he can help me clear his name and bring him home with me," the Witch explains. Anarchious scoffs.

"First of all, yes, I am a Rebel, but more specifically I am a Body-snatcher." The tank continues his fiery glare directed at Anarchious.

"Body-snatcher," the Mutant repeats.

"It's a division within the Rebels that specializes in securing or terminating bounties that are a threat to human life," the blue-eyed brute explains.

"You're still General Dimps, bitch," the fired-up Mutant states, maintaining eye contact with the tank.

"Please, in garrison he may heavily outrank me, but in the field, my people are on a completely different rank structure. We operate how we want, and he has no say," the tank says, grinning. "Look, I want to hurry up and help her find this shadow guy so I can get back to being human because that is all I've ever been or will be, for that matter." He continues to glare at the Mutant.

Anarchious turns to Ace, then looks at the Witch, who is grinning as she looks at her bodyguard.

"OK, well, we will be leaving soon. Maybe we will all meet again," Ace says, sitting down in a chair next to the front door.

"Fine with us," the Witch replies, returning to her meditative state.

"It's obvious to me that none of you knows a blessing when you see it," the woman states as she enters the room, carrying a platter filled with many different types of sandwiches. The Lycan pops up, grabs several, and sits back down.

"What do you mean?" the Mutant replies.

"Well, you guys are all looking for the same individual while you all are now wanted by the
URA. It's slapping you in the face, and you don't even know it!" the middle-aged woman says, placing the platter down on the table in front of the brute, who grabs a sandwich and begins devouring it.

"Nope, ma'am, we've learned our lesson. Never trust her kind," Ace exclaims, jaws full of chewed-up meat and bread.

The Witch, ready to throw down, turns and screeches, "Got more derogatory things to say about my people?! Say it to my face!"

The Lycan swallows his food and wipes his mouth. As he stuffs his face with more sandwiches, he says, "I don't mean your dirty, murdering, hag-raven, matchstick, finger-wiggling, tree-huggers club. I mean you women who know Abel. We've have a bad track record with you, so we are staying away!"

The Witch gives Ace the evil eye but decides to ignore his insults.

"Why are you helping us, ma'am?" Anarchious asks Joyce, enjoying his first sandwich.

"I hate the URA just as much as you probably do. To tell the truth, most humans hate the URA. They've committed so many war crimes over the years in the name of 'protecting the human race,' things like genocide, pillaging, robbing, collateral murder, and resource hoarding. All any of it's done is make stuff worse for us civilians. We have all this knowledge and technology but can't even talk out our problems or negotiate like the good old days. The URA jumps to war every time as a result just for economic gain. They are rumored to have a bomb now twenty times more powerful than the ones they dropped on the people of Eden. Rumor says it was built to blow up the moon just to keep turned Lycans at bay." The woman sits down next to the meditating Witch. "How ridiculous can they be? Most of us just want peace, but that loony general of theirs has refused it at all costs while the president does nothing. Also, there's something about him that just doesn't sit right with me at all. I don't like him!" the woman explains to the group.

"You and me both, sister," the tank replies.

"You kids are all great. I can tell. To me it doesn't matter if you are human, Mutant, Vampyr, Lycan, or Wiccan. We all deserve peace—peace of heart, peace of soul, and peace of mind, as the good book says. That brings me to my original point—you guys will need each other," Joyce explains, placing her hand on the Witch's shoulder. "This was no coincidence. Two sets of people searching for the same person for nearly the same reasons who just 'run into each other.' This was destined. You youngsters should band together because I fear if you separate, you'll have much less of a chance against the URA," she continues, looking at Ace's silly stuffed face and Anarchious's straight one. "I do not doubt your powers, but these are the people who have bombed populated villages just to kill one menace. Having two extra folks to watch your back could help. Shoot, if it weren't for that storm approaching or being on this being a national reservation, they would have napalmed this place three days ago," she concludes.

The room grows silent as everyone's eyes survey each other's. Joyce has a valid point, and four people with their ears to the ground can help out significantly. The Mutant looks at the Lycan. Ace looks at the Witch. The Witch looks at the tank. And the tank glares back at Anarchious. They reluctantly agree, still skeptical of each other, but for the time being, sticking together might be for the best.

Suddenly, Ace hops up and swallows his food. "Wait a minute! I saved your life!" He points at the Witch. "I'm not going anywhere till she thanks me!" he proclaims deviously.

"Shut up!" Anarchious says, smiling and slapping his counterpart on the neck. "My name is Anarchious, and this is my annoying but lovable Lycan pal, Ace!" the Mutant says, introducing himself to the tank and Witch, holding his hand out to offer a truce.

The wild-haired Witch stands up and approaches the Mutant. "This blue-eyed devil of a man is my bodyguard, Jasen, and my name is Eva," she says, introducing the blue-eyed man and herself and shaking the Mutant's hand to confirm this team-up.

"Great!" Joyce states, overjoyed. "I am happy for you all, but y'all have to leave soon because it is only a matter of time before they search this entire house, and I suspect it will be soon with the hurricane predicted to hit the coast in a day or so," the woman explains.

"Thank you again for taking us, Joyce. I…we really appreciate it," Anarchious states, reaching out to shake the woman's hand. She rejects it and brings him in for a hug.

“The Spirits are watching over you children, and if you ever need anything, you’re welcome back to my home,” she says, letting him go and hugging Eva, then kissing Jasen on his cheek. “This lake gets lonely sometimes,” she continues. The room becomes quiet and awkward pretty fast. “Yeah, you guys should probably get to work, like, now,” she finishes, stepping out of the room.

17
Dark Reality

The newly formed quartet sit in the woman's home, awaiting the perfect moment to avoid the URA, who are hot on their asses. When the crack of dawn comes, the rebels quicken their search efforts as the wind picks up.

The jets and helicopters are doing fly-bys as tanks and foot patrols begin combing the area more frequently. It is too busy in the area to try to escape. Eva continues her spell over the cabin, concealing the presence of her comrades, while Ace uses his hyper-senses to gain an idea of the patterns the URA is moving in. Anarchious uses his newfound senses to determine the number of bodies surrounding them, while Jasen uses his extensive military training to map and predict an escape route.

This goes on until dusk, when they decide to move. The foursome move along a river running southeast from the lake. This route has very few troops and not many jets or helicopters strafing near it. The group makes it outside of the URA's reach in less than an hour, moving nonstop. They avoid all patrols, not wanting to bring the humans' hammer down on their heads.

Far out of the reach of the Rebels, they eventually hit a beach town. The beach seems abandoned, and all the businesses along the unkempt boardwalk are boarded up. The waves crash, the wind blows gently, and light storm clouds approach from over the water. Seabirds still seem to be stirring, cawing in the night.

"OK, so what now?" Ace asks the group. They all look at each other, lost, realizing that they have spent so much of the day trying to avoid the URA, they have forgotten to plan ahead.

"We find my brother," Anarchious replies, stating the obvious

"Yeah, but need I remind you? Our strongest lead lived up to her people's name and was a back-stabbing Witch! No offense, Ava," Ace says, reminding his partner of their failures and follies.

The Wiccan rolls her eyes at the Lycan and states, "It's E–va. E-V-A, dog-breath. Curious, though; which Wiccan are you guys talking about?" she asks, looking at the Mutant.

"Mystie" the Mutant answers.

"Mystie? The defector?" the Wiccan asks, cracking a smirk.

"Yeah," the Mutant says with a guilty look on his face.

"It must have been your genius idea to listen to someone like that," Eva says. The Mutant is silent. "Never dawned on you once why a Wiccan was living in a URA city? You never heard the saying, 'Never trust a Witch who wears black lipstick'?" the Wiccan asks, smiling and already knowing the answer.

"See? Told ya!" Ace says, throwing in his own two cents. "But no! Don't listen to the guy who knows what he's talking about!" The Lycan walks on all fours into the warm ocean water.

"You guys have any leads on Abel?" Anarchious inquires of the Wiccan and her companion.

"Well, my buddy here is the best the Rebels have to offer," Eva starts. "He has never ever lost a bounty, so I was following his lead along with nature's sway," she finishes, smiling with confidence.

The Mutant looks at Jasen, whose face is showing slight annoyance. "What is your stance on this?" Anarchious asks, making eye contact with the very tall man.

"He's been a menace all over this continent, and he has been sighted in broad daylight and at night according to URA's reports, attacking everyone from URA camps, Vampyr settlements, Wiccan forests, to Pride nests," Jasen explains.

"What's that supposed to mean?" the Mutant asks, almost taking offense.

The blue-eyed man grunts and says, "Do not interrupt me."

Anarchious's eyebrows lower and his relaxed posture changes as he frowns at the much taller man.

"Reportedly, four months ago, things began to change. Attacks became mass murders, mass disappearances, massive collateral damage with whole cities destroyed," Jasen begins once more.

Eva interrupts her partner. "Yes, but that doesn't mean it was him! Those attacks are the same MO as the Demon-King's! Let's not jump to conclusions, Jase."

Jasen scoffs as the Wiccan and Mutant glare at him harshly. "No. Do not interrupt me!" the Mutant says, mocking the tank.

Jasen steps towards the Mutant. "I'll destroy you, clown."

"Try me!" The Mutant steps towards Jasen, unafraid of his threats.

"Dirty mau-mau!" Jasen retorts, gritting his teeth while getting in Anarchious's face.

one to know one!" the Mutant says, grinning at the tank.

The Witch immediately lodges herself between the two, trying to keep the peace.

"If it weren't for this Wiccan, you and your piece-of-shit murdering brother's brains would be mashed within the grips of my boots!" Jasen yells, balling his fists.

Anarchious's eyes immediately turn violet as he states, "No one threatens my brother! I'll kill you!"

Ace stops his frolicking in the ocean and gets a very familiar feeling as he glares at his partner.

"It must hurt your little feelings to know your brother is a murdering sociopath bent on genocide!" Jasen says, almost wanting the Mutant to go off.

"Stop it! That hasn't been proven at all!" Eva snaps fiercely at Jasen. The tank is taken back but isn't surprised at her reaction.

"So I am guessing you guys were in North Torious after you heard about the attack, like us," Ace says, still in the water. "Arrived to find the city had been destroyed like the others that were possibly attacked by him."

"Yeah," the Witch replies, directing her attention to the Lycan.

"Good news. It wasn't him!" Ace yells, riding the waves back to shore.

"How do you know that, Ace?" the Mutant asks.

Ace gets back on all fours and shakes all the water and sand from his body. "Before and after they caught you, I did a li'l investigating of my own," Ace begins to explain. "I did a lot of smelling in that city, and I know how a Mutant smells, seeing as I have to smell your mustiness, our master and big guy over here. If Abel attacked that city—it doesn't matter how—he would have left his scent. The stronger scents were a mixture of a lot of things, something I've never smelled before, but none of them were remotely Mutant," Ace states to the group.

Anarchious immediately feels a sense of relief, but that doesn't explain the eyes in Magi's vision or Mystie's testimonial. "I can tell by that look in your eyes, brother, you're wondering about other elements. Allow Ace to help ease those ailments," the Lycan jokingly states. "The Witch didn't know that Abel was the one to attack the city. Abel came to warn her, but it was already too late. All she could do was protect herself...which I think is what might have made her do what she did to you."

The Mutant stands there for a moment and thinks to himself. He ponders on how this must be why his brother was seemingly hiding in the alley in Magi's vision. "Mr. Jasen, you said years ago his MO was just kicking ass, did you not?" the Lycan askes the tank. Jasen nods, making eye contact. "Well, folks don't normally go from a track record of whooping to massacring whole towns. That still doesn't make Abel innocent because the Witch confirmed to me that he knew of this massacre, which means he has some type of contact with the Demon-King," the Lycan continues. "Not too long ago, we found out that one of his old Vampyr acquaintances pointed him to the Demon-King. It's possible he is involved with the Demon, but from a move like this—warning a person he possibly cares about—I think he's having doubts about it all. And it's not like he'll be able to stop someone like the Demon-King. Hell, even that hag-raven knew he wasn't strong enough to devour the entire city," the Lycan says, finishing his long-winded explanation.

"That all sounds like a huge assumption to me," Jasen blurts into the conversation.

"That all sounds like hatred coming from you," Anarchious replies.

"Self-loathing—why do you hate your own kind, Mr. Rebel tank, sir?" Ace follows up. At that moment, Jasen gets in the face of the shorter Anarchious, and Ace gets in the face of the slightly shorter tank.

"Enough! This is ridiculous! All this alpha male crap isn't going to help any of us get this done!" the Witch says once more, separating the three. "We need to figure the fastest way of finding Abel and proving his innocence," the Wiccan states. "Or disproving it," she follows up with a stern look at her partner.

Everyone backs off and relaxes. The waves continue crashing. The wind blows harder, creating a tiny sandstorm as it begins to drizzle. "I think I know where he may be, but I fear what will happen to us if we go there," the Lycan says to the group. Anarchious immediately becomes attentive. Ace looks at his partner and sighs. "When I interrogated that Witch, she also mentioned the Red Desert," Ace explains. The Wiccan's eyes widen as the tank shakes his head and chuckles.

The Mutant looks at their reaction, curious. "What is the Red Desert?" he asks the Lycan.

"It is said that in this desert, the only oases are pools of blood. The red sunrise rebirths the billions of restless souls, and the sunset afflicts them. The nights are freezing and filled with the screams of tortured souls. It's basically the worst place on this planet besides Post-Nuked-Eden," Ace explains.

Jasen laughs while Eva just covers her face, trying to hold in her building emotion. Anarchious glares at Jasen. "What's so funny?" he asks.

Jasen continues to laugh. "That's a far-fetched 'legend.' The Red Desert is just barren, like most deserts in this world. That was made up from a bunch of crazy people who saw mirages."

"It isn't a mirage if more than one person describes the same experience! That 'legend' is true, Jase!" the Wiccan says. "I crossed that desert as a little girl, and I witnessed its horrors. We set out with fifty, and only ten of us came out alive." Jasen chuckles once more, taking the conversation very lightly.

"As I recall, your precious URA has bases all over the world in every 'friendly' territory, it seems, but they don't have one near that desert," Ace intercedes. Jasen stops laughing and huffs at the Lycan. "If that's not enough for you, tank, it's also rumored to be the home of the Demon-King. Are you willing to risk your life?" the Lycan asks, looking him in his eyes. The tank stares him down for a bit, but his eyes fall as he turns away and walks towards the boardwalk.

For a moment, everything is silent. The waves aren't crashing, the wind has calmed, and the birds are settled. "I am," Anarchious states. "If there's the slightest chance my brother is there, I am willing to take that risk."

"You know me. I've got elsewhere to be," the Lycan quickly follows up.

The duo look at the Wiccan, who looks worried. She nervously looks back and forth at the Mutant and Lycan for a moment. She then turns and glares at her partner, who is now sitting on a banister separating the boardwalk and the beach. "All for Abel?" she asks the duo. They both nod. "I'm in, but I must consult my bodyguard. Be right back," she says as she quickly walks over to Jasen.

"I don't trust them," Ace whispers, pulling Anarchious close to the shoreline.

"Me either," the Mutant replies, glaring at the Wiccan and her comrade. "Especially pretty boy," he states, disgusted at the tank's presence.

"So let's ditch them and make the run there. It's a ways away, so we should run-fly combo like last time," the Lycan says.

"No, we'll use them," Anarchious replies, still glaring maliciously at Jasen, who's reluctantly conversing with Eva. The Lycan looks at his partner, getting another odd vibe from his friend. "I know how stupid it sounds, but..." the Mutant begins to explain.

"No, it's not that," Ace replies, thinking of their master. "I completely understand what you mean," he suggests. "Just make sure your heart is in the right place, bro." Anarchious glares back curiously.

"Hey!" the Wiccan shouts, gaining the duo's attention. She jogs back as Jasen follows her. "Jasen is in too!" she says, approaching them.

"OK, well, we should probably split up to find supplies and stock up on food now," the Lycan suggests to the group. "That way we can go straight there with no stopping." The Mutant nods, agreeing to Ace's plan. "We should also find a shelter for the rest of the night over in that town. That hurricane is near," Ace adds. Jasen, Eva, and Anarchious all agree. "All right, find some stuff and meet back here in an hour," the Lycan says as everyone disperses in different directions.

Everyone seems to be in a hurry while Anarchious flies casually through the town, searching for a place to settle for the night. He can't help thinking of his brother, knowing he is close. He's about to find his brother and then help rebirth his people. With that thought, he begins to hurry, quickly sweeping through the debris-littered streets. He feels something odd, as if he is being watched. He spots several sets of tiny eyes peeking from behind a window.

The Mutant stops midflight and glares back. The eyes quickly retreat, seemingly startled by his appearance. He surveys his surroundings closely. This town seems abandoned due to all the boarded-up windows and doors, but it occurs to him that that isn't the case. Someone is peeking out of just about every peephole and free window. This is bad. It is a human town, so all it would take was its inhabitants to alert the URA and it would be all over.

Just then, the skies rumble viciously, the tiny drizzle turns to heavy rain, and lightning strikes on the shores of the water. Anarchious notices that the wind has become very violent, and the tide is at the boardwalk, crashing into some of the businesses. The clouds now sit menacingly over the town. The presence of an unknown force becomes immediately clear to him. He flies into the sky, fighting the gale as lightning begins to strike more frequently. The wind speeds have picked up significantly since the group reached this beach.

Anarchious adjusts himself, forcing his own air current to circulate more frequently to balance out the storm's overwhelming force and speed. He can feel the wind currents swirling, not just physically but almost through their own life force. He closes his eyes to feel the storm out, to feel the energies it is giving off. As clear as day in his mind, he feels an extremely destructive force approaching. This force could push a train of giant waves into the town, flooding and possibly killing everyone, most importantly his brother at arms, if it isn't contained.

The wind currents push at him. Anarchious's eyes turn purple as he pushes the storm with his own storm. His purple aura emanates from his body, surrounding him as he battles the hurricane. His power is throwing the storm out of whack, but it isn't enough to stop it. It is winning as the waters begin to flood the streets and destroy everything. Lightning violently strikes all around him, hitting streetlights and sidewalks, while the gusts of wind blow out signs, bust unprotected windows, and uproot trees and carry them away.

The Mutant knows if the storm doesn't end soon, it will take the whole city with it. He continues to push his powers to their limit, but it is of no use. He seems to be only making it worse. He stops fighting and calms himself, feeling out the storm again. He lets the storm carry him. It pushes him away, then pulls him in other directions. Right away, the Mutant begins feeling the presence of an unknown force once more, and he grabs a hold of it.

It is as if the essence of the hurricane is merging with him as he commands it. It is monstrously powerful, but Anarchious is unyielding. Lightning strikes him several times, but it only empowers his will. He can feel the power and the spirit of the storm as his very body becomes lightning itself. The powerful gales stop tackling him, and the storm seems to be withdrawing back to sea. The harder he pushes, the more quickly the storm falls back. The waters even retreat back into the sea where they belong.

The Mutant gives one final push, and the hurricane is no longer causing any destruction on land. Anarchious watches as the storm heads back east. He lands on top of a building, feeling proud of himself. The skies are calm as the moon and stars shine brightly on the now-safe beach town. Anarchious can't wait to brag to Ace and tell José that he became a hurricane and then sent it all back with plenty of Ki to spare. He just breezed through the five Mutant lessons and can't figure out why he was so intimidated about it all during training.

"Impressive." The Mutant hears a very familiar voice from behind him. He shudders at the tone.

"Abel?" he exclaims, turning around.

"Least you didn't forget my voice, sloth," the voice confirms, stepping towards the Mutant. Anarchious looks at the carbon copy of himself bathed in the night sky. He embraces his brother tightly.

Abel hugs back, chuckling. Anarchious steps back and surveys his brother. "Yo, you're still the same with the stars in your skin and eye's just like mom's," the Mutant states, overjoyed and smiling widely.

"And you're still the same too—not knowing how to use your power effectively and making idiotic mistakes," Abel replies, looking his twin brother in the eye. Anarchious's excitement falls a bit. "Don't get me wrong, though," Abel states, placing his hand on his brother's shoulder. "You fixed it. Instead of fighting a storm with a storm, you became the storm as you were supposed to. Great problem-solving skills. Honestly, I didn't expect that from you. You've come a long way! That's great. That is really great!" Anarchious's confidence is still shot, even with the compliments.

"Why are you out here?" Abel asks.

"Looking for you," Anarchious replies. "I've been looking for you for some months now. It's a crazy story, man. First Marie got kid—"

"So I'm guessing you have that gut feeling too?" Abel says, interrupting his brother.

"Well, yeah, but you have to hear this story, Abby," Anarchious says, wanting to tell his brother his story.

"It doesn't matter. All that matters is that you're with me by my side where you need to be!" Abel says, looking his brother in the eye. Anarchious raises his eyebrow in confusion. "It's been some years, Anarch. I know a lot of things have happened. We can catch up soon, but for now I need you to accompany me," Abel explains, pulling his brother by the hand.

The Mutant holds his twin's hand tightly but doesn't budge from the spot he's standing on. "I can't," the Mutant replies, thinking of Ace.

"Why not?" Abel asks, raising his eyebrow in confusion.

"I'm a part of something big, sort of an investigation of our peoples and a possible rebirth."

The dark twin waves off his brother's grip and looks at him funny. "What?"

"Yo, that's what I was trying to tell you. I met this older Mutant. He helped me with my powers. Then I kind of inspired him to pursue the truth of the Eden bombings," Anarchious explains.

Abel laughs loudly as his twin looks on, surprised at this reaction. "Look, I'm sure I know more than anyone on this planet about the Eden bombings, and I'm in the process of fixing it all by myself. No 'investigation' needed!" Abel proclaims condescendingly, chuckling some more.

Anarchious gets a weird vibe from his brother as he stares him down, not knowing what to think. "You work with the Demon-King," Anarchious states.

Abel is taken aback for a moment and glares harshly at his brother. "Who told you that?" Abel asks, approaching his brother aggressively.

Anarchious's eyes widen as his twin stands with him face to face. "Zera and that Mystie character. They both mentioned him and pretty much said you work for him," Anarchious explains.

Abel steps back, crosses his arms, and huffs. "Well, I wouldn't say 'work for.' It's more like 'running errands' than anything," the dark twins explain.

"What?" Anarchious the Mutant replies, squinting at his brother.

"Put it like this. This guy claims to be a God. He is no God, nor a Demon. I see through his faulty claims. Once an opening presents itself, he will fall, and I will restore order to this world. I will bring Judgment Day, and I will rebirth our peoples!" Abel proclaims to his brother.

This gives Anarchious goose bumps. He doesn't know what Abel means exactly, but he definitely likes the sound of it.

brother's hand once more, opens up a dark void, and
alk through it Anarchious is ready but resists once
the need to at least say goodbye to Ace. "What's your
probl... el asks.

"Look, I made a friend. I need to say goodbye. So give me some time before I join your crusade, yo," the Mutant states reluctantly to his brother.

"No humans, right?" Abel asks with an evil look in his eyes. Anarchious shakes his head no, disgusted. Abel sighs heavily. "Look, I'll give you until tonight, but I have to go for now, Anarch. Say your goodbyes, sloth, but after that, you're coming with me!" the dark twin says as he walks into the void. It melts away.

This has to have been one of the happiest yet most confusing days for Anarchious in a long time. His brother he hasn't seen in five years has found him and even accepted him despite their history, but he isn't about to just ditch the Lycan, who has grown to be family. This has all been so surreal, and after hours of standing on that roof watching the sunset, he questions whether what has happened was real or not.

The Mutant descends from the roof and lands in the street. People are breaking down their boarded-up homes and emerging onto the streets confused while others are praying loudly, thanking the Spirit. "That was a sham of a superstorm," some people state, disappointed with all the preparation it took to stormproof their homes.

"It was him, Momma!" A group of children approach the Mutant, pointing at him. "He did it. He fought the hurricane and made it go away. We saw it!" The children grab at the Mutant and some imitate his actions from his short clash with the storm. Soon a tiny crowd has gathered around him, inspecting him. "You're a Mutant like in the books," one kid squeals after jumping on Anarchious's back.

That instant, Ace, in his human form, grabs the Mutant and puts him in a headlock. "You're gonna get us found out. Even the kids know you're a damn Mutant!" Ace whispers.

The Mutant looks back in the eyes of the people, feeling their joy. It reminds him of the feeling he'd get after seeing his mother after a few days. "Yeah, I have a feeling they're not going to care. I saved the town from being ripped to shreds a few hours ago," Anarchious says as Ace releases the headlock. They gaze at the crowd as it gets bigger and approaches the duo.

"Hey, is it true what my son says?" a woman asks curiously, staring at the Mutant. Anarchious scratches his head and opens his mouth, about to explain, but the Lycan reaches up and slaps his hand over the reckless Mutant's mouth.

"Where do you people stand with the URA?" Ace asks.

"Fuck the URA! Those assholes only care about the rich. They denied us aid and supplies even though they've been tracking that storm for days! If this had been North Torious, we would've gotten a full escort through the rancid lands," one of the townsfolk replies while another in the back of the crowd yells, "Too fucking important to track down hoax fugitives!"

Hearing this, Anarchious and Ace look at each other wide eyed. "In that case, this guy right here did save your butts!" Ace replies as the crowd engulfs the Mutant with hugs and pats on the head. They eventually carry him off, parading him through the streets.

"Hey! What is this?!" a voice calls out to Ace.

Ace turns and sees the Wiccan and the tank rolling up, looking like they have gone through hell. The Lycan scoffs and walks towards the crowd. "I honestly have no clue, but just go with it!"

The townspeople spend the entire day pampering the Mutant. This has been the first time in his life a group of human strangers has treated him as if he mattered. Anarchious's mates try to pull him away so they can get on the road to the desert. He refuses and blows them off, enjoying the limelight too much. So instead, the group spends time exchanging stories with the natives.

It is true the URA abandoned their own, ironically in order to find the foursome. It is also true that when they broke the news to the town about the storm, they advised them to move westward, but it just so happens westward, beyond the marshlands, are feral Vampyr and rancid Lycan lands. So most of the townspeople chose to take their chances here and not in the wilderness, where they were surely going to lose their lives.

As the day drags on, the Lycan notices little things that are different about his partner. He is happy but seems more distant than normal. The Mutant has spent the entire day thinking of ways to say goodbye without making Ace, José or his new friends feel completely abandoned.

The townspeople throw a luau to celebrate some more and light the beach up as the sun ducks behind the horizon in the west. The people dance all evening around several bonfires, yelling and screaming, banging on drums, and enjoying life.

The Mutant approaches his best friend, looking for the words to say goodbye. He tries to speak, but only an incoherent mutter comes from his lips. He thinks about his brother's statements, not really understanding anything he meant. If he knows his brother, he is aiming to kill this Demon-King, and from the stories he's heard during his journey, the king deserves it. Yet the end result, the king's death, couldn't be any better he didn't know what comes after that. He needs to know the details, and now.

The festivities cool down near midnight. Ace has gone to sleep. Jasen and Eva remain on the beach, drunk. Using this opportunity, Anarchious slips back into the heart of town. He flies back to the roof where his brother appeared the night before. Sure enough, Abel is back in that spot, patiently waiting and looking ominous as his large black cape blows in the wind.

"Let's go," Abel says immediately.

"Not so fast, man," Anarchious says to his twin. "I need to know some things before we go."

Abel, annoyed, breathes heavily. "Shoot, sloth."

"Yo, after you kill the king, what are your plans?" the Mutant asks, looking his brother in the eye.

Abel smiles mischievously. "Good to know you know me well enough to comprehend my statements. Haven't gotten that part of the plan just yet, but before I do that, I am going to go find the last of the families of our people and slaughter them," Abel states, smirking at his brother.

Anarchious's eyes widen. He thinks of the mission with his master as he says, "You know about that?"

"Of course I do. I also know their importance and how they are supposed to be the strongest, purest leaders of our race, but they abandoned us and hid from the humans instead of imposing their wills on those cockroaches," Abel says as he approaches his brother, who is standing on the ledge of the building.

Anxiety takes over the Mutant, and he begins to shake. "Why would you do that? We have a chance to reunite and rebirth our people! We could finish what Mom and Pop didn't get a chance to do!" Anarchious explains to his brother, not understanding his logic.

"Do not be naïve, Anarch!" Abel says sternly to his twin. "As long as there are humans, our land won't be safe, our way of life won't be safe. We will not be safe!" he exclaims passionately. "Simple fix is to kill them all too. This is all part of a greater plan. Trust me, Anarch, you'll understand it all in due time!" Abel says, placing his hand on his brother's shoulder.

Anarchious continues to feel uneasy, shaking and gritting his teeth. He can feel the evil seeping from his brother. Something is eating at him, but he can't accept it. Anarchious jerks his shoulder away from his twin. "What exactly are you going to do after you become the king?" Anarchious asks sternly, remembering his brother's words from the night before about bringing Judgment Day.

"Become a god. Exterminate all the vermin, and enslave the cowardly. Remake Terra Belle in my image!" Abel states, grinning widely. "All in that order!" he adds cockily.

Those words and that attitude severely stress Anarchious. "Why would you go to war with your own kind, though?" the Mutant asks under his breath after dropping his head.

"War? Hmph, it's more like a hunt," Abel replies bluntly with pompous undertones, confident in his power. "Please pick your head up. You're acting like you have no backbone." The dark twin becomes frustrated at the sight of his brother's show of emotion. Abel stares at Anarchious, becoming only more enraged at the sight of his emotions. "I see. I understand now. Living amongst the humans has made you soft. You've groveled for their acceptance but have received only stonings and alienation, and they've broken you," Abel states. "We'll make them pay! Just come with me." Abel offers his hand to his brother

Anarchious feels conflicted. He wants to go, but it is wrong. It is all wrong. For some reason, he thinks about the humans he's met on his journey—Jeb, Joyce, and the townspeople. His anxiety gets worst. He begins shaking, reflecting on the memories of the carnage that took place in North Torious.

"Ask him, Anarch!" a voice shouts from behind the twins. They both turn around, and from over the ledge of the building climbs up Ace in his Lycan form.

"Who's this sloth?" Abel says, unafraid of Ace's natural menacing nature.

"Ask him, Anarch!" Ace yells once more.

Abel scoffs and laughs once more. "Who are you to interfere in my family?" Abel says as he steps toward the Lycan, but his brother stops him by gripping his arm.

"Did you kill those people in North Torious?" Anarchious says. It feels like a ton of bricks has been lifted off his back, but the anxiety does not fully subside. He needs an answer.

and snatches his arm away from his brother and hem. He glares at his brother for a moment, thinking. e. I slaughtered those pigs," Abel says, confirming s suspicions. The Mutant steps back away from his brother, totally stunned. "C'mon, you can't be that surprised, bro. Humans are disgusting!" Abel replies, grinning.

"How?...But why would you? That's horrible!" Anarchious yells at his brother.

Abel gives his brother a glare that could kill. "Are you serious? Who are you to fucking judge me?" he says, getting in Anarchious's face. Ace, being protective of his friend, approaches and growls. Abel waves his hand nonchalantly, and several hellhounds emerge from the shadows and quickly restrain the Lycan.

"These are the same people who shot and killed our mother and father in front of us. The same people abused us both for being different. The same people who nuked our entire race nearly out of existence! For nothing! You do know that, right?!" Abel yells at Anarchious for showing concern for the humans. "You do know that, right?!" Abel yells one more time, looking for confirmation from his twin.

Anarchious hears him but is haunted by images of the innocent slaughtered people from Magi's vision in his mind. He knew all along but didn't want to believe it. And to make matters worse, as if he wasn't haunted enough, childhood wounds begin to bubble up from the back of his mind.

Anarchious understands his brother's beliefs. He feels they are justified. He too shares the same hatred for the humans. Humans never passed up a chance to torture them when they were growing up. Humans were selling each other into slavery before their parents came to the District. Their mother and father ran of the Districts old city council and fixed it, only to have credit stolen from them for rebuilding the city. The humans deserved everything they received from Abel.

Abel grabs his brother by the face. "Humans fear what they cannot understand, but most of all, they fear what they cannot control. They have the Vampyr, Wicca, and Pride all by the balls, but they can't fathom that we have no weaknesses," Abel proclaims to his brother, looking in his eyes. "That's right! They tried to control us, but that didn't work! So they studied us! Dissected us like lab rats! And you want have feelings for them? You want to get all sympathetic for those spineless cowards? Listen, in Notorious, that wretched city, they have an underground facility just for imprisoning and studying us. They've studied us for years! Years before either of our parents were thought of, they found something that separated us from them. It was so defining, it even separated us from the Wiccan, Pride, and Vampyr populations, and it terrified them!" Anarchious can feel all the pain and anguish pouring from him.

"So instead of crushing the URA and that facility, I devoured their families. Those people deserved everything they got!" Abel proclaims, aggressively brushing his brother's face. "You mean to tell me you're still soft and you're going to back humans? You're going to back them before your own flesh and blood?" Abel asks, trying to manipulate his brother's thinking.

"Yo, you're going to kill Mutants too. I cannot be a part of that!" Anarchious retorts, feeling confused.

"Mutants? Humph! Apprime, Anarch!" Abel states.

"Appree-what?" Anarchious replies.

"We are Apprime. Mutant is a human scientific fallacy. That is not what we are!" Abel explains.

Anarchious looks at his brother, still conflicted as to what to do.

"I am enlightened," continues Abel. "Living on my own a half decade has taken me to many places in this world. Most importantly, back home I've discovered our truths. If you come with me, I can show them to you. You won't be alone anymore, brother."

"Yeah he's right," Ace says, still restrained and struggling to get free, but the hellhounds are insanely strong. "You'll never be alone, Anarch! You have me!"

Abel blasts Ace in the face with dark energies, nearly blowing him off the roof. The building shakes as concrete debris riddles the air. "One more word and next time I'll skin you!" Abel yells at the Lycan, then directs his attention back to his brother.

"Listen," says Abel, placing his hand on Anarchious's shoulder once more. "We could rule this world. No more hiding, no more running, no more stones!" The Mutant, angered and feeling awfully conflicted, jerks away from Abel. He collapses to his knees, and his eyes begin shining and turning purple.

"Abel!" comes a womanly voice from behind where Ace is being held down. It is Eva, hovering on a large white feather as she descends towards the reunion. Soon after, the tank lands on the roof as well, seeming to have jumped from the street.

"You?" Abel says, looking at Eva, then back at his brother. "She with you?" Abel asks him.

Anarchious shrugs and answers, “Meh, she found me lookin’ for you.”

The Witch jumps from the feather, lands on the roof, and advances towards the twins. “Stop right there!” Abel exclaims, holding out his hand. Eva stops and opens her mouth to speak. “Shut up” Abel interrupts her. “I’m not in the mood for lies!”

Eva steps closer and speaks anyway. “Those things I said back then in fact weren’t true, but I do still—”

“Not in the mood, bitch!” Abel says as he waves his hand at her. Her own shadow peels off the ground and puts her in a tight headlock. Jasen sees this and advances on the dark being. Abel fires dark energy at him, hitting him dead on, but Jasen is unaffected and keeps coming.

“Hmm, a Lesser?” Abel says as he walks towards the advancing tank. Jasen yells as he readies a clothesline a few steps away from Abel. He looks the tank in his blues eyes as his own turn red. Instantly, Jasen drops to his knees, and his face hits the roof of the building hard.

“Never thought these Apprime still existed,” the dark twin says as he walks past the petrified tank towards the restrained Wiccan. He comes face to face with her as his eyes turn back to their original silver. “You’re as much as a lie as that...beautiful form you’re taking,” Abel says, glaring into Eva’s hazel-green eyes. He leans in closer and says, “But the one thing you were right about is that I am a monster. I hold no remorse and have no sympathy and no conscience, especially for those who cannot stand up for themselves. You are a disgrace, and I wish those Lycan had killed you!”

Eva stops struggling when she hears that, and her eyes began to glass over. The shadow disperses, and she drops to her knees, sobbing. Abel turns his back on her and returns his attention to Anarchious.

"Anarch, I have no more patience for this nonsense," Abel says, vanishing and then reappearing right in front of his brother. "I'll give you one more chance. You come with me and be a God, or I'll deal with you myself." Abel gives his twin a very seriously look.

"Deal with me?" Anarchious says, glaring back.

"Kill you!" Abel follows up with no hesitation.

Anarchious can see his brother isn't joking at all; he is ready to kill. He glares over at Ace, who is still restrained; then at Jasen, who is still face-planted ass up; and then at Eva, who doesn't really look up for any of this anymore. Anarchious looks his brother back in the eye and says, "Well, looks like you've given me a clear choice." The once-reluctant twin sticks his hand out, wanting a handshake from his twin brother. Abel grabs his hand and brings him in for a hug. "Dude, really, bro!" the Lycan yells in a high-pitched voice to his now former partner in crime.

Abel turns with a malevolent look in his eyes and chuckles as he looks at Ace. He conjures dark energy in his hand, laughing hysterically. "So you are Mister Comic Relief Guy, hmm?" the dark twin asks the downed Lycan. "This is a family affair, and out of respect for my brother's clear attachment to you, I haven't killed you. Normally, I behead for disrespect, and that's what I think I'll do!" Abel says as his smile quickly turns to disgust. He holds his arm out, aiming it at Ace, about to end him.

Anarchious grabs his twin on the shoulder. "I choose death!" he grunts as he shocks his brother and aims a lightning punch him. Abel disappears. Anarchious turns around quickly, looking for his brother.

Abel is behind him, aiming his dark energy at his brother with a malevolent look in his eyes. "Wrong choice!" the dark twin states as he releases all his dark Ki in Anarchious's face, blowing him up along with the Lycan, the Wiccan, and the tank and collapsing the entire building.

The townspeople, who had heard the explosion earlier, scream in the street, witnessing the collapse of the building. They are all confused and not exactly sure what is going on. Abel takes it upon himself to make his presence known, landing in the street and observing the chaos he is creating. He laughs as several people point him out, screaming, "The Darkness! It's the Demon-King!" This all amuses Abel, who just continues laughing.

Some people run up and worship him at his feet, asking him not to destroy the town and reciting the God-King's prayer. "I am not your God-King," he states, "but shortly I will bring you all to your Judgment Day!" The shadows all around them transform into hellhounds. Shadows on buildings turn into hell bats as the skies turn pitch black. Some people pray harder, crying and sobbing in sorrow, while others try to flee, but the beach town is quickly surrounded by Abel's dark force fields and creations.

A child escapes his mother's grip, bravely approaches Abel and looks up at the evil being. "You a bad man, but Annie will beat you! He beat a hurr'cane!" the kid says, staring up at Abel.

Abel points at the child's head. Dark energies charge in his hand as he looks down on the child. "Well, Annie is gonna die, just like you and your momma!" A quick gust blows in his face, and in a flash, his brother is standing tall before him, blocking the child. "Good to see you're not as weak as you were as a child, Anarch!" Abel proclaims.

"You're twisted, Abbie, so twisted!" Anarchious retorts, shaking his head.

"Twisted? You're defending the very people who destroyed our lives. No, you are twisted!" Abel replies, still charging his blast.

"Are you blind or just plain dumb? You just threatened to kill a child and his mother!" Anarchious yells at his brother. "Just like what happened to us! You're no better than the soldiers who killed Mom and Pop!"

"No more talking. I'm going to kill you, then kill everyone in this town!" Abel states, aiming the dark Ki ball at his brother's face.

"Try me!" Anarchious yells as he takes his Ghost-face form, lightning bursting forward. Abel fires the Ki ball, and Anarchious shoots a lightning bolt at point-blank range, blowing it up and forcing Abel to roll back through the streets, skidding on the concrete.

The dark twin uses his momentum and skids to a halt in the street as he glares at his brother. Anarchious and the people who were surrounding them before are all encased in a force field of some sort. Abel surveys above Anarchious and spots the Wiccan, who is back on her feather-casting spells. "Anarchious," he says, surprised at his brother's white-faced appearance.

"Ace!" Anarchious calls out. From the side of the decimated building comes Ace, blazing at top speed. He blindsides Abel and uppercuts him, sending him flying through several homes and buildings out of his own darkness dome, heading westward.

"Wooo, I got all of that one! Didn't expect that plan to work," the Lycan states as his best friend approaches.

"Think that landed him near the marshlands?" Anarchious asks him.

"From his trajectory, chances are he'll land a li'l beyond that!" Ace states as the darkness begins to recede, revealing the stars and moonlit sky.

"All right, let's go finish this, guys!" Anarchious says.

Eva and Ace take off towards the west. Anarchious hesitates for a moment and flies off when he hears the child call out to him once more. He turns and faces the kid. "Annie! Kick his ass for us!" The Mutant winks at him and takes off after the group.

18
Countdown to Judgment Day

The Mutant, back to normal, and Eva both cut through the sky, following the Lycan, who is sprinting through the trees and a cluster of ponds, sniffing out Abel's position in the dark of the night under a clear sky and crescent moon. They are several miles away from the beach town, now near the marshlands that separate the town and the feral badlands. Ace lands in a clearing next to a swamp and slows down, sniffing the air. The Wiccan and Mutant carefully descend out of the air, keeping their eyes open for any sneak attacks.

Upon landing back on the ground, the Mutant looks to his partner and asks, "This it?"

"Yeah, I think he might have landed in the swamp over there because his scent doesn't go farther," Ace replies as Eva lands on the ground, waving her feather back to its original size and placing it behind her ear.

"That was one hell of an upper cut, Lycan," Anarchious says as the trio hear Abel's dark, ominous voice but can't determine where it is coming from.

"I didn't expect a runt to pack that much power. I underestimated you, but it won't happen again," Abel states once more.

The group tries to find him, but it feels as if his voice is coming from all directions. They quickly all get back to trying to cover all directions from where Abel could attack. It is quiet now, too quiet. The only thing heard are the chirps of the crickets and hoots of the owls calling out to each other.

"Yo, keep your eyes open," says Anarchious. "He's a Dark Mutant. He can slip in and out of shadows and darkness, so this situation is ideal for him."

"I'm going to find him with the mother's bond. Watch my front," Eva says as she forms her hands into signs and touches the ground. The Wiccan feels out the earth for a moment, then gasps. "He's..." she says as something jumps out from under her and grabs her by the neck.

"Bunch of sloths and jokers," Abel shouts, quickly tossing Eva into the swamp by her neck. The Mutant and Lycan both attack the dark twin. Abel is fast, though, very fast. He uses the darkness as portals, easily spinning and disappearing in and out of them. His speed serves just to taunt the duo, who are pulling out all the stops to hit him.

"This isn't your best," Abel says, dodging his brother's strikes and Ace's sharp claws. "After I kill you three, I'm going to go back and kill every one of those little piggies!" he says, easily slipping the duo's combos. Ace's eye glow hot crimson as he jabs at Abel from the side. Abel hardly dodges it as Anarchious's eyes begin glowing violet. He spins around and backhands his brother, making him stumble back a few steps.

The fight calms for a second as Abel wipes his face and glares at the duo with his shining silver gaze. "You should enter your Shin form, Anarch. You're boring me," he states, shunning his twin.

"What?" Anarchious says, still in an aggressive stance.

"Ignorant as well as a sloth," Abel says cockily, crossing his arms. "That white face of yours is called Shin-Apprime, and your eyes are like stars. That is your Nsoromma. You should probably cherish it, seeing these are your last minutes with such a privilege," the Dark Mutant threatens his twin while educating him.

"You asked for it!" Anarchious replies, wasting no time. He begins to emit electricity as his Ghost-face form returns.

Abel laughs as he claps at the sight of his brother, unafraid. "Much better! So we have a Kanji-Spartan, the last of the Amor de Tierra Tribe, and a Shin-Apprime," Abel states as the Wiccan crawls out of the water, coughing. "I don't think I've had a decent fight since the one I had with the God-King! So it's up to you idiots to entertain me for a few minutes. If you disappoint me, I promise that your deaths will all be slow and painful. Make it fun and I'll make your passing quick and painless," he proclaims, cracking his neck and giving the trio a very evil glare once more.

"Fuck this!" Ace says, shooting forward and trying to clothesline Abel. The dark Apprime ducks it, sweeping his fist back and landing a blow on the back of Ace's knee, tripping the Lycan. Anarchious shoots forward with lightning bursts of speed, only to run into Abel's iron palm. The cocky twin then grabs his brother by the collar and slams him on top of Ace as if he were nothing. The ground shakes and vines spurt up, and as Abel jumps back trying to avoid them, a vine grabs him from behind and constricts him.

Abel looks towards the swamp, and there is Eva casting her nature magic on him. The vine tries to fling him, but he phases into a shadow, slips out, and charges the Wiccan. Anarchious and Ace both try blindsiding him, but Abel dodges quickly, forcing them both off balance. Eva forms a seal for her spells and kneels.

"Tule!" she yells as a giant tree stump pushes up from underground between the two. Abel has no choice but to body right through it. The dark Apprime's strength and momentum send him crashing through the incomplete tree with ease, but he is pummeled hard by one of its branches and is sent hurling into the mild waters of the swamp.

Ace's eyes widen as he witnesses this. "Anarch! The water!" the Lycan screams at his partner. Anarchious sees what he means and ascends into the air, targeting the swamp and blasting it with continuous scatters of giant lightning bolts. Eva moves slightly aside her dying animated tree, watching. Ace lies a few yards from the tree, and Anarchious rises above them, stopping to watch over the swamp. Many fish and water animals float to the top of the lake, some still flailing from the electrical attack.

"My bad," Anarchious says, not really thinking that would happen. At that moment, there is some bubbling from the middle of the lake; then something shoots up from it. It is Abel wielding something big, and he is pissed. He swings his weapon overhead at his brother, slamming Anarchious to the ground. The ground trembles from the impact as Abel turns his sights on Ace, who is charging at him. Ace tries some misdirection, hopping side to side, but Abel picks up the pattern and teleports beside him. Ace turns, picking up the dark Apprime's movements, but it is too late—the object is already inches away from his face.

The weapon makes impact and knocks the Lycan flying to the other side of the field. He hits a tree and violently uproots it from its position. Abel turns to Eva, who is chanting in her language. He shadow-ports towards her as she rapidly summons a force field. He twists in midair, gaining momentum, and swings his weapon like a bat, bashing Eva, who is encased in a light shield. The force is too much and sends her and her shield flying into the woods on the opposite side of the clearing.

Abel then walks over to his recovering twin, dragging his weapon of choice. "Note to self: dead crocs are a great bludgeoning tool," Abel snidely remarks, tossing the massive deceased reptile aside like a child's toy.

"You're a piece of shit, Abel," the Ghost-faced Mutant says to his brother, now standing face to face with him. "Mom and Pop would be so ashamed."

"News flash: the weak die, and soon you will too, but I want you to watch me kill your little buddies first," Abel replies.

"It's sad you chose this. The world could have used someone like you!" Anarchious says, looking his brother in the eye.

"Fuck this world. If you don't like my choice, you can kill yourself!" Abel replies as the Ghost-faced Mutant looks away from his brother.

"Oh, what's wrong? Feeling guilty? Should have never abandoned your little brother to seek acceptance from those humans, should have never let him leave the village, should have looked for your poor twin brother sooner," Abel says to Anarchious mockingly, knowing those are his exact thoughts. "Don't worry about it. This couldn't have happened more perfectly. Think of it like this: the moment they dropped those bombs, the entire human race was destined to be eradicated!"

"Not all humans are evil," Anarchious retorts.

"Doesn't matter! They started this war, and I will end it! No one will stop me!" Abel replies, glaring harshly at Anarchious.

The Ghost-faced Mutant glares back with a hardened look. "I will stop you!" he states, readying himself in a formal fighting stance.

The dark twin scoffs at this sight. "You're really serious about this?" Abel asks. Anarchious responds by balling his fists and staring with a tough look, finally serious about the fight. "OK, if you insist. What do you want on your headstone?! Ooh, I know: 'Here lies shuck and jive,'" Abel says as the two begin engaging in hand-to-hand combat. The Mutants throw all kinds of vigorous combos and fighting styles at each other, and despite being separated for so many years, they know each other well while fighting one on one.

The twins don't have to read each other's moves; they can feel them. Anarchious strikes with combos first while Abel blocks and dodges. Then in the next moment, Abel is more active while Anarchious plays defense. It is no use; they begin frustrating each other because both are trying to land a blow, but neither can. It is clear neither twin has the advantage. They eventually lock knuckles and head-butt each other like two male bucks trying to throw each other off balance. Anarchious's body radiates violet lights whereas Abel smokes with a black darkness. The more physical strength the battling brothers use, the more their auras encircle the clearing.

Face to face, forehead to forehead, they continue to push, trying to throw each other off balance, but neither twin will give in. They eye each other, surprised at each other's strength. "Where did you learn those styles?" Anarchious asks, amazed.

Abel chuckles and replies, "Well, I didn't need a master like some people! My element, the Dark Element has so many hidden abilities that I tapped into!" Just then, Abel can feel the recovering Ace and Eva getting ready to jump in. "Abilities like these," he says as shadows jump out of his aura. They are several hellhounds and hell bats. They go at the Lycan and Wiccan, keeping them from assisting Anarchious. "Three's a crowd. Go one on one with the dark one!" Abel says, smiling.

Anarchious shakes his head and retorts, "Yo, one-liners are so cliché, bro!"

The Ghost-face releases his brother and fires a lightning bolt at point-blank range. Abel weaves his head and body while blasting a dark energy ball into Anarchious's ribs, forcing him back. Anarchious skids and comes to a stop. Then lightning bursts forward, punching his brother in the gut. Abel stumbles back as his brother advances for another strike, but he shadow-steps the attack and appears behind his brother, blindsiding him and punching him in the jaw, then blasts another dark energy ball into his ribs. Anarchious stumbles backwards and lands on his back. He hops back up, grabbing his ribs as he spits up blood. Abel shadow-steps once more, trying to take advantage of his brother, but the Ghost-face has other plans. He discharges lighting in all directions from his body, blasting Abel and stunning him in the process.

Anarchious winds up his backhand and smacks his twin so hard, Abel leaves his physical form on impact and drops to the ground as a shadow. The Ghost-face grabs his tender ribs, turning his attention to his friends. They both are holding off the hell minions separately, but they are both heavily damaged. If it goes on any longer, neither of them will survive. Anarchious quickly blasts some of the minions, dispersing them.

"If you guys do not fight together, you'll both die!" Anarchious shouts to his friends, who seem to ignore him. Suddenly, Anarchious hears his brother's cocky laughs. The Ghost-face turns and surveys his surroundings, trying to pick up his brother's Ki.

"So naïve," Abel chuckles. "The District really is that sheltered," Abel says, toying with his brother. "Don't you know anything?" he inquires as he appears behind his brother, blending with and bending to his twin's shadow like a snake. Abel rapidly constricts Anarchious's neck, putting him in a tight headlock.

"Pride hate Wiccans, especially Black Mamba Cauldron Wiccans. Idiot! They're literally dogs and cats!" Abel says, conjuring a field of dark Ki and surrounding the two with a force field like a shade, reacting to Anarchious's glowing. "You shock me or lighting-burst me or whatever, the shield will stop you, react, and implode, killing us both!" Abel whispers sadistically in his brother's ear. "Now, we're gonna sit here and watch your friends get mauled by my Shadow Knights," he says as they both look on the battlefield where the Lycan and Wiccan are being overrun.

The Wiccan has been surrounded on the edge of the woods with a bubble-like force field, protecting her as the bats and hounds gnaw at it, eating its Ki. Ace is in the middle of the field several yards away from her in a similar situation, only he has nothing protecting him. Eva casts more tree-of-life spells, bringing several trees to the fight and casting her vines.

The Protector-Trees squash some hounds and swat some bats, but they are too slow and quickly are overcome by the Shadow Knights. This weakens Eva's shield while Ace has his own struggles. He can't keep the shadow beasts from overrunning him. He can handle three hounds at once with his speed and maneuverability, but as soon as extras get into the mix, it quickly turns south for him, so he stays in his four-feet defensive stance, taking on the braver shadows who attack systematically. It is all tiring him out.

"Look at this. They'll be dead in a matter of minutes!" Abel says, laughing. Anarchious can't help feeling helpless watching his team struggle. He knows if he charges, that will only cause more of a ruckus and create a storm that will just block the limited light they have, which would make his brother only stronger. He watches Eva's shields buckle as she drops to her knee, running low on Ki.

Almost simultaneously, Ace's arm is broken by a kamikaze attack from a bat; then he is blindsided and slashed behind the knee by a hound. The Ghost-face has to help somehow. His eyes glow brighter, and clouds converge over the battlefield. The wind blows heavily, and the skies rumble as the Ghost-faced Mutant waits for the perfect moment. "Ha!" Abel laughs. "There's no light on the battlefield. Nice you're blinding your friends!" Just then, lightning strikes across the sky, lighting it up every split second. Abel is unimpressed.

The Shadow Knights continue slashing up Ace, but he continues fighting valiantly, unafraid of his impending fate as they finally break into Eva's shield. Everything in front of her charges quickly as she whips some tree vines from underground and knocks them all away, but she is so frightened, she forgets to watch her back. Eva can hear footsteps, and as she turns, a hound is lunging at her throat. Perfect! Lightning strikes from the skies, hitting a bat in the middle of its kamikaze attack on Ace, dispersing it and jumping to Ace, hurling him at Eva, knocking them both back into the woods. Abel laughs loudly. "Yeah, some fucking plan, genius! I should scalp you just for embarrassing me like that." On the other hand, Anarchious, still in the head lock, is stone faced, hoping his plan works.

Both the Lycan and Wiccan quickly recover from the knockdown. "I appreciate the help," the Witch says to Ace as he sits up.

"I'm going to kill Anarch as soon...Wait, what?" Ace replies to the Witch, supporting his arm.

"Lie still. I'm going to fix this," Eva says as she uses hand seals and then blows a chalklike dust in the Lycan's face. "It'll numb some of the pain. Now, close your eyes because this next spell will still hurt!" she says as her hand begins to glow green.

“What the hell is the point, then?” the Lycan asks. He receives no response, so Ace closes his eyes as she applies it to his arm. In an instant, Ace starts feeling pressure building in his arm. There is a quick snap, crackle, and pop, and his arm is back to new. All his major wounds are healed, but he is in extreme pain.

“Best I can do for now, but we need to figure this out together or we will all die,” the Witch says to the Lycan with a quiver in her voice.

Being the quick-minded person he is, Ace thinks up a plan. “That shield…place that shield around me while I fight them. If I can fight them recklessly, I can dispose of them much easier,” Ace states.

“That shield is defensive. Physical attacks cannot be used from within it,” Eva replies.

“Damn it! I can beat most of them with half the energy I have right now. I just need better defense.”

Hearing that, the Wiccan gets an idea. Her hand secrets a thick bloodlike substance. The Wiccan calls attention to it. Ace’s eyes widen as he watches, not knowing what to do. She slaps him, smearing it on his face. “The hell you do that for?” Ace yells at her.

“Shut up,” she replies as the bloodlike substance spreads rapidly, changing into a sap, thickening and encasing the Lycan’s body. Ace grows scared as it begins to harden and yells, “This shit again!”

“Wow, it’s taking them forever,” Abel says to his brother. “I’d like to see them both get mangled, but if they aren’t out here in ten seconds, I’m going to send the knights in. I’m content with just listening to their screams.”

rning you. Don't underestimate them, or it'll come back to the ass!" Anarchious replies, chuckling as Abel tightens his grip on his brother's neck.

"It's cliché of you to threaten me while you're all cornered," Abel replies, chuckling once more. The dark twin then waves his free hand at his minions as they all begin storming the woods.

Immediately there is some tussling and screaming. It sounds like animals fighting in the dark. Anarchious's clouds began to clear out as some of the moon's light returns to the clearing. Abel's minions are being flung out of the forest like nothing. Something big and obscure bursts from the forest line, slamming, breaking, slapping, and slashing back at the Shadow Knights.

The bats begin their kamikaze attacks on this thing, knocking it towards the twins. Whatever it is, the silhouette is wicked, and the bats never recover from the attacks; they just disperse as if they have been defeated. The big obscure being stands up not far from the two. "Abel, may I present to you..." Anarchious says as lighting strikes all around, protecting the being from incoming hellhounds, "my brother and best friend, Ace." Anarchious finishes dramatically as they both witness the Lycan encased in thick tree bark like knight's armor from head to toe. The wicked armor is riddled in short spikes.

Abel's face goes back to stone as he remembers the armor from his past. "She finally perfected the Lignum Spike Armor," he says under his breath. Ace looks his best friend in the eye as they both smirk in the light of the lightning. Ace turns about and begins decimating the Shadow Knights one by one.

"Sometimes cats and dogs can learn to get along just fine!" Anarchious says to his brother smugly.

"It won't be that easy," Abel states as his eyes begin to glow. The Shadow Knights' eyes begin to glow simultaneously. They grow bigger, faster, and more ferocious. This doesn't scare the Lycan, though. It only makes him fight more recklessly. He claws, slams, and clotheslines his way through the Shadow Knights, who are now quicker and more fight savvy. Ace doesn't slow down a bit. He continues wrecking the shadows till their numbers dwindle to three.

Abel, frustrated, releases the chokehold on his twin but keeps holding him with a shadow tentacle. The dark twin directs his attention to the battlefield and raises his hands as darkness begins spilling from him into the remaining two hellhounds and last bat. The knights begin reacting once more; this time their eyes mirror the color of Abel's.

"You won't beat him that way!" Anarchious says, continuing to antagonize his twin. Abel doesn't respond. He commands his knights to attack Ace head on. Their speed is doubled as they all try to decapitate the Lycan.

Ace knows immediately there is something different about these last shadows. They even smell different, almost familiar. A hellhound jumps at Ace as he hops back but then is blindsided by the final bat. The bat even avoids hitting the spikier spots on the armor. The Lycan rolls up, recovering from the tackle, only to be slashed at by the other hellhound.

The Lycan ducks and dodges but notices he isn't as fast as he should be. The armor is a little heavy and on the clunky side. Suddenly, a hellhound blindsides Ace, slicing him in the creases of the armor right between the biceps and forearm guards.

"Looks like it's not exactly perfect, Ms. Eva!" Abel says, laughing as the Shadow Knights continue their assault in the same fashion. The hell bat comes back around, swooping down at Ace. He watches and waits for the point of no return, then turns his back to the bat and balls up. Suddenly, the spikes along his armor shoot out, stretching enough to impale the bat and disperse it. One hellhound bull rushes Ace as the other seems to be charging a dark Ki ball with its mouth. Abel tries to overpower the hound, but it is freakishly strong. He has no choice but to leap over it. Ace jumps. He is hit hard by the dark Ki and is repelled back towards the forest, smashing into a tree, destroying it.

The Lycan gets back on his feet while the whole left side of his armor is crushed and destroyed. He rips it off, tosses it back, and gets into his four-point stance, ready to tango with the hellhounds once more. He shoots forward towards the hound who shot the dark Ki blast but is only cut off and bull-rushed again by the other one. Ace fights back valiantly, battling with all his strength, but the hellhound ultimately begins winning. Ace then peeks over at the other hound, who is charging up again. The Lycan leaps up once more, and there is the Ki blast once again back in his face, but he is ready for it this time. The Ki blast makes impact once more, explodes, and quakes across the entire swamp.

"Sloth," Abel states, lowering his hands, grinning, knowing he just blew the Lycan to kingdom come. "They're always so tough, yet this one has made it too easy!" Abel continues, looking at Anarchious, who is staring into the clearing as the dust settles.

"Looks like you're the sloth on this one, Abel," the Ghost-faced twin says to his brother. Abel turns and witnesses the Lycan holding a distorted hellhound out in front of him as it disperses.

"Ooooh, time to go one on one with the dark one," Anarchious proclaims sarcastically, picking on his brother's nerves.

Abel turns once more to constrict his brother's throat with the shadow tentacle. "I've had enough of that!" Abel says, trying to choke his brother.

"So has he," Anarchious grunts, being choked while pointing at the battlefield. Abel turns to witness his last knight getting its back broken over the Lycan's armor-spiked knee. The hellhound disperses as Ace turns his attention to Abel.

"Too easy!" Abel says, still confident in his ability to kill them all.

"Yeah, too easy," the Mutant agrees as lighting strikes down from a reserve cloud, hitting Abel in the head and detonating the dark Ki surround them. That instant, Anarchious charges a lighting burst and shoots forward, just missing the explosion radius by a foot. The Ghost-faced Mutant and Lycan both are still pushed back to the other side of the clearing by the force. Half the field is decimated and now resembles a moon-sized crater.

Ace looks at Anarchious and slaps him extremely fast and hard, knocking him on his butt. "Stop fucking shooting me with lightning! It's not fucking cool!" Ace yells while raising his hand to his forehead. "I've had it up to here with that!" he finishes.

"Yeah, but—" Anarchious starts, holding his face, but is interrupted by his partner.

"I get it. You got the Witch and me to work together. Yeah, yeah, thanks, whatever! No more bang-bzzzt-shocky," Ace says, grabbing his partner by the collar.

"Where'd she go?" the Ghost-faced Mutant asks.

"Probably to frolic somewhere in dead foliage. I don't know," Ace replies to his partner like a smart-ass.

"I'm done with you sloths! Playtime is over!" Abel's angry voice calls out from the crater. The duo watch him as he strolls out from the crater, seemingly unscathed. The dark twin rushes towards the duo as they stare in shock. Ace hops out front as Anarchious defensively focuses some of the scattered clouds' lightning at his brother. The bolts strike all around him, but he is too fast. The dark twin then shadow-melds and rapidly rematerializes between the duo.

Abel, with a big smile on his face, sidekicks Anarchious in the injured ribs, thrusting him back. He hops back, sweeps the Lycan's back knee, and blasts him into the ground with a giant dark Ki blast. The terrain shakes as the Ki detonates, shooting grass, mud, and earth directly into the air. Abel turns his attention to his brother, who is on one knee. He conjures another Ki ball and points it at his brother's face, ready to blast him to kingdom come once more.

"Goodbye!" Abel says, looking his brother in the eye.

"Abby!" A womanly voice shouts from the treetops above. Abel looks up, and there is Eva, descending towards him, arms and hands pointing at him, glowing like a prism in the sun. "Usanisinaru," she yells an incatation as a bubble of light and rainbows shoot out and impact a surprised Abel, absorbing and trapping him. Abel yells as the energy from the sphere crushes and cuts, then swirls and implodes around him. Harsh winds sweep through the area, and Abel's body drops to the ground like a rag doll.

The night is now silent as Eva walks towards Anarchious and helps him up from his kneeling position. He stares at his brother's body, replaying the blast and his twin's reaction in the head.

"Hell just happened?" the Lycan says, appearing from the crater Abel blasted him into.

"The Witch just wrecked my brother," Anarchious replies, helping pull Ace from the hole.

"Without your help of course, Lycan!" Eva replies.

"Without your help, shut up!" Ace mocks the Wiccan. "I still hate you, but this armor is pretty badass. Without it, that blast would have killed me!" Ace says, pulling the rest of the mangled armor from his limbs.

The trio look over the unconscious body. He is bleeding everywhere and twitches every couple of seconds. "The hell was that attack?" Anarchious asks, looking at the Wiccan, who doesn't seem to be very proud of the sight of her ex-friend's body.

"That's the energy I drew from the living things in the swamp that they took from the sunlight. It's actually the attack I was going to hit you with at the lake. Didn't have enough time, Ki, or living energy to finish it, though," Eva explains, making the Mutant ponder more. "Abel was the strongest being I ever met when we were younger. Knocking him out was much easier than I expected," the Wiccan states loudly, kneeling in front of Abel's body, caressing his hair.

"For the love of the Spirit!" Ace exclaims, turning about dramatically, pulling his hair.

Anarchious looks at her with dead eyes and sighs. The Wiccan stands up and glares at her partners. "What?" she asks.

"Yo, you never, ever do that!" Anarchious says seriously, looking the Wiccan in the eye.

"Do what?" she yells back.

"Say some typical bull crap like that. It's a jinx!" Ace yells at the Wiccan, kicking up dirt.

Just then, Abel gasps for air and sits up. "This dude! See!" Ace screams in the Wiccan's ear, pointing at Abel.

"No attack like that would have ever been able to put me out for the count, sloths!" Abel says as he sways back onto his feet as the opposing trio slowly backs away from his position.

Ace approaches Anarchious from behind and whispers, "How much do you have left?"

"About half," Anarchious whispers back.

"You have to end this now, bro. I'm almost out, and I'm pretty sure Eva's done too!" Ace replies, letting the Ghost-face know he is on his own.

The Mutant looks at his stumbling brother through his four-pointed star eyes and sees a dying light within him. He can only think of one thing to do. He can't fathom actually killing his brother, but putting him in a coma could buy him time. He shoots forward as hard as he can and strikes at his brother's sternum. He makes contact, stunning his brother and initiating his hidden power. Anarchious's arm is immediately repelled backwards with great force and resistance. His eyes widen as Abel turns about, backflips, and flash-kicks his stunned brother on the crown of his head, drilling him to the ground.

Abel places his foot on his twin's head and shifts his weight on it, applying pressure to try to crush his skull. "Strange, your Nsorroma hasn't matured. Good idea to go after my spirit, but allow me to demonstrate the correct way to do it," Abel shouts as his power swells, causing the winds and sky to change. Eva and Ace try to keep from being carried away by the force of Abel's power. Keeping their eyes glued on him, they watch as dark Ki is emitted from his body and his face begins changing like his brother's. The Wiccan pulls a feather from her hair, enlarges it, and surfs it into the sky, avoiding most of the pressure from Abel's power.

The dark Apprime's face is ghostly white like his brother's with similar black markings. His eyes are still silver, but his pupils are also the same as his brother's. His long black cape becomes big black bat wings. He is definitely more sinister looking than his twin. Abel's power has risen and is still rising to a level they all thought impossible.

"The amplified senses, wicked strength, godly eye perception, and massive Ki size don't even match up to the power to manipulate someone's fighting spirit, but if you're like me, you can remove their very soul!" the dark twin yells, reaching down while stepping harder on Anarchious's head. The Lycan hears this and thinks of the Shadow Knights, making him uneasy. He shoots forward full speed towards Abel. The wicked Apprime's massive black wings rear back and then frontward, gusting a massive black gale at Ace. The Lycan dodges and rolls out of the way, then attempts to recover, but instantaneously Abel appears from thin air above him.

mumbles to himself, realizing he isn't going to be able xt blast. Abel grins and quickly waves his hand, Ki ball at the Lycan. The ball increases speed with the l the Lycan, but witnessing this Anarchious lightning-bursts to the Lycans position, knocking Ace out of the way. The Ki makes impact and explodes, forcefully flinging the duo's bodies towards the tree line, but they are caught by several of Eva's bushy vines.

Ace and the Ghost-face recover, trying to find Abel, who isn't in sight. Eva swoops behind the duo, who are both banged up from the shrapnel of the blasts. She places her hand on them, whispering an incantation, healing some of the damage.

"Did you hear what he said while he was emasculating you?" the Lycan asks his partner, keeping his eyes on the field.

"Yeah," the Mutant says, squinting at the Lycan.

"You know what he means, right?" the Lycan follows up.

Anarchious continues feeling the field for his brother, thinking of everything. "Not really."

Ace, keeping his crimson eyes surveying the field as well, speaks out. "Your brother steals people's powers through taking their souls."

"What?" the Ghost-face replies.

"That new power you have—he knows it too. Those hell bats and eye power he knocked Jasen out with were both Vampyric, and we've seen them before," the Lycan explains.

That moment, Abel appears in front of them, smiling and looking up at the Lycan. "Tell him, fleabag!" he says, nodding at his brother.

"He took Lycan souls to make those hounds. I could tell by their smell in the town and their style of fighting during our scrap," Ace explains to his partner.

"I specifically hunted down the Kanji-Spartans!" the dark twin says, grinning at Ace still.

"He could have easily killed us in the town," Ace says, "but instead he drew this battle out to see our powers to see if it would be worth absorbing our souls, but I think his real aim is to take yours because without you around, he has no more weaknesses."

Anarchious replays the hand-to-hand combat his brother engaged in and his brother's explanation of how his hand-to-hand was so good.

Abel nods with approval, laughs, and slowly claps at the Lycan's explanation. "Hey, you're smarter than most typical canines. I am truly impressed. Your intelligence will make a nice addition to my many talents," Abel says, shooting forward at Ace with blinding speed.

Ace rears back. Anarchious feels something familiar in his brother. The dark twin strikes at Ace's sternum, but he is stopped inches before he reaches him. Anarchious has grasped his brother by the wrist. "You were gonna take my soul?" Anarch asks his twin.

"Precisely sloth, I was gonna devour your soul, then watch your body wither away!" Abel replies, smiling. He rips his arm away, then slaps his brother across the mouth. He blasts Ace in the chest and Eva out of the sky.

Abel whales on his brother, rushing him and not giving him any openings. Anarchious can hardly fight back because his twin's reflexes are too fast. Anytime he gets a chance to strike, Abel shadow-steps and flanks him, with more flurries targeting his injured ribs. The Ghost-faced Mutant can only defend himself, and even that isn't enough. He shoots electricity and electrifies his body, but that doesn't seem to be doing any damage either. His infuriated twin is unaffected by anything that lands.

Soon Anarchious isn't able to defend or fight back as his brother literally beats him into the ground. Every punch shakes and every stomp craters the ground. Injured and out of Ki, Ace recovers from the blast and gallops forward, trying to intervene, but is swatted to the ground like a fly.

The dark twin blasts the Lycan in the back, but the Ki bounces off Ace and rebounds into the woods and explodes. Abel turns his attention to Eva, who placed a force field around Ace. She swings her arms in a quick dancing fashion, striking vines at Abel. The dark Apprime strikes back, shattering each vine with his bare hands. He is completely unfazed. He walks towards her slowly as she begins chanting in her language.

"You sure you want to do this, midget?" Abel says with a straight face.

"I love you, Abby," Eva says with tears in her eyes as he shadow-steps towards her. She blows a thick black cloud of smoke at the ground, concealing them both. Abel appears in the cloud, coughing, not expecting it, and blows the smoke away by beating his big black wings.

"Abby, I wish this could end the way we imagined," the Wiccan says as the smoke clears.

Abel turns and spots Eva, her hands glowing like a pris
him. He shakes his head and replies, "Me too," under hi
fires off her giant Usanisinaru bubble of light and rainbows. Abe
twists out of the way, seemingly missed by a hair, but the beam pulls a v-line, reverses, and hits his leg and begins sucking him in. Abel faces the bubble and quickly blasts it with dark Ki, knocking the bubble of light into the dark skies and imploding like a dying star.

The dark Apprime gets to his feet, legs scarred and bleeding, boots missing, and limps towards the exhausted Wiccan. Eva drops to her knees, having no energy to escape the advancing Abel.

"No, Abel!" Anarchious yells, trying to stand up but falling over, unable to take the pain of his many broken bones. He is not about to give up, though, so he continues crawling towards his brother. The Lycan is also unable to walk and crawls towards Abel's feet at a quicker pace than Anarchious.

Abel picks up Eva by her neck and begins to squeeze. His shadow power begins to overtake her body, spreading like a virus to her limbs. Ace grabs at Abel's shin and squeezes as hard as he can, puncturing his legs with his razor-sharp claws. The dark twin doesn't even flinch. He continues choking her as he rears his free arm back, ready to rip out her soul. Suddenly he feels a hard tap on the back of his neck. It vibrates his body, and the whole ground shakes.

Abel turns still grasping Eva by her neck, and it is Jasen. He had hit Abel as hard as he possibly could, but it didn't hurt or move him an inch. The brute's eyes widen as Abel's eyes turn red once more. Abel's gaze drops Jasen, rendering him useless once more. He turns to find himself face to face with a set of amber eyes that have a look that could kill in them, "Eye of Ra!" a woman yells as her eyes turn blood red, stunning Abel.

He drops the woman and grabs his eyes, screaming and shaking in pain. "What have you done, bitch?!" the dark twin yells as his mind wanders to a desert of burning light.

"Those eyes belong to the Spirit Order's Cardinal Vega, not you, monster!" the voice of Magi replies as she conjures her katana and swings it, slicing Abel across the chest. He slaps her and knocks her back, still grasping his eyes in pain, realizing the woman switched places after Eva's attack. "Tricky little..." he grunts in great pain, still blinded by the attack.

The Lycan sees this opening and looks at his best friend, who is still crawling towards his stumbling brother. "Anarch! The moon," Ace says, still hanging onto Abel's foot and looking in Anarchious's purple, worn eyes. Anarchious knows what he means and directs his hand at his brother, who is still blinded. The Ghost-faced Mutant reaches deep, summons the energy he stole from Ace, and forms it into a ball, blasting at his brother. The ball of light makes impact on Abel's back, explodes, and fills the whole swamp with blinding moonlight. All that is heard are the yells of the dark Apprime and the Lycan as water, rock, dust, and smoke shoot in the air, creating a mushroom cloud.

Miles away from the swamp in the beach town, people are on their roofs watching the light show in awe, not really understanding what is happening. They can see the beams of light and the mushroom cloud stretching towards the heavens. The children cheer, dance, and jump around, having the utmost faith in the foursome who went to battle the Darkness. The adults share looks of horror on their faces, expecting the worst.

Back at the swamp, the landscape has completely changed once more because of the fight. The swamp is now a giant crater filled with muddy swamp water. A lot of the trees in the surrounding forest are bent out of shape or completely uprooted from the soil. The Lycan seems to be the only living being up and is treading water in the new pond. He has the Wiccan, who is out cold and blown to hell, draped over his shoulder as he continues searching the waters, smelling, trying to find Anarchious.

He catches a familiar whiff, follows it, and spots Anarchious's shredded plum vest and black hoodie floating in the water. He grabs it and pulls it up. It is Anarchious, back to normal and also out cold. The dark-chocolate-toned Mutant skin is losing its life and color. Ace snarls harshly in his face. The Mutant, startled, opens his eyes and coughs up swamp water in the Lycan's face.

Ace laughs, shaking the wetness from his face. "I see you're not dead yet," jokes Ace, placing his friend on his feet.

"Only a matter of time," Anarchious says, leaning on the Lycan, still weak. "How did you know that would work?" he asks Ace, surveying the field with his fatigued eyes.

"Because I know everything," the Lycan says jokingly once more.

"No, seriously," Anarchious says, looking up at his partner.

"The only two attacks to do a thing to him were this one's 'Oosa-ni-ni' bubble," Ace says, nodding his head towards Eva on his shoulder. "Those attacks were life Ki she drew from the forest plants, and all plants get their energy from the sun," Ace continues. "Now, that moon ball you made from the Ki you took from me—without my permission, I might add—was from the moon, which also—"

"Is light!" Anarchious says, catching on. "But if that's so, why didn't the lightning work? I put way more into all of that than the ball."

"I don't know. That's a technicality and a question for Master José," Ace replies, laughing. "But don't beat yourself up about it. You're an idiot who doesn't pay attention to detail very well." The enthusiastic Lycan continues laughing some more as his partner joins in, but grabbing his still broken ribs in pain.

"Truth is, if he were my brother, I would have avoided fighting hard too!" Ace says, looking down at his counterpart. Anarchious drops his head, humbled. His best friend can read him like a book.

"We both had it tough growing up, but he had it tougher," Anarchious says. "He deserves some sort of understanding. I was hoping to change him or talk some sense into him."

Just then, there is some movement in the water thirty meters away. With a quick splash, a person emerges from the water. It is Abel, and he looks as if he hasn't been touched by the devastating attack. He has hate in his eyes and is shaking uncontrollably. The dark twin is clearly pissed.

"Change me?" Abel yells as the winds begin blowing and waves begin forming on the water from the force of his power. "Change me? Change me?!" he yells emotionally, eyeing Anarchious. "Don't patronize me! There is nothing wrong with me, you see. It is you. You with this…skewed view now. They committed genocide on our people. They killed Mom and Pop, alienated us, and put us through hell, just for being something they're scared of, not knowing we were their greatest allies. So growing up, we both hated humans. Why you decided to protect them now, even after you knew it was they who wiped out our kind... it sounds as if you were the one who changed for the worse!" Abel eyes his twin as his preaching becomes more agitated. "And do not give me that shit about all humans or any other race not all being the same. Twenty-some odd years now and leadership hasn't changed for most groups, even for the 'defenseless' humans. They chose leaders who all were elected to eliminate the Apprime while their common populations stood by idly," Abel continues, enlightening his brother, who now remembers his recent history with humans as well as his experiences in the distant past.

"There is no one on the planet Terra Belle who is innocent, not even the children, as you and I both know from the stoning. So now I am giving them exactly what they wanted—a monster, someone or something they're so terrified of that they will act against each other. I'm going to take the God-King's method and perfect it, and I shall erase anyone who opposes me out of existence, and that includes you and your merry band of clowns," Abel says as he walks towards his twin, surrounded by a dark aura.

Ace tries to step in front of Anarchious, blocking him off, but the intrigued Mutant refuses to let him do so. The Lycan strikes a defensive position, ready for the ruckus, feeling the Ki levels of the wicked Apprime continuing to grow. Suddenly, Abel stumbles as if something has pushed him, and he begins to cough violently. His face turns back to normal, and his wings transform back into his long, flowing cape. He struggles to move forward. He takes one last step and collapses into the swamp water, falling to his knees and hands. Anarchious walks towards his brother but is too weak and collapses.

"I swear, I'll kill you all, sloths!" Abel yells, feeling a deep pain in his chest. "Especially you! You're a traitor to all worthy Apprime, Anarch, and I will spill every ounce of your blood for choosing those monsters over your own!"

Anarchious chuckles. "Forgiveness, Abel," he says, grabbing at his ribs. "I'm sorry, but I couldn't continue holding on to this...hate. All it has done is cause problems. I accept this, Apprime, just as you have, but I have learned something from Marie. You should have too. Forgiveness. I forgive them and will not hurt them or anyone else. You see, I've seen the best and worst of them all and believe I can show them through my actions that I am not their enemy, and I believe you can too," Anarchious explains to his twin. He tries to make it back to his feet but is unable. He coughs as well.

Abel laughs and begins to speak but gags and regurgitates a great amount of blood. He holds his ribs. "Yeah, that sounds like 'The White-Faced Warrior' they sang about," he replies, grunting in pain.

"What?" Anarchious asks, not knowing exactly what he meant.

"Mark my words, Anarch; your new buddies and your precious humans won't understand you. They will turn their backs on you like you did to me, and I'll be there. I'll be there to put you out of your fucking misery!" Abel promises his brother.

"I've almost died a thousand times. One more time won't hurt," Anarchious states with a giant smirk on his face.

The look of tranquility on his twin's face enrages Abel. His dark Ki surrounds him, rippling the water as he sticks his hand out, aiming it at the duo. He tries summoning all his Ki, ready to destroy the duo, but in an instant it recedes. Abel glares dumbfounded, not sure what is happening. Just then, lightning strikes out of the clear sky and hits the space between Abel and Anarchious, blinding them.

"It's not time yet, Master Abel," a dramatic voice echoes from the light.

"Apophis! Stay out of this!" Abel yells.

"I humbly deny your request, Master Abel," the voice calls out as the light dims and a pale old man wrapped in red drapings and holding a staff floats before them. He waves his hand at Abel, and the dark Apprime begins warping away.

"No! Apophis, you son of a bitch!" Abel yells, unable to fight what is happening as he shoots into the sky. The old man turns, looks at the duo, and grins.

"I suggest you all stay far away from Abel because next time, this fight will be different, and he won't hold back," the old man says as he warps away into the sky as well.

The duo isn't sure what they have just witnessed. Ace approaches his partner and touches his shoulder, trying to help him up. The Apprime begins vomiting blood harshly as the Lycan continues trying to help him. The world around him starts to blur out and his body goes numb as he tries to stand up. Ace speaks to him, but it is all muffled, and in seconds, Anarchious loses consciousness in the arms of his best friend.

19
Dawning

"Shh. He's coming to," a woman's voice says as Anarchious's eyes slowly open, trying to adjust to the bright light.

"Take it easy, bro." Anarchious hears the voice of his best friend as he slowly sits up, surprised that he doesn't feel the pain of his shattered ribs. "How you feeling?" Ace asks from beside him.

The Apprime turns his attention to the Lycan. Anarchious's eyes are still adjusting, but he can see the silhouette of his pal. "Yo, I feel like a newborn, stool!" the Apprime replies, chuckling and looking around with his blurry vision. He sees several people—his trio of friends with one new individual, all looking at him in relief.

"Ribs still broken?" Ace asks with a surprised undertone.

"You runt! I kept him from flatlining once, so I can fix some ribs, idiot!" Eva retorts, annoyed at Ace.

"I don't believe it. Let me check," the Lycan says doubtfully, slapping his partner in the belly. Anarchious feels no pain, but the sting of the slap hits his bare skin.

"Yo, where am I?" Anarchious asks as his eyes finally adjust to the light. He now clearly spots the whole team, including Jasen, who is sitting in the corner and glaring out the window with a mean mug. He also spots some very familiar faces.

"Salisbury, the beach town you saved from the hurricane," the woman says, answering Anarchious and placing a warm rag on the Apprime's forehead. The warm sensation sends a great feeling throughout Anarchious's body as she gently assists him in lying back down.

As Anarchious lies down and inspects the room, he sees it is big and very luxurious. Everything is colorful silk, down to the sheets he is lying on. It all reminds him of José's robes. Every chair reminds him of thrones in Zera's castle. Books are on every shelf and beautiful red drapery on every window. It is a room fit for kings.

The Apprime thinks back on the battle he survived with his brother. Everyone else seems to be in better shape. Then he recalls someone who had appeared during the fight. "What happened to Magi?" Anarchious asks, looking at the team.

Eva looks at him, drawing a blank. The Lycan looks at him and begins to speak, but before he can, there is a pink flash. Magi appears, sitting on top of a bookcase.

"I'm here," the Vampyr says, eyeing the Apprime with her stunning amber eyes.

"Oh, look, she talks!" Ace says, mocking the Vampyr.

She jumps down from the bookshelf, walks past the Lycan, ignoring his sarcasm, and leans on the giant bed. She keeps her eyes on the Apprime, and a grimace forms on her lips as she speaks. "I don't know how you feel about Abel, and I don't care. I just want you to be the first to know your brother is a dead man." Anarchious looks on, confused, not expecting that. The Vampyr looks appalled at his reaction. "You mustn't know. Allow me to show you," she says as her eyes change to sea-blue. She forces her hand out to him.

Images are forced into Anarchious's head. He sees Glen Haven at peace, total peace. He can feel no tension, no hate or distrust. It is completely different from when he and Ace left. People from every racial group are in the town dancing, laughing, conversing, and having a good time. There is food, drink, colorful lights, confetti, and a live musical performance going on. He can hear the lyrics to the music playing loudly and harmonically, over and over again. "There's a white-faced warrior in all of us." He gets goose bumps, remembering his brother's words.

Magi, seeing where the Apprime is, fast-forwards the vision. Anarchious now sees Darkness taking over as people are screaming and running away. Some drop to their knees and pray to the God-King. Hellhounds overrun the streets, killing anyone. He then sees a hellhound grab, rip apart, and devour the young Lycan he saved from the mob. Then he flashes away and sees a look of worry and urgency plaguing the cardinal's face as he yells to teleport the people out. The vision then speeds up again to the sight of Vega's body being ripped apart by the hellhounds and a dark being he knew as his brother stick his hand in the helpless Vampyr's chest, rip a red light from his body, and absorb it into his being.

Magi pulls away from the bed as tears slowly roll down her cheeks. Anarchious wipes his face and nods at the Vampyr. "I'm sorry," Anarchious says to Magi as her eyes return to normal.

She lifts her head and looks down on Anarchious with confidence. "He destroyed peace, so I will destroy him. If you and your pathetic little boy scouts should run into him, I advise you to speak my name. You'll need my help," Magi replies to Anarchious.

Ace grunts, not liking her last statement. She turns to him and grunts back, mocking him, and flashes away in an instant.

The Lycan then surveys the room with a look of disgust on his face and says, "I don't like that bitch!"

The Apprime chuckles for a moment, but his mood takes a quick nosedive as he thinks of the good times he had with his twin brother. The Wiccan notices it and asks, "What did she show you?"

Anarchious gazes at the ceiling for a moment, thinking to himself, knowing what he saw, but his subconscious still doesn't want to believe it. Through his battle and brief interaction with his brother, he witnessed Abel's blatant disdain for life. Yet something deep within the Apprime wouldn't accept it, even after knowing for a fact his brother was a mass-murdering psychopath. It was surreal, but he was going to have to accept Abel for what he was.

Anarchious glares at Eva. "She showed me Abel destroying Glen Haven and murdering thousands of people during a...peace festival or something like that," he replies.

Ace shakes his head at the news. Jasen scoffs while grinning, keeping his eyes focused out the window as the Wiccan looks surprised. "What? He wouldn't do that! He knows that town is protected by the Church of the Spirit," says Eva.

"Unfortunately, this isn't the first time I was shown memories of him killing innocent people. Just like you, I couldn't accept it, and not until a few moments ago could I accept it either." Anarchious breaks it down for the Wiccan as she drops her head, fighting the tears. "I'm not sure about your relationship with him, but I know for sure you saw the side of him I lived with. But that Abel is dead," Anarchious continues.

"No! You don't get it! I still felt him. I know he's there," the Wiccan says, in denial.

"Idiots," Jasen grunts, drawing the attention of everyone in the room. "The Darkness is evil. There's no changing him. Only way to stop him is to kill him, and this is what I've been trained to do," Jasen continues. "Whether you all are in or out like that Vampyr chick, I'm going to kill him and take satisfaction in doing it, twin brother or not!" Jasen states, glaring at the other Apprime in the eye, purposely trying to aggravate Anarchious. They stare each other down crudely for a moment.

"Ahh, shut up. You're just mad that the 'strongest' person in the room and 'the best bounty hunter ever'—you—wasn't able to touch hurt him!" the Lycan says, once again easing the tension in the room.

Jasen looks confounded for a moment but soon rebuts, still staring Anarchious in the eye. "If not me, the URA and our weapons, or someone looking to be a hero," Jasen says, irritated, leaving the room, purposely bumping the much smaller Lycan on his way out.

"No. If I may interject..." A petite human woman, possessing the face of an angel with brunette hair and one braid encircling her head like a halo enters into the conversation. The room focuses on the woman, unsure of her intentions. "Hi, I am Senator Organa, Carrie Organa. Nice to meet you, Anarchious," she says, shaking his hand and bowing. "I represent a small movement of folks. Up until a few days ago, they were just a group of humans seeking change and peace. We believe we've found what we're looking for—better protection than the URA or nukes. It's best I show you."

The woman walks around Anarchious's bed and draws back the drapes, exposing the bright sun shining through the several windows and a balcony. She slides the screen door open and gestures for Anarchious to follow. Not knowing what's really going on, he cautiously follows, stepping onto the balcony as Eva and Ace follow. They are many stories up, beachside. Then Anarchious hears a lot of chatter—an enormous amount of chattering in fact. It sounds like people. He walks closer to the railing and peeks over it. The entire beach, which stretches many miles in both directions, is filled with people. It has to be thousands, maybe more.

"It's him!" a voice comes from the crowd, pointing up to the balcony. Everyone in front looks up and begins to cheer, scream, and hop joyfully. In seconds, a domino effect causes the entire crowd to cheer from one end of the beach to the other.

"What is this?!" Anarchious yells at the group behind him, confused, as the noise becomes overpowering.

"These people are here to see you. Two days ago, it was just the people of Salisbury, but by this morning, people from all over the coast started pouring in, waiting for you to show your face!" the woman states loudly.

Anarchious looks down on the crowd, spotting several familiar faces. A lot of the faces are those of people who helped him or people they've helped along their journey. A lot of the people aren't even human. There are many Vampyrs (who are covered head to toe), Lycans, and Wiccans. A lot of the faces are from Glen Haven.

The crowd begins chanting something harmoniously. The melody gives the entire group in the room goose bumps as the massive crowd sings the song from Magi's memory, "White-Faced Warrior."

The Apprime is dumbfounded, not really understanding what is going on, but all he can think of is Marie's letter.

"My organization has been watching you guys," the woman says. "You all have been all over the Internet these past few months. I mean, a rogue Mutant and Lycan working together as a team—something like that has never happened in these times. There is too much backstabbing. Most have thought those stories were a giant hoax, but when the footage of 'the White-Faced Warrior' saving the Lycan kid from humans actually showed up, and then people heard about the hurricane and saw footage of you fighting the Darkness in this very town and winning, they flocked here," she continues to explain to the trio.

"That song has inspired hope, something that has been missing for a long time on this planet, especially with the emergence of the Demon-King," she says. "Hope is something you guys have given all the people on the beach right now." The woman tries to rally the trio. She looks each of them in the eye intensely. "So I humbly ask you, please lead us in this revolution. You're our only hope to end this great oppression," the woman pleads.

Anarchious looks at Ace, Ace looks at Eva, and Eva looks back at Anarchious. They all look unsure, but their hearts and minds are moved by this show of peace. They all look down on the crowd as the song continues.

Eva can feel the crowd's life energy. It makes her smile as it reminds her of the better times with Abel. The Lycan almost feels at home in front of all these people but worries about Anarchious's true thoughts. Anarchious feels hesitant but doesn't want to let the crowd down. He feels he owes it to them for his brother's deeds.

The Apprime Anarchious nods as he glares at Carrie. The small woman throws her hands into the air and thanks the Spirit. The crowd reacts to her, cheering and singing even louder, knowing what this means for them all.

"Yo, not to interrupt," Anarchious yells at the woman, breaking her prayer, "but what the fuck is the Internet?"

Made in United States
Orlando, FL
03 December 2021

11048704R00195